Summer Sky

Lisa Swallow

Copyright © 2014 Lisa Swallow

All rights reserved.

ISBN: 1497508819
ISBN-13: 978-1497508811

No part of this book may be reproduced in any form or by any electronic or mechanical means including information storage and retrieval systems, without permission in writing from the author. The only exception is by a reviewer, who may quote short excerpts in a review.

Cover designed by Najla Qamber Designs
Photo by Lindee Robinson Photography
Models: Madison Wayne & Chad Feyrer

This book is a work of fiction. Names, characters, places, and incidents either are products of the author's imagination or are used fictitiously. Any resemblance to actual persons, living or dead, events, or locales is entirely coincidental.

Summer Sky

Dedication

For Louise - thank you for your feedback,
encouragement and friendship.

Summer Sky

Chapter One

You know that moment when you meet someone, only to discover they're the most arrogant, self-important asshole who you've had the displeasure of colliding fates with? Somewhere, on the edge of my normal life, this just happened to me.

Three hours driving non-stop from Bristol to Broadbeach, and I'm in a crappy mood. This trip would take three hours if every traffic cone in England wasn't blocking the motorway, therefore forcing all the cars into a 'traditional English traffic jam'. Or if I didn't get stuck behind the slowest tractor in the world, after I had the bright idea of leaving the motorway for country roads to speed things up.

I whined when I was dragged to Broadbeach on summer holidays with my parents as a teenager, every time. At that age, the quiet seaside town was the armpit of the universe and no longer the sandy playground by the beach I loved as a little kid. There's no place I'd rather be now, than the small house on the edge of the dunes. When I finally bloody get there.

Frustration mounts as the afternoon grows late, and skipping lunch to get away from Bristol as quickly as possible hasn't helped. I took a wrong turn thanks to my stupid decision to take a short cut, and I'm lost on a narrow country lane looking for a road sign. So when a fricking dog runs across the road in front of me, I'm not exactly calm about the car behind rear-ending mine when I hit the brakes. There is one screech of tyres, one exchange of alarmed looks between the black and white dog and me, and one loud metal crunch.

I glance in the rear-view mirror. Some guy in sunglasses hastily puts down his mobile phone and starts gesticulating in a way that demonstrates he's as happy about the collision as I am. Like this, is my fault? I throw open the door and slam it closed. Heading to the back of my small, silver car, I'm aware of his scrutiny as I inspect the damage. Great. There's a broken light and a bloody huge dent.

I turn to his. I know nothing about cars but I'm sure this is going to cost him more than me. Sleek, black some-kind-of-penis-extension prestige vehicles like this costs more to fix than my I-have-no-money-and-a-crap-job ten-year-old hatchback.

The guy remains in the car, so I stomp over and indicate he should lower his window. The tinted windows seem a bit excessive in the English climate, but I guess this adds to the image of the car. All I can see of the man is dark sunglasses and spiked brown hair, with his hand waving at me to stand back. I huff and back away.

Out of the car steps a guy with an attitude as big as the dent in my bumper. He doesn't speak, but his body language indicates an apology isn't coming anytime soon. Six feet of tightly drawn muscles and a hard set mouth. I'm immediately drawn to the sleeve of colourful tattoos disappearing under his greying black t-shirt. Why do people get so many tattoos? They're plain ugly when there's so many they merge into one canvas of colour.

I shift my gaze to his face. His sunglasses remain in place, and I can't see much beyond his sharp jawline and the fact he really needs a shave. My first impression is he's trying to cultivate some sexy, edgy image to match his sexy, edgy car. The guy whips off his sunglasses revealing bright blue eyes circled by tired black marks. The looking rough is more than an image then. I figure he's in his twenties like me, but his exact age is difficult to tell beneath the exhausted face.

Without a word, he stalks to the front of his car and rubs the dented paintwork, sucking air through his teeth. Flakes of silver paint from my car drop to the road. I take the opportunity to size him up. He's grungy in an attractive way; or the way attractive people can be as scruffy as hell and still look okay. He looks more than okay. I'm momentarily distracted by how his dirty jeans hug his backside but blink the image away.

"It's your fault if you ran up the back of me," I inform him.

"You stopped without any indication!" he retorts, straightening and turning back to me. His accent is odd – English but as if he's lived overseas too long and lost part of it.

"A dog ran out in front of me."

He looks into the road. "What dog?"

"The dog's not here now. I don't think the dog realised it needed to be a material witness and ran off!" I narrow my eyes at him and he deliberately looks me up and down. I'm wearing a short floral summer dress. Hardly sexy, but his scrutiny makes me feel exposed. I cross my arms over my chest.

He hesitates, tapping his fingers against his teeth. "I wouldn't normally do this, but I'm in a hurry. Forget the insurance, I'll give you the money. How much do you think it'll cost to fix your car?"

Do what? "I don't know."

Cocking his head, he studies the car. "Not much, I think. It's an old model. Was the paintwork that bad before I hit you?"

Cheeky bastard. "I'm not taking your money. Repairs might cost more than you have! If you give me your name and number, we can sort the insurance out the proper way."

He laughs. "Very fucking clever. Do you think I would?"

I'm taken aback at his attitude and language. "Swapping details is a strange and ancient custom which occurs when dickheads on mobile phones rear-end the car in front."

For a moment, he looks as if I slapped him across the face, and he's rendered speechless. I mentally clap myself on the back. If he can afford a car like this, I bet people in his life rarely call him a dickhead. At least not to his face anyway.

"I don't give people my personal details." As he speaks, he scrutinises my face and something in his ocean blue eyes prickles the back of my neck.

Oh, I see, turn the smouldering on and get me eating out of your hand. Forget that, buddy; men aren't my favourite species currently.

"What makes you so special?" I snap.

A slow smile spreads across his face. "Nothing, what makes you so special?"

He traps me in a well-practiced seductive gaze, accompanied by the grin sharpening his stubbled features.

Not going to work... "Do I have to call the police?"

His brow tugs together and he responds with a sharp. "No. Wait. Okay."

As he turns and goes back to his car, my heart rate picks up. Shit. Maybe he's a drug dealer. Or has a body in the car. And he's got a gun. And he's going to shoot me. Or maybe I watch too much CSI. Time to leave.

I attempt to memorise his number plate as I jump back into the driver's seat. Jamming the car into gear, I take off as fast as my not very fast car will take me. Through my mirror, I see six feet of muscled, tattooed, blue-eyed hotness (possibly with a gun) watching me drive away.

*****

The house by the sea never changes, inside or out. Or in my mind it doesn't. The whitewashed building belongs to my grandmother, and has been in the family for years. The house nestles between the sand dunes and the town, isolated from the neighbours but close to the track running up the hill to Broadbeach.

My heart rate won't slow following my accident and encounter with the other driver. Why is my day going from bad to worse? I push the incident out of my mind; I'm here now, things will change.

I park my poor, mistreated car on the side of the track and climb out, inhaling until my lungs are full of the sea air. Odd how somewhere I resented so much is now a symbol of sanctuary. The sandy front garden is overgrown, weeds now resident in the huge terracotta plant pots full of geraniums. I tip the largest to one side and pull out the spare key. Gran needs to learn spare keys under plant pots don't equal good security, but I suppose security isn't as big a concern in Broadbeach as in Bristol.

A musty, familiar smell greets me as I push open the front door. Old books, lavender perfume and the seaweed smell of the sea. The mix of scents transports me back to summer days playing in the sand dunes and getting into trouble for sneaking off to the nearby shop for ice creams. The house is a few hundred metres from the beach. A small path and the dunes I rolled down until my knickers were full of sand, lies between the house and the shore.

Nobody has rented recently, and the house is cold and clean. I'm lucky to be able to stay here, especially as I phoned and asked to stay at short notice. Early June and heading into summer holiday season, Broadbeach is quiet. A week's solace should help with the break-up from Grant.

Grant who took me for granted; who I changed for, morphing into someone I didn't recognise. I came home one day last week and found him with someone else. Such a fucking cliché, Grant knew I was due home, so he either decided to live dangerously or didn't give a shit. Personally, I think being told the relationship is over beats coming home to find a girl wrapped around your boyfriend of five years.

I left him (and attached girl), and slept at my best friend Tara's for a couple of nights. But this wasn't far enough away from Grant. So I walked away from my job at his parents' finance company and headed to Broadbeach for some 'me' time. Some 'find me' again time. I've left behind the consequences of losing my boyfriend and probably my source of income.

I head upstairs with my stuffed blue rucksack and dump the bag on the bed. The duvet cover is seashell patterned, and the curtains match, the same bedding has been used for years. A local painting of the coast hangs on the cornflower blue wall. In a fit of glee, I tip the contents of my rucksack on the bed. Clothes go everywhere. I giggle. Grant hated my mess. Picking up underwear, I drop items around the room, and then scrunch back the bed covers. Now, the place is lived in. Imperfect. A little voice in my head whispers: "Fuck you, Grant."

The view from the window is what I dreamt of in the traffic jams on the way down. Unspoilt after all these years, the sandy beach stretches to the sea. Closing my eyes, I imagine I can hear the waves but I'm too far. The absence of sound is somehow louder than the traffic noise from my house back in Bristol. My ex-house.

One disadvantage of being the first guest of the season is there's nothing in the fridge or freezer. Zilch. Nada. I once came at the end of the season and the assortment of items in the cupboards and fridge kept me going for days. Unopened packets of cold meats, frozen bread and UHT milk conveniently located next to the teabags in the cupboard. One year someone left frozen pizza and two bottles of expensive wine. Win. This time? Big lose.

Pouting, I open the plastic bag I packed my lunch in. Pulling out the banana peel left from my emergency refuelling as I was driving, I discover the bottle of juice I packed has leaked all over my cheese sandwiches.

I don't want to drive anywhere again in a hurry, but a trip to the new out of town supermarket is needed. I need supplies. Lots of unhealthy, relationship break-up goodies. Guilt follows me out of the seaside town, away from the local shops in need of my money. However, I'm too tired to face twenty questions from Mrs Hughes or see the weird guy at the newsagents who never speaks. I'll spend money there too, of course; I'm here for a week. But tonight, I need bulk amounts of chocolate, crisps, ice cream and wine. So Asda is the place to go. Sorry, Mrs Hughes.

Chapter Two

Evening encroaches as I return to the house; I spent more time and money than I expected at Asda because choosing the right wine for wallowing is important. And don't get me started on the number of ice cream flavours to choose from. I bought the hottest pre-packaged curry I could find because I couldn't eat curry around Grant. He didn't like the smell. Add wine and a juicy new book for an awesome evening ahead.

When I get back, the lights are on, shining through the downstairs window at the front of the house. I halt, the plastic carrier bags digging into my hands. *What the?* I push open the creaking front door and peer inside, aware the isolation I craved is not so good at this point. Unable to detect anything strange, I step inside and close the door, hand on my phone. Just in case. In case of what, I don't know. A projectile weapon? Setting the bags on the table, I listen. Nothing. Maybe I left the lights on before I left.

First things first: wine. I open a bottle of red, and rummage around for the biggest glass I can find. After a satisfying gulp or three, I pull my curry out of the pre-packed box and shove the container in the microwave. After only a minute, the smell pervades the house.

The sense of relief and freedom from being here, away from someone else's scrutiny or criticism, engulfs as I slump on the sofa. The wine glass empties quicker than the curry cooks, and I close my eyes, soaking in the moment.

"Is this your underwear?"

I snap my eyes open, spilling my wine as I jump to my feet. Psycho-sexy driver stands at the bottom of the stairs with a pair of my knickers hanging off his long fingers. Not even nice underwear. The sort reserved for unsexy times of the month.

The mortifying sight of a stranger holding my flowery underwear is joined by the eye-popping sight of him standing shirtless in the house with damp hair. My look travels from the knickers to his low-slung jeans and the tightest six-pack I've ever seen, in real life anyway. At least he's not spoilt his sculptured chest and abs with the ugly tattoos on his arms. Um. What the hell? Calm down, Sky.

This man has broken into my sanctuary and stolen my knickers. I snatch the offending item from him, mind scrambling to form a coherent sentence. "Get out of my house before I call the police!"

"Your house?"

I clear my throat, not impressed with the squeaky tone I'm favouring. "Where the hell did you come from? Did you follow me?"

"How is this your house? This place is a holiday rental."

"Well, my Gran's house but I'm staying here," I say, unsure why I'm justifying myself to a knicker thief.

The tired, ocean blue eyes fix on mine. "That's a problem then."

"Why?"

"Because I'm renting the place for a month. I arrived about an hour ago and thought the last guests must've forgotten some items of clothing." He points at my knickers. "Then I get out of the shower and find you here."

"Gran never said when I asked to stay..."

I vaguely remember Gran's distraction when I asked. She was shouting at her dog - I bet she wasn't listening.

Crap.

"Well, I was here first! You have to leave!" I retort.

He raises an eyebrow. "I have to leave? I've paid for the place. Have you?"

He already knows the answer judging by his growing smirk. Fine. I change tack.

"You can't kick me out!"

"Stay then. But I'm having the main bedroom, and you'll have to remove all your clothes and underwear." He pauses, fixing me with the look he tried when we were in the country lane. "From the bed I mean."

Damn my blushing cheeks. "I'm not staying with you; you could be a psychopath or something."

"Or something? What's worse than a psychopath?"

An arrogant but disarmingly attractive barechested man stirring things that should remain unstirred, that's what.

"You have to go," I repeat.

"Where?"

"I don't know. Get in your penis extension of a car and find somewhere expensive."

The man laughs. Really laughs, not just a chuckle. He looks at me as if I'm the weirdest thing he's seen; but with a genuine, open, and 'non-frowny' expression for once.

"I got a taxi," he says. "Didn't you notice my ah…penis extension wasn't parked outside?"

"Why get a taxi?"

"I didn't want to park my car here."

"Why?"

"Why do you think?" His smile leaves.

"If I had an idea, I wouldn't ask." The microwave beeps and I glance over, stomach reminding me drinking red wine when it's empty isn't smart. "If you could get your T-shirt on and go now, please. I want to eat my dinner."

I stalk over to the microwave and pull out the carton. Underestimating the heat of the plastic, I drop the container and watch in disappointment as my beef madras decorates the linoleum.

"Fuck."

"Quite."

The amusement in his face does nothing to calm the situation. "If you hadn't freaked me out by being here, I wouldn't have dropped it!"

"Do you like pizza?" he asks.

"What's pizza got to do with anything?"

The man sits on top of the table. "I'll order some for us. If you'll put up with my company until I can find somewhere else to go."

I eye him suspiciously. "You'll leave?"

"Yeah, I can always sleep on the beach."

I'm not a hundred percent sure if he's serious or not, and I'm still very wary. "Hang on."

Rooting around inside my handbag for my phone, I walk away and turn my back, dialling Gran's number.

When she answers, her West Highland terriers are yapping in the background, matching the volume of her television. "Hello?"

"It's Sky. I'm at the beach house and there's someone here saying he's rented the place for a month?" I half-shout.

Man-whose-name-I-don't-know-even-though-he's-seen-my-underwear cocks an eyebrow at me.

"Why are you there?" asks Gran.

"You said I could stay for a week."

"In July."

"No, now."

Gran shouts at her dogs, forgetting to take the phone from her ear and I wince at the volume. "I thought you said July."

Great, I knew she wasn't listening when I asked. "I told you about..." I almost remind her about Grant, and then realise I don't want the guy knowing my business. I lower my voice, "The thing with the thing."

"Thing?"

"Yes, the thing that's made me want to come here for a week. Remember?"

"You're making no sense, Sky. Have you been drinking?"

So much for escaping everything. "Has he paid?" I whisper. "You've got his details? Is he...you know...genuine."

"I spoke to him myself. He transferred the money straight away and paid over the odds. And yes, I have the usual: drivers licence number, bank details and such. They were definitely him. Bit cagey about giving them to me, maybe he has a mistress he's bringing down, wouldn't be the first time..."

She's burbling; Gran loves red wine as much as I do. Hmm. Paid in full, so definitely not someone she wants me to kick out. "Oh."

"I'm sure you'll work something out, sweetie! Listen, I have to go. Monty is eating the curtains."

As she hangs up, I stare at the phone. Why me?

"And?" he asks with an eyebrow still cocked.

"Fine. I'll pack."

"Where will you go?"

"No idea."

He looks at me with *that* look again, curious and amused. "I won't kick you out into the night. We can stay together for one night?"

I splutter. "Yeah, right."

"Is my reputation bothering you?"

"Reputation as a bad driver?"

"No." Shaking his head a little, the guy holds out a hand. "I haven't introduced myself. I'm Dylan. Dylan Morgan."

I stare at his hand, and wonder why he has so many rings on. Big solid silver things. When we shake hands, I'm aware of a weird, but not unpleasant, tingling continuing up my arm and somehow hitching my breath.

"Um. Sky."

His mouth tilts at one side. "You're funny. It's refreshing."

I have no clue whether he's insulting me or not, but for some reason, under his scrutiny, heat creeps across my cheeks. Am I supposed to know who he is, or something?

The curry congeals on the floor next to me, and as if on cue, my stomach rumbles. I cough to try to disguise the sound.

"Pizza," he says as if forgetting himself. "You will share a pizza with me? I don't often get to share pizza with funny chicks."

I scowl, but he's earnest. Do serial killers have a detectable aura? I always thought I was a good judge of character, though that's cast into doubt recently, thanks to Grant wearing a girl on his head. Dylan has a presence. Confident, a little arrogant, but I don't feel unsafe. He's tired, and I think something is dragging him down too. How do I know? I don't, but something in his presence reflects my own state.

What bothers me more than his possible psycho status is how those eyes have brightened since we spoke and how they've disarmed me.

"I think I'll eat a whole one. Meatlovers." I promise myself I'll eat less chocolate tomorrow.

*****

I lied. Despite my best attempts, there's no way I can finish a whole pizza. Not with half a cow on top, and a fair bit of pig too. Plus, Dylan studies me with barely concealed amusement. Again.

"What's so funny?" I ask, swapping a slice of pizza for my wine glass.

"You're not pretending."

"What do you mean 'pretending'?"

"It doesn't matter." He finishes his last slice of pizza and stretches. Thankfully, he put a T-shirt over his way too distracting toned chest, but the faded black T-shirt rides up revealing a washboard stomach I have only ever seen in pictures. Or on Facebook. He grins at me as he drops his arms. He so knows I'm checking him out...

More wine. I tip the bottle but only a dribble comes out. Tapping my fingers on the table, I debate whether to open another. Dylan refused a glass of wine, telling me he's having a dry spell, drinking one of my cokes instead.

"So now what?" he asks.

I wipe tomato sauce from the edges of my mouth. "I'll pack my bag?"

"Already? We've hardly spoken."

"What do you want to talk about?"

He places his elbows on the table, and fixes his baby blues on mine. "Why you came here."

"Why did you come here?" I shoot back.

"Same reason as you."

"How do you know what my reason is?"

"Coming to a two-bedroom seaside house on your own? You're taking time out from something. Running?" Dylan cracks another can of coke with slender fingers and watches for my reaction.

"So what are you running from?" I ask him.

"Life's a bit intense. I need to pull back, unwind. Disconnect from the people around me." His expression darkens.

"Oh, well, at least you didn't say the police," I say attempting to lighten the mood.

Dylan laughs, the dark look blowing away from his face. "Funny, Sky. So who are you running from?"

"No one." But the speed of my retort doesn't fool him.

"It's none of my business. That's cool. We can ignore each other's business together for a bit if you like?"

The way he trails his hand up and down an arm, long fingers stroking those unfortunately tattooed biceps distracts me. The expression on his face as he looks at me suggests he's thinking, not trying to act seductive. Is this seductive? I really can't remember because Grant never was.

"A bit?" I ask.

Dylan spreads his ringed fingers on the table. "How about we chat about stupid stuff, irrelevant stuff, not the real life crap? We know nothing about each other, no preconceptions. What do you think?"

His eyes shine at the idea and I scrunch my nose. "No preconceptions isn't true. You did ram your car into the back of mine. Your expensive car. Then you wouldn't give me your insurance details so I've already formed an opinion." *Great, here comes the wine-induced burbling.*

"Which is?"

"Straight up?"

"Straight up."

"Not the kind of person I'd sit and share pizza with." Telling him, I think he's a serial killer with an underwear stealing fetish springs to mind.

"Fair enough, but you just did share pizza with me. Anyway, I haven't formed any opinion of you."

"Liar."

Dylan tips his head. "You're not transparent enough. I can't see through you. I think you're one of those people who are more mirrors than windows."

The wine fuzzes my head, lulling me into a possibly false sense of security. So, I get up and open another bottle. God, I love the glug sound, even if drinking alone makes me feel a little judged. Who cares? I'd open another if he weren't here.

Dylan watches me walk over, elbows on the table, chin in his hands. He can't be a serial killer. Surely, serial killers aren't six-feet of searing hotness, are they?

"How about if you agree to stay and chat with me for a few hours, I'll leave and you can have the place for the next couple of weeks."

"But you paid to stay here."

He shrugs, curling his fingers around the can. Well, who am I to argue? My options are limited and I don't want to go back to Bristol.

"Okay. But I'm not talking about anything to do with my normal life."

"Oh, that's such a good idea." Why do his eyes darken when I mention reality? "Ask me something. Anything."

"Um. What's your favourite colour?"

He splutters. "You can do better than that! Black. If you could go anywhere in the world, where would you go?"

"Here. I came here every year as a kid so I see this house as my happy place. Where would you go?"

"Here."

"I don't believe you."

Dylan frowns. "I've travelled a lot and seen a lot of places. But I always came here too, when I was a kid."

"Oh?"

"My summer childhood too, Sky. We rented this place."

He stands and wanders to the tall bookshelf in the corner, stacked with books I doubt anyone has read for years. He pulls one forward and drags it out. "I left this here one year."

Dylan places the book on the table, a book about animals and the seaside. He opens to the first page. "See."

In childish scrawl is his name - Dylan Morgan.

"Huh." That's not what I expected.

"Funny, how we're attracted to the places of our childhood when we need to get away."

The guy standing in front of me has a strange vulnerability, and for a moment I imagine him as a ten-year-old boy fishing in rock pools and collecting shells on the beach. Carefree.

This is not what I expected, from today, from him, or from fate. He's a mirror too, when I think about his ten-year-old self, I picture mine. He has to be who he says or has concocted a lie worthy of MI5, which would be a bit extreme to commit a crime against a broken-hearted girl from Bristol.

"Did you go to Mrs Hughes for ice creams?" I ask.

He sits back down. "Yes - and she made those ice lollies, great big ones in cups that melted down your arm before you finished."

"Yes! And she had a dog - I think she might still have it..."

"...has one eye. Buster."

We grin in unison, and suddenly, we don't seem as far apart as we once did.

Chapter Three

Firstly, I'm aware of the drool creeping out of my mouth. Next the sensation of being scrunched into a bed half a foot too short. And the smell of bacon.

I open an eye and ground myself. I'm lying on the sofa of my gran's cottage with a blanket over me. Sitting, I turn towards the kitchen area. Through the door, Dylan stands over the stove, pushing sizzling bacon around the pan and singing to himself. Shirtless. I have never seen a back like his, how does anyone have muscles in their back like this? Sinewy, strong and sexy as hell.

Who is this guy? And why is he still here? I stumble to my feet and creep past him, up the stairs and into the small bathroom. I study my bleary-eyed self in the mirror. Dark smudges rest beneath blue eyes, flushes of pink on my cheeks contrast pale lips. The night of pizza, wine and sofa slumber hasn't improved my generally tired appearance. Or my hair. I pull the straw-coloured blonde mess through my fingers, wishing I'd left my brush in the bathroom, not in my rucksack in the bedroom.

Peeking around the corner, Dylan is nowhere to be seen, so I sneak into the bedroom to recover my toiletries bag. A sinking in my chest accompanies the realisation I have to pack soon. Or is Dylan going? I can't remember; the evening is hazy. The bedclothes are scrunched, so he slept there last night. I wonder if he sleeps naked. *What the hell? I need slapping.* My clothes have been piled into a corner, and my cheeks flare red again at the thought of him picking up my underwear. Dylan's bag is a black rucksack, placed under the window and unpacked.

"Please tell me you're not throwing your knickers around the room again."

I spin round. Dylan leans on the doorframe with mussed hair but a brighter expression than yesterday. I've no idea if he's changed as he's wearing similar clothes, but I'm in a creased up and not so pleasant smelling summer dress.

"No," I squeak.

Squeak?

Rubbing a hand across his face, Dylan scrutinises me. "You look tired. I should've woken you. Let you go to bed."

"Doesn't matter."

"The sofa is shorter than you - can't have been comfy?"

"I didn't really notice; I was so... tired."

He grins at my embarrassment. "Okay. Well, I made breakfast."

I gape at him as he wanders back downstairs again. Grant never made me breakfast. He'd get a bowl and spoon for my cereal and stick a teabag in a cup but that's as far as his culinary skills went. I follow the inviting smell and equally inviting body downstairs.

"I hope the bacon's okay. Kind of been a while since I cooked." Dylan scrunches his nose, looking as if he's a kid trying to make a meal for the first time.

"I like bacon crispy..."

The image of a tall, tattooed, shirtless guy holding a spatula and a concerned expression amuses me and I giggle.

"What's so funny?"

I don't think he's used to people laughing at him. "Nothing. Well, you."

He purses his lips. "I guess we're both funny then."

As we eat our surprisingly good bacon sandwiches, I'm aware of a new aura around this guy. Dylan's loosened physically but also in his demeanour. Maybe, because he got a good night's sleep unlike some of us.

"Why was I asleep on the sofa?"

"Ask those empty bottles of wine." Dylan tips his head to the two by the sink.

"Ah." *Shit*.

"Don't worry; all you did was fall asleep with your mouth open. Nice look by the way, the little drool hanging down the side of your mouth was special."

I refuse to blush every time he teases me. "So you left me and went to bed?"

"The bed I paid for, yeah. Once I removed your underwear." He pauses, and a glint of something appears in his eye.

Now that is what I think is termed a 'panty-dropping look'. Involuntarily, my mouth parts and a soft breath escapes. In response, Dylan shifts his eyes and frowns at the floor. I should be relieved he left me on the sofa and didn't take advantage. Not that I think I'm his type; something tells me he's not into girls with a natural look. And there's nothing more natural than the state I'm currently in. As a teen, I dreamt of long legs and a skinny body like my friend Tara, but I ended up average height with plenty of curves. Nowadays, I'm happy with my size and shape and have no desire to emulate the girls in magazines. Looking like that would take sacrifices I could never make - such as not eating the food I love. I exercise and I'm a healthy weight, and that's all I want to be. Why try for the unattainable and be miserable? The one thing I would change is my hair - I can never get it to behave unless I have the wild blonde waves captured in a ponytail.

"Anyway, what should we do today?" He slaps his large hands on the table and smiles.

"We?"

"I thought we could revisit some childhood haunts and see if ours match?" he continues, as if we're best buddies.

"No, I mean...we? I thought one of us was leaving?"

"Hmm." He taps his ringed fingers on the table. "Later? I'd like to spend some time with you."

No 'panty dropping' look accompanies these words, and a secret happiness this man wants to spend time with me sneaks in. Okay, so I came here to be alone and lick my wounds but I'm flattered. And intrigued.

"Spend time doing what?"

"Like I said, revisiting some of the places we chatted about last night."

I clench my teeth and squeeze my eyes shut. "I don't remember a lot of what was said last night."

A knowing smirk crosses his face. "Yeah, you ramble on after a few glasses of wine. Mostly about your childhood though, I still don't know why you're here."

That's one good thing, I suppose. But the drool, that's downright embarrassing.

"How about a walk to the beach?"

"I smell. I need a shower," I say.

Dylan smiles the kind of smile I rarely see on anyone, happiness filling his face. I have no idea why.

"Get your shower, summer Sky. Then you can come to the beach and search for shells with me."

*****

Pulling my damp blonde hair into a ponytail, I head downstairs in my denim cut-off shorts and plain pink T-shirt. There's no sign of Dylan in the kitchen or lounge and my stomach sinks a little. Did he leave?

The sea breeze blows through the open front door, the salty scent of the ocean pulling me back to childhood. The sun decided to shine today, and the breeze is warm. One of the rare and perfect English summer days to match my brighter mood. I stand in the doorway and close my eyes, letting the sound and smell wash over me.

A noise around the side of the whitewashed house alerts me, and I wander around. A pile of shells rests against one the house walls, a white and pink mix of flat and spiralled, some intact but mostly broken. Dylan crouches on the sandy ground, pushing through the mound, and spreading them across the floor. He's swapped his jeans for blue board shorts and the colourful, mash of tattoos on his legs catch my eye.

"Why do you have so many tattoos?" I ask.

"Don't you like men with ink?" He straightens, holding a shell in his hand.

"Doesn't matter if I do or not. I'm curious."

"I like them." Offering no additional explanation, he returns to his digging.

The sound of shells scraping together as he digs around triggers another childhood memory. "I think I made this pile," I say

"Or you added to it. I think I made the pile," he says not looking round.

"No, I'm pretty sure it was me. Look."

I crouch next to him and scoop to the bottom of the pile. There's a small, rusty steel tin that once contained shortbread biscuits. I prise open the lid. Inside are three spiral purple and white shells. These are intact and bigger than the others in the pile are; and they have vibrant purple winding around the edges. Perfect specimens I sought for days on the beach. My forgotten treasure.

"That's what I'm looking for," he remarks holding a hand out toward me.

I grip the box in a childish manner, like I did to stop my brother getting hold of my prized finds years ago. "Why?"

"I remembered finding the box one year. I thought it was someone's secret stash." He peers inside. "I left a shell in here too but it's gone."

I know where the shell went. I blamed my brother for stealing my secret treasure box and contaminating it with his inferior shell. Then I yelled at him never to touch my stuff again and in a fit of anger, I stomped on the shell until it broke. Okay, so I was eight. That's normal, right?

"Oh?" I ask innocently.

Dylan picks one of the shells from the box, and I'm hyperaware of his proximity; his freshly showered smell with a hint of Dylan. His toned arm is almost touching mine, and I picture myself licking him. I've no idea why. I'm not often overwhelmed by an urge to lick strange men's biceps.

"I was eleven and spent hours combing the beach for unbroken shells," he says. "The perfect ones you find in the souvenir shops. It was the summer my parents spent the whole holiday arguing, and our last summer we came as a family. My Dad left us later that year." He pauses and inhales. "Anyway, after a week of finding half-broken ones, I finally found this huge shell - as big as these. The purple on the spiral was awesome." He curls his hand around the one he picked out of the box. "I left the shell here, because it seemed right to leave it with the other treasure."

I want to cry, which is totally weird. I feel so guilty, picturing the sad little boy searching the beach alone for something I later destroyed.

"We can look for one now?" I suggest.

Gently placing the shell back in the box, he snaps the lid shut, fingers brushing mine. I jolt, his touch sparking something odd but not unpleasant when he lingers his fingers on mine. I stare back into those gorgeous blue eyes and I'm gone. He's a part of my past I never knew about, and now he's here. And I think I like him. Just a little.

*****

The shell search isn't fruitful. The tide is in so most of the shore is covered by seawater. We trudge through the sand, waves dragging seaweed across my feet. Dylan laughs as I jump away from the slimy tendrils, but seaweed has always grossed me out.

We reach the rock outcrops blocking the end of the beach. I suggest we come back later, when the tide is out and we can see the rock pools too. Dylan grins like a kid and suggests we get nets to catch crabs. I can't tell if he's serious, so I explain we have no nets. He informs me there may be one in the attic so we head back towards the house.

We've known each other twenty-four hours – less than – but I feel I already know Dylan. Even though I have no clue who he is, the absence of the outside world and the natural, easy-going atmosphere between us means as each minute ticks by, I want him to stay around.

"Where are you from?" I ask, as we stand in the foaming sea. The beach is empty, apart from a solitary family camped out under windbreaks on the tiny part of available sand, the children squealing as they run in and out of the cold water.

"Wales."

"You don't sound like you're from Wales." His accent is a strange mix – sometimes, he sounds English, at others, he has an American twang.

"I left a while ago. I've been living overseas quite a bit."

This I'm interested in. "Oh? Where?"

The amused smile I don't understand reappears. "In LA, Sky."

"Why's that funny?"

"No reason." He walks away, sloshing through the breaking waves and I stride to catch up, aware the conversation is over.

We reach a part of the beach where the path leads through the low sand dunes towards roughly carved stone steps. Souvenir shops and cafes border the street at the top.

Close to the top of the stairs is Mrs Hughes's shop. A metal ice cream sign perches at the edge of the brow of the hill, waving and squeaking in the breeze.

"How about you get us ice creams?" asks Dylan.

"How about *I* get them?"

"I made breakfast," he says, biting away a smile.

His look knocks the breath from me for no other reason than I'm struck by how beautiful he is. I know beautiful isn't a word used for guys but Dylan is. If I had any artistic skill, I'd draw the classic lines of his face but struggle to find a colour to match his eyes. They're blue but edging towards green and seem to change colour with his mood. Due to my lack of art skills, if I tried to draw him, he'd end up looking like a Muppet; his sensual mouth would be lost in translation. I stare at his mouth and wonder what his lips would feel like on mine.

"Are you okay?" He frowns and I get the impression he knows what I'm thinking and isn't impressed.

A young couple head towards us, hand in hand, interrupting the charged atmosphere between Dylan and me. Dylan swears under his breath and turns towards the sea, his broad back to the passers-by. The young woman reins her long brown hair in and doubles her head back as she looks at Dylan. Yeah, a tattooed Adonis doesn't adorn Cornish beaches often, I guess.

The crunching footsteps on the sand fade as they move away, and Dylan turns back and glances at them. "I think I'll go back to the house. You okay to get the ice creams?"

I dig my hands into my shorts pocket and study the coins I pull out. "I've only got enough for small ones."

When I look up, Dylan's tall figure is retreating, back down the beach, towards the house.

*****

The inside of Mrs Hughes's shop never changes. I swear there are items on her shelves that have been there since I was a child, such as tinned stew and butter beans. The half-empty rack of postcards contains faded pictures of the town in the 1970s and postcard views of the beach that could lead to the creators being sued for misrepresentation. Colouring the sea blue will not make Broadbeach a tropical paradise.

I spend ten minutes in the small shop attempting to extricate myself from Mrs Hughes, who also never seems to age; she seems to be stuck at sixty in appearance and clothes. The dog Dylan mentioned pants heavily as it lies at her feet.

Mrs Hughes bombards me with 101 questions about my life, followed by 101 memories of me as a child. Of course, she asks where Grant is, the last few times I came here was with him. Surprise cracks the foundation in her wrinkled face when I tell her we're over, and I pray she doesn't start prying – or even worse – commiserating.

"Never liked him," she remarks, scooping vanilla ice cream from the ancient fridge and mashing it into cones. Well, that was unexpected.

When we came here, Grant never wanted to collect shells on the beach, or visit Mrs Hughes for ice cream. All he wanted to do was eat, watch TV and have sex. Thinking about it, that's mostly what he wanted to do even when we weren't on holiday. You'd think with all the practice he'd be good at it, but he isn't. The sex I mean, he's a master of the eating and TV watching.

I bet Dylan knows what he's doing in that department.

What the hell? I admonish myself. Just stop this. Now.

Leaving the grey-haired Mrs Hughes and her one-eyed dog, I walk back to the house along the beach as quickly as I can. I'm puzzled by Dylan's sudden desire to go back to the house. The ice creams melt, sliding down the cone and across my fingers. Outside the house, Dylan reclines on one of the slatted wooden chairs, looking as if he's in a beachside photo-shoot. Like the magazine ads for underwear. An image of Dylan in underwear pops into my mind. *Ohmygod, Sky, stop.*

"Here." I hold out his semi-melted treat.

He takes the cone and his eyes zone in on the action as I lick the melted ice cream off my fingers. When he switches *that* look to my eyes, I'm positive the heat ignited inside me is enough to melt the rest. I have never been looked at like this before; I don't understand the meaning, not fully. Desire, yes, but there's something more.

"Thanks," he says in a low voice, shifting his scrutiny to the flaking wooden table.

Silently, we sit and eat; something just shifted in our atmosphere and a different kind of energy flows between us. I twist my body away slightly, so he can't watch me eat because Dylan's reaction when I licked the stickiness from my fingers added something sexual to the action.

"So, where are you from, Sky?"

I drop my train of thought. "I live in Bristol."

"What do you do there?" He bites halfway down his cone, ice cream smearing his lips. An urge to lick him reappears; his mouth this time.

"I thought we weren't going to talk about this stuff?"

"Just curious. Can I guess? And if I guess right will you tell me?"

A game. I like games. "Okay."

Finishing his last mouthful of cone, Dylan stretches his long legs out. He cocks his head and taps his fingers on his lips in a deliberately thoughtful way.

"Teacher?"

"No."

"Hmm. Nurse?"

"What? No."

"Do you work in an office?"

The realisation strikes - I don't have a job anymore. "No. Not really."

"You do work?"

"Yes!"

"Lion tamer?"

"Ha, ha."

He shrugs. "No idea then."

"How about you?"

Dylan's eyes widen. "You're serious, aren't you?"

"About?"

He sits forward, resting his elbows on his knees, hands under his chin as he scrutinises my face. "I thought you recognised me but were pretending you didn't."

I knew it. "Are you famous or something?"

He laughs a belly laugh that annoys me. "A little."

I scour my mind, trying to match this man with anyone I've seen on TV. Unfortunately, this means I need to study him again and trip the switch allowing my attraction to him back in. "Are you an actor?"

"Nope."

"Musician then?"

"Correct." He straightens, as if he's waiting for me to reveal I know who he is.

"I don't listen to much music so that's probably why I have no idea who you are."

"Never heard my name?" His amusement grows, his smile sharpening those amazing cheekbones.

"I don't know band names, never mind the people in them." I bite down on my cone, getting annoyed.

"Seriously? Well, I'm glad then." He reclines in his chair, lacing his hands behind his head, "because now you'll keep being you."

I think back to Grant's Sky, the one who attempted to mould herself to someone's ideal and lost herself in the process.

"So what sort of music?" I ask.

"Loud. Guitars."

I wrinkle my nose. "Heavy metal?"

"Hmm. More rock than metal."

"Which band?" I could pretend I knew if he tells me.

"Guess."

"I told you, I don't know band names."

"Then why ask?"

I shrug. "Maybe so I can tell people about my secret holiday with the famous rock star." I snort and Dylan's amused look disappears. "Or not, I really don't care."

Dylan fixes me with his ocean eyes. "And that, summer Sky, is why I like you."

We sit silently, and I concentrate on eating while ignoring the giddy, giggly feeling of sharing ice cream with someone famous. Even though, I have no clue who he is.

Chapter Four

After our beach walk and snack, we make lunch. Well, I make lunch since apparently it's my turn. I complain that I bought the ice creams and Dylan says this doesn't count. The relaxed banter continues, but beneath the laughter, I catch his intrigued looks. Does Dylan believe I don't know who he is? I inform him he's just an ordinary man with a few too many tattoos as far as I'm concerned. He seems happy with the opinion, and munches on the cheese sandwich I reluctantly make him.

I spend the afternoon lazing around the house, curled up on the lumpy brown sofa with a book and endless cups of herbal tea. Dylan tries a cup of raspberry and mint, holds the tea in his cheeks with a pained expression on his face before swallowing and tipping the rest down the sink. Now he sits in the matching armchair opposite with a pen and A4 pad, scrawling words. I glance over occasionally, at the crease of concentration on his brow and the way he mouths words as he writes. The calmness of the atmosphere and the lack of need to fill this with awkward conversation are odd.

Inexplicably, after such a short period of time and the underwear situation last night, I'm more comfortable with him than people I've known years.

Who is he?

I am clueless. I, genuinely, pay zero attention to the music scene. I mean, I know the famous bands - the old ones who hang onto their stardom by the fingernails - but modern ones? Nope. I went to clubs when I was younger, before Grant decided the places were a waste of money, but even then, I'd recognise the songs and have no idea who the artists were. The only time I see musicians I recognise is if they're X Factor winners. Dylan must be moderately successful if he's lived in LA and drives a fancy car. And if he felt the need to run away on the beach this morning.

Of course.

"Did you think I was a groupie when you first found me in the house?" I blurt.

Dylan looks up from his writing, blinking in as if I've dragged him back to the here and now.

"When I discovered a girl's underwear strewn across the bed, I was suspicious. Although normally, the underwear people throw at me is a little...lacier. And smaller."

Sofa, swallow me up. Now.

"That would be some determination, tracking you to a Cornish seaside town in the back of beyond."

"You'd be surprised. They've done a lot worse." He clamps his mouth shut, and returns to writing.

When we finished lunch, I hoped he'd go out somewhere because I itched to sneak off with my phone and search Dylan's name on the internet. He never left and I resisted anyway. I like my bubble with the mysterious, sexy guy; I don't want to know who he is.

There is one big issue hanging between us.

"What do we do about the house?" I ask.

He sets his pen on the pad. "I'll leave if you want. How long are you staying?"

"I don't feel comfortable kicking you out. You've paid." I pause. "Where would you go?"

He stares at the paper, a muscle twitching in his cheek. Dylan came here for a reason. Like me. "Are you hiding?" I ask.

"Kind of."

"And if you stay at a hotel..."

His distant blue eyes squeeze my heart. "I won't be hidden anymore."

I can't afford a hotel, or particularly want to stay in one. I'd need to go back to Tara's. "I can come back down here next month when you're gone."

I stand and he does too. "But you're hiding as well, Sky?"

"Not from knicker-throwing harpies, no. I'll be okay."

"Fuck, you're funny." I frown at his language and he puts his hand over his mouth, eyes shining again. "What if I want you to stay around? There are two bedrooms."

His voice is soft, pleading almost. Not suggestive. Unfortunately. I'm sorely tempted, partly because I don't feel like facing the no Grant and no job situation and partly because well... Dylan. Who would say no to a hot as hell, famous whatever-he-is who personifies sex on every level?

Sensible people, Sky, that's who.

"Why do you want me to stay?"

"For the same reason I think you want to stay. I feel like I've escaped to a different time and you remember that time too." He bites his lip before continuing. "And you don't know how refreshing it is to meet a girl who'd rather talk to me than fuck me."

I reel at the word - the strength of his tone when he says 'fuck'. Stunned into silence, I pick my book from the sofa, and take my red-faced self into the kitchen. Dylan follows. Turning and leaning against the sink, I watch him warily. He runs his hand up and down his tattoo-sleeved arm, studying me with the intensity I can't cope with because the look is too damn sexy.

"Even though I'm tempted to kiss that sarcastic mouth of yours, I promise I won't," he says in a low voice.

Holy crap. Can one person's words really unravel me like this? Forget about the ice cream earlier, I'm about to turn into a puddle on the floor.

"Good," I squeak. What a lie.

"Just so you know, so you can feel safe." The intensity of the sexual energy from him contradicts his words.

My stomach tightens as the image of his mouth on mine, and my stupid breathing speeds up. I part my lips and of course, he recognises my reaction; if girls regularly throw themselves at him for sex, he'll have a pretty firm handle on reading female body language. Dylan moves forward, and I grip the edge of the sink behind as he holds his face close to mine. What the hell is he doing? Why say this when he's just said he doesn't want me to react like this to him?

Dylan smells amazing. Amazingly amazing, with amazing sprinkles on top. Male with a hint of shower fresh. His cheek is millimetres from mine, a strange static in the tiny gap between, and I can feel him as if we were touching.

"But if you change your mind, let me know." His breath is warm, mingling with the short bursts coming from my mouth.

Pulling back again, he waits for my response and it hits me what he's doing.

I'm pretty sure Dylan's testing me.

Does he think I'm lying and I'm really a clever groupie? No, he can't believe I am. That's insane someone would go to this amount of trouble and pretence to um... fuck him.

I shake my hair and pull a nonchalant face, sidestepping him. "Okay, so I'll stay if you cook."

And he laughs, dropping all pretence of seduction. "So, pizza again?"

Why am I disappointed? And I don't mean about eating pizza again.

*****

I move my pile of clothes and rucksack into the second bedroom, across the creaking hallway from the bright and sunny bedroom facing the sea. Dylan supervises as I transfer my things from his room. Is he worrying I'll go through his bag and take something to sell on eBay?

He follows me into the room where two sets of bunk beds and a wardrobe are crammed. I dump the clothes on the bottom bunk nearest the window and pout at the lack of view from the window. Then I hoist myself onto the top bunk I slept on as a grumpy teen, back then the height implied superiority over my younger brother sleeping in the other. Dylan looks up at where I'm perched on the edge of the top bunk.

There's the sexy, amused smirk again.

"What?" I ask.

"I'm trying very hard not to say something," he says in a low voice, "about you preferring to be on top."

"Jeez! Captain Cliché!" I throw a pillow at him and he catches it. Then I jump down, and start sorting through my clothes, so he can't see my dilated pupils and heavy breathing reaction to him as easily as he did last time. Why isn't he leaving the room? God, please make him leave because every moment he stays in the confined space with me, the harder my heart beats.

"I'm glad you decided to say," he says softly. "I like being around you. Here."

Straightening, I turn back to Dylan, thankful he's in the doorway and at a non-gravitational distance. "But this is weird."

"Yeah, but it's good weird?"

"My life is beyond boring and nothing like I imagined. It's safe and predictable, or was until this week when everything turned to shit." He makes a mock gasp at my swearing. "So I guess sharing a holiday house with some guy who may or may not be famous is weird. But I feel like it's time I did something weird."

I can't have a conversation with him now; I need this man to leave the bedroom so I can stop picturing what he said about being on top. In my imagination, I'm not on the bunk beds, I'm on him running fingers across those muscles while he...*I need to stop this.* "I want to unpack."

"You already did."

"Tidy then."

"You mean you want me to leave you alone?"

"I'm a bit tired; I've had a long week. Think I'll have a rest while you make dinner. Oh, wait, sorry. Order pizza."

He purses his lips. "I can cook!"

"Yeah?"

"There's not much I can make with bread, cheese, crisps, chocolate and wine, Captain Cliché," he teases.

"Cliché?"

"Girl going through a break-up? Eating her way through the pile of junk food in her cupboards."

Now, he's hit a sore spot. "Fine. Whatever. Leave me alone."

Dylan backs off. Literally and figuratively. If I'm in my happy bubble of weirdness, he's not bursting it.

Chapter Five

Day Three of Weirdness. I'm still alive, so it seems unlikely Dylan Morgan is a serial killer even though he shares the same initial and surname as a fictional one.

We missed each other for the rest of the day yesterday. My rest turned into several hours, and the house was quiet when I woke up at 10pm. Downstairs, half a pizza sat on the table with a note from Dylan informing me he'd eaten and gone for a walk. Then this note was crossed out and he'd written he'd gone to bed beneath. Half asleep, I munched on the cold pizza considering the strange domesticity of this arrangement, and how I didn't imagine rock stars (or whatever he is) went to bed so early. My phone beckoned me towards googling him, but I resisted. Bubble walls are very thin.

This morning, Dylan's bedroom door is open, bedding scrunched into a pile. He's not downstairs but a dirty bowl rests in the sink. No bacon sandwiches this morning then. I sit and eat toast, in the silence of the house I came to be alone in, a house with an unwanted emptiness without Dylan, the man who shares my summer memories. I rub my eyes, fighting thoughts of Bristol and dickhead, cheating boyfriends. And wondering if I'll have sex with Dylan before I go home.

Oh, wow.

Does he have this effect on every woman?

I suspect so.

But do I really want him to, as he so subtly put it, fuck me, and then leave? There's adventurous and then there's shameful. I don't know. I'm being a little presumptuous he wants to do *that*; he said the reason he likes me is because I don't. Then he teases me by saying things about wanting to kiss me. Can he relate to women on a non-sexual basis?

I pack up my confusion and head for the beach.

Today, the sun fights with grey clouds, the idyllic summer weather gone. Instead of walking between the sand dunes, I scramble up the side, grasping onto seagrass as I do. The dunes aren't high, but elevated enough for a better view of the area. The almost-empty beach stretches between two rocky outcrops, and I can count the number of people in the surf on one hand. The grey sky turns the seawater to the colour of lead, the break of the waves higher than yesterday.

The wind whips my untamed hair across my face and goosebumps rise on my arms, so I clamber back down towards the beach. The tide is out, and I fix my attention on the damp sand, hoping to find shells as I walk along the shoreline. Half an hour later, I have a sandy pocketful but none to match those in my treasure box. I stand in the break, enjoying the sensation of waves lapping my toes and wriggle them into sand. With or without Dylan, this trip to Broadbeach was the best move; there's something raw about the sea that pushes away thoughts of the world I left behind in Bristol.

I've walked a long way from the house, so I head back, holding my hair wishing I'd tied it back. As I get closer, I notice a male figure in the waves. The man lets the waves carry him to shore, then swims back out to repeat the process. As I continue walking, this happens three times. The only other people in the sea are the same two kids I saw yesterday, who are getting into trouble for copying this swimmer.

I stop near the spot where the waves sweep the swimmer. Dylan, who else? I wait for the foaming waters to carry him to me. Emerging from the surf like some kind of movie scene, Dylan's chest gleams from the water trickling across his abs, and his board shorts hang lower, revealing the tantalising line of dark hair disappearing into his shorts.

Breathtaking doesn't even begin to cut it when describing this guy.

"Morning, summer Sky," he says, out of breath. "Having fun?"

Of course he is; the guy's face is lit up like a Christmas tree. Water shines on his face, drops landing on his lips, which he licks away. This fires the desire to touch my lips to his, igniting the slow burn inside so I tear my gaze away.

"The water's a bit colder than the beach near my house…"

"Your house?"

He shakes water from his hair at me. "Forget I said that."

"The water's bloody cold!" I step back and rub the water off my arms. "How can you stand swimming in this?"

"Because it makes me feel alive! Free. Fuck, I'd forgotten how awesome this place is. I can breathe again." Dylan's half talking to himself, I can't help but smile too. His happy enthusiasm is contagious. "Come in the water!"

But not that contagious. "I'm okay. Not my thing."

The waves pull at my feet, as if joining Dylan in persuading me to let my inhibitions go.

"I thought you said you wanted to do weird stuff that wasn't your usual thing?"

"I draw the line at hypothermia. I'll see you at the house." Despite the overwhelming urge to continue staring at the water dripping down Dylan's chest, abs and into his shorts I take a deep, calming breath and turn away.

"The water's not that cold!" he calls after me, as I traipse across the beach.

I don't get far. Footsteps thud across the sand, as he races towards me. Before I can register what's happening, Dylan grabs me around the waist, lifts me over his shoulder and turns back to the sea.

"What the hell are you doing?" I shriek.

I'm half upside down, face against his damp back and my legs gripped by strong arms. The body

I've lusted after, in an 'I will not lust after' way, is closer than I ever imagined. Wet. Cold. And almost naked. My breasts squash against his back, nipples hardening as his skin dampens my t-shirt.

"Put me down," I demand unconvincingly.

"Come and have a swim with me."

His behaviour spins my mind, reckless and free. "No!"

I wriggle unconvincingly, but his grip is steel. "Yes."

"Stop behaving like a cave man." I slap his backside, secretly pleased to get a chance to touch him.

He slaps mine in return, "Stop being boring!"

"I'm not! I have all my clothes on!" I say through a giggle. This is insane, freeing and a huge turn on.

Until, he tips me over, dumping me in the middle of a cresting wave. My backside hits the sand and water pours over my head. Bloody cold water. Dragging myself upright, before another wave covers me; I wipe my hair from my face and shake water from my arms.

"Oh, my God! I can't believe you did that!" I yell.

Dylan laughs; the sound pushes through my irritation to the freedom of the situation. I screw my face up, attempting not to laugh.

"Don't! I'm annoyed with you! Look at me!" A wave drags my footing and I stumble. When he doesn't catch me and instead lets me fall into the sea, I'm disappointed. I sit in the wet sand and cross my arms.

"Here!" he holds out a hand, to pull me up.

Gripping his wrist, I give him a hard stare as I stand but I'm not convincing anyone. "I'm soaked! If I'd wanted a swim, I'd have put my swimming costume on!"

"You don't have a bikini?" he asks, looking me up and down.

"Who the hell would wear a bikini on an English beach?"

"Plenty of people."

I won't tell him I haven't the confidence to parade my pasty body covered in scraps of material for the world to see. Oh, my God, he's staring at my tits. I pull forward my T-shirt, loosening from where it's sticking to my chest, and then cross my arms across my protruding nipples. Dylan bites his lip, turning darkened eyes back to mine.

"Sorry, I was just picturing you in your bikini."

Which is pretty close to him imagining me naked. So now, I'm imagining him naked. *Jeez, Sky.* "I don't have one."

"You do in my imagination," he says in a low voice, leaning towards me, "You're lots of things in my imagination."

I can't do this - have him suggest things like this to my sex-starved brain. "Well, you can keep them there!"

If we were on TV, or maybe somewhere warmer, and I was a foot taller, we could pretend to be a romantic couple playing in the sea and using the water as an excuse to get skin to skin. But we're not. And I'm bloody cold. I turn and wade out of the sea before I'm pulled under again - by Dylan or the waves.

I need a shower, but now I'm unsure whether to go for cold or hot.

*****

Dylan stays out most of the morning; and when he gets home, I remain buried in my book world and ignore him, despite being hyperaware of his every move. Following a shower, he makes me a sandwich and tells me to stop sulking. I carry on sulking. With a darkly muttered, "Fuck this." Dylan disappears upstairs for the rest of the afternoon.

Hours later, a pen lands on the book I'm reading, thrown by Dylan who's holding his writing pad under his arm.

"Fish and chips?" he asks.

So engrossed in the peace of the world around and the hot sex occurring in my book, I hadn't noticed Dylan reappear. He's back in distressed jeans, and a black T-shirt stretching across the ridges of his chest. I point at the band name and symbol printed on the front.

"Is that your band?"

"White Stripes? No. I wish. We opened for them on a tour though, a few years ago."

I give him a blank look. He's speaking a different language. He smirks and shakes his head. Reading about red-hot sex in my book while Dylan is in the house is not a great way of controlling my um... urges.

"Are you okay? Your face is flushed."

"Fine," I tuck the book under a cushion.
"Ah! What's this? Fifty Shades?"
"No!"

He roots under the cushion then pulls the book out. Momentarily, he appraises the semi-naked kissing couple on the front, and then flips over to the blurb on the back. *Ground open up and take me now.*

Dylan's eyebrows shoot up. "Sounds ... interesting. Any good?"

I pull a face. "Guilty pleasure."

A snaking grin almost reaches his ears. "We all have guilty pleasures."

Oh, holy crap. Is he going to switch up the seductive looks now he's caught a glimpse of the Sky who wouldn't exactly say no if he offered? Were the beach and the dip in the sea another test?

I clear my throat. "Fish and chips?"

"My guilty pleasure? Nope, way off the mark, Sky."

"Ha ha. Shut up. I mean, you said you wanted fish and chips."

"Oh, so I did. Sorry, got a little distracted." He puts the book on the coffee table. "How does fish and chips on the beach sound? I don't want pizza again; it sends you to sleep."

"Maybe I'm still pissed off with you," I say.

"I don't think you are. I think you secretly liked it earlier."

"Oh, yes? Which bit?"

Dylan smirks. "All of it. Get changed; otherwise, we'll miss the sunset."

"The sky's too cloudy."

"She is today."

Unable to find a good retort, I stalk upstairs.

As I change into jeans and a fitted blue T-shirt, I peer at myself in the mirror. Flushed cheeks and brighter blue eyes - a couple of days without tears, living in my fantasy world and the layer of sad is peeling off my face. I touch my lips, visions of Dylan's lips dancing into my mind's eye. When his stubble touched my legs before, it scratched lightly and sent a not very chaste tingle through my body. Will he kiss me if I ask him? I snort at myself. He said he liked me because I didn't want to…ah...screw him. But he did say something about changing my mind.

Deciding all this is having a bad effect on my heart rate, I head downstairs vowing to think only pure thoughts for the rest of the evening. And not admit to anyone (including myself) that every word of the hot sex in the book downstairs involved a man who looked uncannily like Dylan.

Chapter Six

Warm English summers often lead to cool, cloudless evenings, and I shiver as we walk along the beach towards the town, wishing I'd brought my jacket. When we reach the stone steps, Dylan waits on a low wall at the bottom, and I make the five-minute trip to the fish and chip shop. We don't discuss why he decided to wait, but we both know why. Dylan wears a navy hoodie, and sits with the hood over his face, hands burrowed into the pockets.

What would it be like to live his life? The fact he may be more famous than he's making out pushes on the edges of the bubble. I like my bubble; I won't be the one to burst it by pushing to find out if he is.

I wrap my bare arms around the welcome warmth of the paper fish and chip packages as I carefully climb back down the steps. Eating straight from the greasy paper used to be a tradition of our holidays. Is this Dylan's too? I stand in front of him, hugging the meal.

"Where did you used to go to eat your fish and chips as a kid?" I ask.

"Normally, we'd sit here on this wall. You?"

"We used to sit on the beach and watch the sunset."

"Sounds like a plan." Dylan holds his hands out for the food but I keep hold, passing him the cans of orange Fanta.

We find a sheltered spot and sit against the tall rocks at the edge of the dunes, looking over the beach. If I'd planned this better, I'd have brought a blanket. I unwrap the parcels, and peel the greasy paper back. The smell is heaven. Heart attack inducing, celestial goodness. I close my eyes and inhale, making a satisfied noise.

Dylan chuckles. "Funny, Sky."

I open an eye. "What?"

"Nothing, at least you're not obsessed about what you eat." With deft fingers, he unwraps his bundle too. "Forks?"

"Umm. I forgot."

He rolls his eyes. "Fingers it is then."

As much as I love fish and chips, the sensation of Dylan's hard thigh pressed against mine interferes with my appetite. We're touching, his soft cotton hoodie warm against my goose-bumped arm, the material rubbing me as he eats. Whatever his presence fills my stomach with; it won't be chips. Damn. I pick at the food, attempting to quell the shaky excitement of being close to this man.

"We can go back to the house and get forks if you don't want to use your fingers?" he suggests through a mouthful of chips.

I wrinkle my nose. "It's fine, I'm not as hungry as I thought."

Dylan shrugs and returns to his food. As the sun drops behind the horizon, the temperature drops to match. I gaze at the red and orange clouds streaking across the sky and touching the grey sea, and focus very hard on not getting aroused by Dylan.

"Wow, it's a long time since I've had decent fish and chips. Not quite LA style," he grins, rubbing his belly.

"I suspect if you had too many fish and chips, you wouldn't have the body you do..." I trail off. *Nice one, Sky, lay yourself open.*

He lets me off. "True. Being on stage burns a lot off though. If I stay in Broadbeach and eat junk food for a month, I'll be sporting a party pack instead of a six-pack."

I giggle and fight my overwhelming urge to check out his six-pack, in case he needs any advice on the intactness.

"So why did you really come here?" I ask him, twisting around as I sip from the can of Fanta.

Gaze fixed on the sea, he doesn't reply for a few seconds. "I want to remember what life was like before all the crazy shit. Coming back here, I can block out the rest of the world without using alcohol and drugs."

"You had an alcohol problem?"

"Yeah. For years, it was great until alcohol became the way I coped with my weird reality. I stopped drinking and drugging and had nothing else to fill the hole with." He pauses, then continues quietly, "The hole gets bigger every day."

Was I filling my emptiness in the same way and craving affection from Grant, a man who only gave me love conditionally? Is that what's happening here - my need for affection rebounding me into Dylan like a huge jump on a trampoline?

"So you came back here?" I ask.

"A couple of days ago, I got up and thought 'fuck this'. So I cut my hair and left."

Forgetting myself, I reach a hand and touch the short hair above his ear. "You had long hair?"

My hand slides across Dylan's face as he turns to look at me, his cheek smooth above his stubbled jaw. "For the last eight years, yeah. I'll show you a picture sometime. You might recognise me then."

"That's a long time. It must be weird looking in the mirror and not recognising yourself."

"I didn't recognise myself for a long time even before I cut my hair." He picks at his food and looks back to the sea.

Despite avoiding talking about each other's lives, things slip in. Like this explanation for the tightly wound Dylan I met a few days ago.

"Maybe I should cut mine, I can recreate myself too. This is the longest my hair's been for a few years."

Dylan strokes my fringe from my face, fingers trailing across my forehead. The touch ignites nerve-endings across my face. "I'm sure you'll look great whatever you decide to do with your hair."

"Grant said girls with short hair don't look right."

"Who's Grant?"

I clamp a hand over my mouth. Real life things. Secrets. "Just some dickhead who used to be my boyfriend."

"I wouldn't think you were the kind of girl to date dickheads."

I huff. "Yeah, some of them slip through the net and I don't realise until it's too late."

"How can it be too late? You weren't married, were you?"

I splutter Fanta over my cooling chips. "Hell, no."

"Then what?"

"Once you fall in love, it's harder to let go; even with dickheads."

"But you let go? Is that why you're here?"

This isn't fair. He's poking at what I came to escape from - letting things into our bubble world. I set the meal onto the sand next to me. "I don't want to talk about this."

Dylan's scrutiny traces a pattern over my face, leaving a trail of heat. How does he do that?

"Such a shame I'm a dickhead," he says in a low voice.

"I'm sure you can't help it. Part of the Y chromosome disability, unfortunately," I say lightly.

Reaching out a finger, he brushes salt from my lips. An embarrassing sound escapes my throat as he rubs the rough fingertip along my lips.

"Remember what I said about your sarcastic mouth?"

Of course, I remember, how am I going to forget? But all I can do is stare back like some wide-eyed idiot and nod.

He removes his finger and licks the salt off the tip; the move is impossibly sexy and fires arousal through me.

"I know kissing you is the wrong thing to do to you, but I'm starting to get obsessed."

My brain struggles to keep up. "Wrong?" I ask.

"When you look at me the way you do, I love and hate it at the same time. When you *don't* look at me the way I want you to, that's even worse. Every funny thing you say, every time you blush, even just being in the same room fills me with an unexpected urge to kiss you. I don't understand, because this isn't what I want."

"That makes no sense."

"It doesn't, does it? But nothing in my life makes sense to me." He moves the fish and chips from his lap onto the sand.

Excruciatingly slowly, Dylan leans towards me. My heart somersaults and cheerleads in my chest as his mouth approaches mine.

"So about kissing your sarcastic mouth...?"

The words are spoken millimetres from my lips and as his mouth moves, his lips touch mine. He's good at this.

"Yes."

"Yes, you remember, or yes, you've changed your mind and want me to kiss you?" Dylan rubs his cool nose along my cheek towards my ear.

"Both. All. Whatever." I'm losing the ability to process words.

Cupping my chin with his rough fingers, he rubs my cheek with his thumb. My breath comes in such short bursts. I'm convinced I sound like I've run a marathon.

Dylan replaces his fingers with his mouth, a hesitancy in his kiss I didn't expect. Because he's not sure I want to or he's not sure he wants to? I push my lips against his, tasting the salt and Fanta. Dylan winds a hand into my hair and gently holds my face to his. His lips are firm and warm, softer than I imagined. When he runs his tongue along my bottom lip, the tingle spreads across my face and I'm gone.

I want Dylan to kiss, touch, whatever he wants. Because with one kiss, he's shot my brain into orbit and left my disintegrating body falling into his arms. I grab Dylan around the neck, steadying myself, and unashamedly kiss him back. Hard.

Dylan drops his hand from my hair and runs his fingers along my bare arm, adding to the goose bumps from the cold night. A small part of my brain asks why the hell this god of a man wants to kiss average me but who cares? He does. He delves his tongue into my mouth, snatching my breath. With Grant's kisses, I couldn't breathe because he suffocated me with bad positioning, but Dylan takes my breath away with the sheer expertise. I have never been kissed like this. Ever.

I slide my tongue to meet his and as the intensity of our kiss grows, I relish the burn of his stubbled jaw on my sensitive skin. He makes a low sound in his throat, and the fact I caused this arouses parts of me I've tried desperately to ignore around him.

Dylan pulls his mouth away, a tiny space that feels like a gulf opens between us, and his breath comes in warm bursts against my face. Shifting his attention to my neck, Dylan plants a row of tiny kisses before he flicks his tongue into a sensitive spot I never knew I had. I curl my fingers into his short hair press myself into him, not wanting this over any time soon.

With the sound of the sea in the background, and the cool sand beneath my legs, I'm pulled back to my first teenage summer kiss on the beach. Everything is new and forbidden - the excitement and illicitness of what might happen next adding to my arousal. Fourteen-year-old Sky takes control of my thoughts. Will he touch me? Or just kiss me? Where will he touch me? Should I touch him?

Dylan does touch me. Possibly, because I dive my hands beneath his hoodie first, eagerly scrabbling under his T-shirt to touch the lickable abs I need to inspect. He winces at my cold hands on his heating skin.

"Sorry," I murmur.

If I sounded like I'd run a marathon before, I'm pretty sure I sound as if I just finished a triathlon.

"No problem," he breathes.

Dylan snakes a hand under my shirt, the sensation of his feather touches on my lower back flicking some kind of switch. Heat streams through my body. To. Every. Part. Of. Me.

When Dylan slides his hands up my sides, towards my breasts I ache for him to explore. I don't care I'm on the beach. But Dylan pulls away again and rests his head on mine. He sounds as if he's joined me in my marathon, rapid hot breath against my mouth.

No, no, no. Don't stop. For a heart-aching moment, he doesn't speak and I need to know what he's thinking.

"Did you have summer crushes when you came here in the past?" he asks, his breath ragged.

My ability to form a coherent response left minutes ago. "Mmhmm"

"Will you be my summer crush?"

"Mmhmm." I don't care how stupid I sound, or what a weird question this is, I want him back to kissing me again.

Dylan lifts his head away, and strokes my cheek with the back of his hand, placing a final kiss on my forehead. Then he takes my hand, laces our fingers and pulls me close. I lay my head on his chest as he wraps the other around my shoulders, rubbing my cool arm.

My disappointment at the end of passionate, teenage-style kissing on the beach edges away as I enjoy the comfort of his embrace. Nothing else is said for some time, as if everything is communicated by us being here in this moment.

I don't think rock gods cuddle much, or ask people to be their summer crush, so now all I need to do is figure out what being his summer crush entails.

Chapter Seven

We walk back to the house along the beach, and I'm pretty sure the fizzing inside is from holding this guy's hand and not the can of orange soda I just drank. Dylan dressed me in his jacket and I surreptitiously burrow my nose into the soft material, inhaling 'scent of Dylan'. Sandalwood and male. Absentmindedly, I wonder if he has his own brand of fragrance. Then giggle.

"You okay?" he asks, pushing the front door open and flicking on the lights.

"Everything's great," I say staring at his mouth, wishing it were back on mine.

But something's odd. Dylan's looking too intense, and not in a sexual way. As if he's considering what he's done and is unsure about the kiss now we're back in the light and he's seen who I am.

"What about you?" I ask cautiously.

"All good."

I don't believe him and rather than stand and stare at each other awkwardly, I head for the kitchen. Cup of coffee? I don't think so. I pull out my last bottle of red.

"Do you want a wine?" I call.

"You know I'm not drinking."

I turn and he's resting on the edge of the doorframe, one hand above his head holding the top of the frame. This exposes his lean stomach and the 'v' shape Grant definitely never had disappearing into his dark jeans. Why did he have to do that and set my mind wandering into his jeans?

"Okay." I pour myself a generous glass and his eyes zone in on my mouth as I sip.

Dylan's phone rings upstairs.

"Is this where we get awkward?" I ask him.

"Awkward about what?" He glances towards the stairs.

Like he doesn't know. Jeez. I'm not having elephants in the room. "You kissed me."

"And you kissed me," he replies with a small smile.

"And...?"

"And...?"

I narrow my eyes. He's playing games. Was the kiss a game to him? "Nothing."

"I'll be right back. I've been waiting for a call about...something." He heads in the direction of the incessant ringing.

I thought he was hiding?

I sit at the table, body still wired from our kiss, and struggle to decide what to do if he wants to take things further. Such as to bed. Or against the wall.

Or wherever. Maybe the walk along the beach and phone call defused a situation heading towards explosive. The murmured conversation Dylan has upstairs grows louder. Being the nosy person I am, I sit on the bottom step and listen.

"I don't give a flying fuck what he wants!" He sounds different. Not just the swearing, but his accent has more of the American twang.

Long pause.

"Yeah, well, tell him to go fuck himself. I'm not doing what he says. I'll do what I fucking like with my life!"

Even when our cars collided, and I was rude, he didn't show any sign of this kind of anger. The vehemence in his tone shocks me.

"I don't think so," he continues, "and don't think about trying to find me or I'll fucking leave for good!"

Another pause.

"Fuck the contracts, so sue me! I don't fucking care!"

That's a lot of fucks. He's definitely a different Dylan. I retreat to the lounge with my glass of wine and retrieve my book from earlier.

The conversation stops and there's a fair bit of banging around upstairs. Suddenly, I'm not sure I want to be in the house with Mr Angry, remembering I don't know much about this guy at all. The worry empties my wine glass so I find the bottle and set it on the coffee table, curling up with my book.

I lose track of time, lost in the world of the billionaire and the PA. Why do I read this stuff? Oh, yeah, escape. Fantasy. Like holidays with mysterious men, who kiss in an unimaginably skilful way.

I'm aware of Dylan's presence in the room again and turn my head. He's watching me; the idea he may have stood there for a while sends a shiver through. Maybe this guy is unstable and I haven't seen his true self yet.

I wish I knew what was behind those ocean eyes. They've regained some of their guardedness - worry etched back on his face. The aura emanating towards me isn't anger or danger, but stress in his slumped stance.

"Is everything okay?" I ask, attempting nonchalance.

"It doesn't matter." He sits in the chair opposite, not next to me. Damn.

"Liar."

Dylan looks genuinely taken aback. "Okay, no. But that's my shit to deal with. The other world we're not living in at the moment."

I'd like to say he's deluding himself; we're not closed off from the real world, but I've joined in the illusion so I can't.

"Want to talk about it?" I suggest.

"I said that shit's not part of this world," he snaps.

I pull a face, not impressed by him talking to me like this. "What world are we part of, Dylan?"

"The world where the man from the sea meets the summer sky."

"Pardon?"

"My name. That's what it means. I love the ocean so my name's pretty apt. And you're like the sky."

Okay, did he take something illegal when he was upstairs? "Expansive and empty?"

He leans back and places his feet on the coffee table. "Where the sun's hidden behind the clouds, and some days the sun shines through and fills the sky with warmth and brightness."

I'm beginning to suspect he might be the band lyricist.

"How do you know what I'm like? You've known me two days."

He watches as I gulp more wine. "I know you're hurting. And I know you hide behind your sarcasm because you're vulnerable underneath."

"You don't know me at all. You know a girl you met, who shares a childhood past. You know the childhood me."

He inhales, and then exhales slowly. "Fine. I don't want to argue with you."

I shrug and return to my book, considering why I'm so irritated. Because he kissed me, set my body on a collision course with his, and then backed off? Or because this real Dylan poked his head out?

The front door closes as Dylan leaves the house.

I'm confused. After our tryst on the beach, every time I meet his eyes, I want to throw myself at him. Maybe I should. Isn't that what he's used to? Is that why he's annoyed? Because I haven't?

Still wearing his hoodie, I follow Dylan out of the door expecting to follow him to the beach but he's in the shadows, leaning against the house and looking at the stars.

"Are you sure everything's okay?" I ask, touching his arm.

"We can't escape really, can we?" he asks quietly, eyes fixed on the stars still.

"Not everything. But we can control some of what happens to us."

"I don't feel like I can." He takes my hand and squeezes. "I don't feel like I have any control over my life."

The happy guy from the beach, the summer boy who ate fish and chips with me on the sand, left when he went upstairs. This Dylan is dejected, shoulders slumped, and he tears at my heart because he's touched my life in a way that makes me feel the opposite.

"Of course you do, and if you don't, change things."

Dylan looks at me and makes a soft sound of derision. "That's why I came here, but I can't run forever."

I want to hold him, but his body language creates a barrier I don't want to cross, and be rejected.

Gently, I stroke the back of his hand. "Then enjoy the freedom and control you have now, and when you go back change what you can."

"Yeah, maybe." He runs a hand through his hair, and turns to me sliding his arm around my waist. My scalp tingles as he nudges his cool nose into my hair, and I place my hands on his chest, desperate for him to kiss me again, filled with trepidation of what happens next.

"I want to kiss you again, Sky. But I don't think I can stop there and I don't want to spoil this," he says, voice muffled in my hair.

"How would you spoil this?" I ask, pulling back.

Dylan releases his grip on my waist and quietly says, "Because when I fuck a girl, I don't want anything to do with her afterwards."

Anger flashes across my mind and I shove him hard in the chest so he stumbles backwards. "I wouldn't let you! I don't fuck people, you arrogant bastard!"

Dylan straightens. "I told you I was a dickhead."

"And now I believe you," I snap, shaking with a mix of anger, disappointment and arousal.

"Sky," he says, softly, closing the charged space between us, hovering his mouth close to mine in his annoying seductive way. "If I took you upstairs to bed, I wouldn't fuck you. You're worth so much more than that. You have no idea…the things I want to do to you…"

The heat from my anger dives straight to my core, arousal by his words taking me by surprise. But I keep a grip and don't meet his mouth or touch him.

"And if you'd let me finish what I was saying, I would've explained what this would do to my head is the problem."

I step back, to reinforce the impression I don't want him anywhere near me. "I think we'd better stop now, you're right, this is going to spoil…whatever this is."

Rubbing both palms across his face and down to his neck, Dylan appraises me one last time. "Suit yourself. I think I need to go for a walk."

That's a typical male shutdown response there. His tall, but hunched, figure strides away, hands buried in his jeans pockets. I watch him go, guilty about my overreaction to this troubled guy.

I already have a problem caused by 'whatever this is': the inexplicable need to be around Dylan.

Returning inside, I grab my book and a glass of water, and then traipse upstairs to bed. I can't be wrapped in Dylan's arms, but I am wrapped in his hoodie still. I drift to sleep, arm across my face, his scent following me into my dreams where we do more than kiss.

Much more.

And he doesn't use the word 'fuck' once.

Chapter Eight

I wake early, and listen for movement downstairs. Nothing. I never heard him come back last night, but I presume he did because where else would he go? Apart from back to where he lives and I don't think that's likely. I look out of the window hoping to see the sun but I'm greeted by a cloudy day. Summer here is so hit and miss; the sunny childhood day replaced by grey for a second day. The floorboards creak as I leave the room. Dylan's bedroom door is closed and he leaves it open when he's not inside so he must be in bed still. Good. I don't want to see Dylan; I don't know what to say to him.

I grab my remaining banana from the table and peel it, dropping the skin in the bin on the way out of the door. The solace of my beach walk yesterday helped, and I don't want to be in the house facing awkward conversations. Maybe I should leave and go back to Bristol.

As I wander towards the sea, I realise the weather is colder than I first imagined and my legs smart from the cold breeze. I remove my shoes anyway, and stand in the sand at the edge of the breaking waves. The water gradually buries them beneath the sand. Then one by one, I pull my feet out and move to a new spot, repeating the exercise. The sensation of being sucked down and trapped is odd. What would it be like to be dragged under quicksand?

A man walking a large, scruffy black dog passes and I nod hello, but the beach is almost empty again. I'm happy I remembered to tie my hair back today, not so happy about the huge drop of rain landing on my nose. So much for enjoying the seaside holiday weather. This isn't any different to my childhood summer, rain is very much part of the experience. Good thing I have plenty of books to read, because today is a TV and books day.

On the short walk back to the house, I find Dylan walking across the sand towards me. He's wearing his jeans and T-shirt but his feet are bare. In his arms, he holds his hoodie, the one I wore last night and left neatly folded over a chair in the kitchen this morning. I pause, debating what to do or what to say.

As he approaches, I study him with new eyes. The confident, lithe movements and his easy-going stroll are back. This Dylan is miles away from the uptight guy who rear-ended me, the one who reappeared last night.

When he stops short of me, blue eyes searching mine I want to ask him why. Why did he kiss me and say those things?

He's wearing a sheepish look as he hands the hoodie to me. I stare at it blankly.

"Why are you giving me this?"

"I saw you on the beach from the window and I think it's going to rain."

"Very chivalrous."

"And this is an excuse to talk to you and apologise about last night. We should talk about it?" He's wary, which doesn't suit him.

I lean down and pick my sandals up. "It doesn't matter. Forget it."

"I didn't mean to upset you. I was upset about something and that kind of took over."

"Really?" I ask sarcastically.

Since I woke, I've debated packing and going. I'm not sure I want to get involved in dramas with this person. But the fantasist inside wants to stay.

"I shouldn't have said the stuff. About sex," he continues.

Oh, God, don't talk about sex again, not when you're standing there in all your Dylan glory.

"You mean fucking? That's what summer crushes do, right?"

He winces. "Not always. I never did, mostly because I was too scared to ask."

His admission disarms me. This guy? Too scared to ask? I bet that hasn't happened for a long while.

"Don't tell me - you were a spotty teen boy who didn't know how to talk to girls?"

Tensions ebbs away as he laughs. "No, I was too polite."

"Right...of course, because you weren't ruled by your hormones like every other teenage boy?"

"I'm not saying I didn't do anything, just not all the way."

"I bet you've made up for it since, with all these girls you fuck."

He closes his eyes. "Okay, I said I'm sorry about saying that."

"I came for a walk to be alone," I tell him, but take his jacket and shrug it on. The scent immediately triggers memories of last night.

A second drop of rain hits my nose and I glance up. The darker sky rolls in. Great.

"It's raining," he says.

"Very perceptive."

"What's wrong? Is this all because I said stupid things last night? Or because I kissed you? Can we forget what happened and rewind?"

"To before we kissed? So it never happened?"

Dylan's eyes glint as he reaches his hand to touch my mouth with cool fingers. "No. To the point we got home."

I shiver at the suggestion beneath his meaning, but pull myself into the now. "Why?"

The rain falls, hard drops seemingly from nowhere; they're so sudden. "I thought summer crushes lasted more than one evening?" he asks.

"You do more than one night stands then?"

He drops his hand. "Sky, what the fuck is going on? How many times do I have to say sorry?

Seriously, if you don't want me to touch you again, I won't. But let me back in."

"Back in where?"

"Your life. Here. This."

I wipe the rain from my forehead. "This? What is this? You're not in my life because this isn't my life. Or yours."

"Right here and right now this is our life, and I'm pissed off if I fucked that up last night. I guess I need to find a new way of relating to women."

"Apart from seeing them all as a potential fuck you mean?"

Dylan pushes his hand through his wet hair, as the rain grows steadier around us. "What is your obsession with fucking?"

"You're the one with the obsession! One kiss and you presume I'm going to say yes to sex with you?"

"Wow. Just wow. I don't know what's going on here but...wow."

"It doesn't matter. I'm just glad I didn't," I retort.

"So am I." His words sting. Yeah, I get that. I'm not exactly his usual type. "Not for the reason you're thinking. I told you that last night; it's because I think sex would spoil this."

We watch each other warily and I don't know what to say or do. He confuses me; the whole situation is surreal. I can't get my head around what he wants - or what I want. One minute I'm staring at his killer body wanting him all over me, and the next I'm telling him to leave me alone.

Why did he have to kiss me and drag us up to this level?

I turn back to the waves tumbling in, willing him to walk away. The white surf rolls over but never quite reaches my toes. Shells have washed in with last night's tide and are dotted around, stuck in the sand as the sea retreated. Ignoring Dylan, I walk along the shore towards the shells and dig them from the sand. Something about the possibility of finding a perfect shell draws me to them every time. A large patterned tip protrudes from the sand and I wander over. Bending down, I dig around with my fingers and pull out a huge purple and white spiral shell. Twisting the shell in my hands, I check the intactness. Perfect.

"Sky! Waves!"

I have my back to the ocean and a wave crashes against my legs, destabilising me. I regain my footing and attempt to move before the retreating water sucks my feet into the sand. At that moment, a larger wave wipes me completely, dragging my body underwater. I panic at the confusion of being pushed and pulled out of my control, seawater swirling hair into my face and the bubbles rushing into my ears. The shell remains tightly gripped in my hand.

As water draws away, I push my head free. Dylan stands on the edge of the shore, water lapping his ankles, laughing. I spit out seawater and stagger to my feet. The weight of the damp hoodie threatens to pull me down again as I push hair from my eyes.

"That was fucking funny! You should see your face!" He wades towards me, arm outstretched to help.

Attempting to keep my footing, I lunge at him and slap his hard chest with both palms. "It was not! Screw you!" Dylan catches my arms as I make contact, and pulls me towards him.

Scrutinizing my face briefly, Dylan takes my cheeks in his broad palms and crushes his lips against mine. I gasp again, but it's not the sea snatching my breath this time. A new wave sways us, and Dylan holds my face tightly, his own footing steady, as his mouth claims mine. A small voice in my head asks what the hell I'm doing, but I ignore it. Dylan overwhelms all common sense the moment I have any physical contact with him. Losing myself in his mint-flavoured kiss, in the slide of his tongue, I yield to the power he holds over me. Dylan curls his fingers into my wet hair and pulls me closer; I respond with a deep kiss, running fingers across his face.

Fierce or gentle, his kisses mould my soul to his as perfectly as his body shapes with mine, as if we're in a place created by our coming together. Kissing Dylan last night pulled me into his orbit, and when I see stars again, I swear his kisses will always take me away from the real world. If Dylan can remove me from reality with only this, God knows what anything else he's skilful at would do to me. The thought of us skin on skin, united through more than a kiss, lights a fire deep inside that would take more than the cold Cornish sea to extinguish.

Dylan loosens his grip on my hair and slides his hands across my damp back. He closes the final gap between us as our bodies meet; the soaked clothes annoyingly in the way. "I have never met anyone so…" He grasps for a word, but then gives up and rests his forehead on mine. "I feel as if I've waited my whole life to meet you and then suddenly you're here."

For a moment, I consider whether he's teasing me again, but I guess I'm very different to the people in his real life. "I can honestly say I've never met anyone like you, Dylan Morgan."

He wipes water from my cheek with cool, damp fingers. "No one's met Dylan Morgan apart from you, not for a lot of years, anyway."

I stare at the truth reflected in his pale blue eyes, unable to believe any of this is reality. His grip on my back loosens, and I step back. Rain drips down his face, soaking through his now damp T-shirt and clinging to his body in a way that does nothing to help my mounting desire to get my hands on him.

A subject change is needed rapidly, before I begin drooling. I hold out the shell in the palm of my hand. "I was getting this."

"For your treasure box?"

"Kind of." To replace his; the one I destroyed thirteen years ago.

He takes the shell from me and inspects it. "Oh. A good find, definitely worthy of the secret box."

"Not worth half-drowning for though," I mutter.

A seagull shrieks overhead, I could swear the bird is laughing at me.

Dylan shoves the shell in his pocket. "Let's get you home."

We tread across the soaking sand and as the rain switches to a vertical sheet of water, I pick up the pace. Dylan strides to catch up.

"I'll carry you?"

I speed up. "Don't you dare put me over your shoulder again."

"Piggy back?" He turns and bends slightly gesturing with his arms.

"You are one big kid."

"Yep. And loving every minute! Come on!"

Every time I think I can avoid physical contact with this man, I'm in a position to get my hands on him. And how can I deny myself? I jump onto Dylan's broad back and wrap my legs around his taut waist, arms around his neck. Dylan grabs me under the legs and runs.

"You'll drop me!" I shout, alarmed by his speed.

"You're not heavy! But stop strangling me!"

I shift my arms, crossing them over his toned chest instead. Close contact with Dylan, even through my soggy clothes, sends the butterflies in my stomach into a frenzy. My damp cheek rests against his, and I fight the urge to bury my face in his neck and kiss him.

We arrive at the house in half the time walking would've taken, and he sets me on the floor.

"So we rewound to last night after the kiss. What now?" he asks, eyes shining.

A mess of arousal from his holding me, and shivering from my soaking, I can't think straight. "What did you intend to do last night?" I ask

"I was leaving that up to you. I didn't want to scare you off. What would you have done?" His eyes search mine as we puddle water onto the polished wooden floor.

We've stepped over the line so far now, I don't think there's any point holding back. I'm pulled in and locked into Dylan whether I like it or not.

"Probably, I'd have kissed you some more and finished my fish and chips. Maybe not in that order."

"Sky, you are the funniest girl..." He wipes water from my face with his palm.

The kiss Dylan gives me next is brief and soft, rather than the all-encompassing one from the beach. I attempt to control my chattering teeth but fail.

"I think you need to get changed," he says, peeling the hoodie from me.

Before I decide to let him undress me completely, I head upstairs.

Chapter Nine

When I return downstairs, Dylan has changed into jeans and a T-shirt, and sits crossed legged on the sofa. The brightness of his tattoos contrast his dark clothes, adding the edge of exotic to the ordinary.

"I don't know how you'd ever hope to blend in anywhere," I say.

"What do you mean?" I indicate his tattoos. "Oh, I cover up sometimes. I look pretty fucking hot in a suit too, you know?"

His slips back into foul-mouthed do-I-give-a-fuck Dylan amuses me; they're as big a contrast as the ink and the dull English summer day. I want to say he'll never blend in because there's something about him that fills the world around with colour as bright as his tattoos. Is this how some people become famous and others fail? Do they have an aura like Dylan's, sucking everyone in?

He tips his head at me. "What are you thinking about?"

"You."

"Oh...?" He moves and crosses his leg over his knee, stretching an arm across the back of the brown sofa. And gives me *that* look – the one worming its way past my anti-male defence system, the system blown apart by Dylan Morgan.

I poke my tongue out. "Don't presume I'm thinking anything good."

"Sky, I can read your face, and your eyes."

Ignoring him, I walk to the window and peer out. The rainy weather has taken hold, the bright world of yesterday muted into greys.

"It wouldn't be a summer without this," he says from behind. "What did you used to do here on rainy days as a kid?"

I turn back and shrug. "Stay home and read. Fight with my brother."

"None of those sound fun to me."

"TV?"

Dylan's eyes flick between the TV and me. "Do you like snuggling?"

Here we go again, Mr Random. "As in?"

"Cuddling with someone, relaxing, maybe watching TV together."

Like I did with Grant? Watching TV together with a Chinese takeaway was his idea of a hot date. His snuggling involved groping when he was drunk - or decided I was drunk enough. I scrunch up my nose but before I can respond, Dylan disappears, jumping upstairs two steps at a time. Seconds later he reappears with his duvet, the seashell covered pattern looking out of place in his inked arms.

"Do you know how long it is since I've snuggled?" he asks.

"Umm...?" Actually, I can imagine. "Not rock star behaviour, I guess."

He narrows his eyes. "Reality stays at the door..."

"Okay. No, I don't."

Dylan resumes his seat on the sofa and picks up the TV controller. "Choose a DVD?"

There's something about Dylan, which makes him hard to refuse. Apart from what my mum would call devilish good looks, he has an odd presence. The presence of someone used to people agreeing with, and never questioning, him.

The DVD collection stacked in the TV cabinet is eclectic and I attempt to find one he'll hate.

"Twilight." I hold up the box and fix him with a 'don't disagree' stare.

After an initial tug of the eyebrows, he shrugs. "Sure. I've never seen that one."

"That's what I thought."

"But I know..." He stops himself.

"You know who?"

"Do you have popcorn?"

Again, the subject change. He'll give me whiplash. "No, why would I?"

"But you have crisps? Lots." He grins teasingly and stands.

I load up the DVD and settle on the sofa. Dylan returns with a huge plastic bowl of crisps and some cans of coke. Setting them on the table, he curls his long legs under him and pats the sofa. I get up from the floor and hesitate.

"Live dangerously," he says and smiles.

Snuggling under that duvet with him *is* dangerous - to my heart rate, my hormones and eventually my modesty.

But I climb onto the sofa with Dylan anyway.

Compared to the cool outside, Dylan's hard, muscled body is warm. When I cuddled Grant, there was a lot of loose flesh; I don't think Dylan has an ounce of fleshiness on him.

I extricate the controller from under the duvet and hit play. Dylan leans forward, drags the bowl of crisps onto the duvet between us and sighs. I smirk. He's sitting through the whole thing, whether he likes it or not. This is pay back for my second dunking in as many days.

Me, I've seen *Twilight* around twenty times. Don't judge. There's something about Edward - so what if he's pale, skinny and the antithesis of the man I'm currently lusting over? Maybe I like the unattainable. Every now and then, Dylan makes a soft scoffing noise in his throat but masks the sound with a mouthful of crisps.

As the movie progresses, Dylan's behaviour confuses. I thought 'snuggling' might be secret code for 'I'm going to make out with you', but looks like I was wrong. I have my body buried as far into him as I can without sitting astride him and begging him to touch me (which becomes more of a possibility as the minutes pass) but all he does is rest his head against mine and drive me mad with gentle touches on my arm. Under this duvet, I'm getting hot and bothered; I'll be a gasping heap of hormones by the end of this.

Halfway through the movie, Dylan shifts around to face me. "How am I doing?"

"Doing?"

"At snuggling."

"I don't think snuggling is an art form." Now he's locked me in his sights again, my pulse rate goes haywire.

"But this is how it's done?"

I rub loose hair from my face. Sometimes, I feel like I'm sharing the place with an alien. You know, 'teach me how to love, earth girl'. The thought plasters a smirk on my face.

"What's funny?" asks Dylan.

"Nothing. Snuggling. Whatever." I lean towards the table and grab a handful of crisps, shovelling them in my mouth.

As I munch on the crisps, Dylan strokes my head, fingers setting off a soft buzz across my scalp. "What are you thinking?" he asks, in a low voice, gaze moving to my mouth.

"What are you thinking?"

"Honestly?"

I wrinkle my nose. "Okay. Tell me. Honestly." *Please, don't let it be something I can't say no to.*

"I'm not thinking; I'm fighting." Dylan traces my lips with his index finger, the abrasive touch shivering down my spine. "I'm fighting with the overwhelming desire to show you what you're doing to me."

"Oh…" *Crap*, I sound like some stupid, breathless teenager. Again. I can't ask him to elaborate; otherwise, I'll have no control left.

I touch his face in return, dragging my nails through his stubble, remembering the burn against my face last night. I shift closer and his hand closes on my knee, gripping as if stopping himself moving his hand elsewhere.

This weird connection pulling us together also pulls my insides tight – attraction, apprehension, lust. I don't understand how I feel as if I've known Dylan months instead of days, but I do.

The way Dylan's looking at me right now, I don't think I've ever been looked at before. Lust is clearly in his darkened eyes, but something is behind that expression I can't fathom.

"I know I pissed you off last night, Sky, but I really want to kiss you again."

The hesitancy in his words amuses me - I bet Dylan Morgan doesn't usually need to ask for permission.

"Really?" I say and bite my lip in a deliberately coy gesture.

His grip on my knee tightens. "Really, because your mouth on mine feels fucking amazing."

"Don't swear at me!" I say, slapping the hand sneaking up my leg.

"You're also fucking funny." He kisses my nose.

Secretly, Dylan's colourful language is a turn on. The swearing reinforces his bad boy image - his ink and the strength in those muscles he could use to hold me down and do bad boy things to me.

Jesus, Sky...

"And you're unbelievably, fucking sexy." He moves towards me and I brace myself for a suffocating, urgent kiss. Instead, Dylan kisses me softly, his lips barely skimming mine. This is not what I want. I brazenly hold his face and meld his mouth with mine.

Embarrassingly, I tremble the minute he responds and encircles me in his arms. Either he, politely ignores this, is used to girls reacting the same way, or thinks I'm cold. I don't explain. I can't, because his lips are locked on mine and I don't want to stop.

He captures my lip between his teeth, tugging gently and eliciting an embarrassing groan from low in my throat. I feel him smile against my mouth and nip his lip in response. His lips harden as he presses them against mine, thrusting his tongue into my mouth with a low growl.

There is no mystery to how this man gets girls into bed. With or without his name, he'd manage to seduce with a kiss, a touch and a blast of that panty-melting sexuality he can't control. One I doubt he tries to control.

Dylan laughs against my mouth, and then pulls the duvet over our heads, landing us in a shadowed world of sensation. The warmth and scent of him emanates around in the airless space between the duvet and us, drowning my senses.

The heat from our breath and bodies stifles, intensifying the intimacy beneath the duvet as we hide like kids who've made a den from their bedding. Dylan runs his fingers along my lower back, a shiver shooting from the sensitive spot at the base of my spine to my toes. Sliding his hands around to my waist, he pulls me closer, hands igniting my skin where he touches. We explore each other with the urgency of teenagers, mouths locked together.

Dylan pulls his head away, and places his hand against my cheek. His hooded eyes are dark in the dim world of our hiding place. "Is this part of the snuggling process? I wasn't aware…"

"I think this is optional," I say and curl a hand around his neck to draw his face to mine again.

"I think this should be compulsory," he says hoarsely.

"Fine, but I can't breathe." I pull the duvet from over our heads, drawing a huge breath as the cooler air hits. If I remain under there with Dylan, I might never come back out.

Damp hair sticks to my head and Dylan pushes his hand beneath a tendril, twirling the hair around his finger. He looks down, eyes glazed and distant.

"Okay?" I ask. *Please don't stop now…*

"This is strange. Good strange, but strange." He nuzzles my neck, hot breath against my sensitive skin.

"Strange?"

"This. Slow. Not all about me." Dylan pushes the duvet away and pulls me onto his lap so I'm straddling him. I look into his darkened eyes, convinced I'll faint due to hyperventilation. "Restraint – it's different."

I'm glad one of us has restraint; because now I'm on his lap, Dylan's arousal is evident. Because of me? *Wow*.

"You, umm, don't have to be totally restrained." I close my eyes, *stupid croaky voice*.

Dylan sighs and tugs the neck of my T-shirt to one side, darting his tongue into the hollow of my neck. I jerk at the intensity, so many places he knows to touch, and Grant never did. Grant had two or three places he zoned in on - the obvious ones.

"I can tell this is okay with you. But tell me when to stop," he says.

We lock gazes. Dylan slides his hand beneath my T-shirt, and strokes along my side until his hands hover below my breasts. He pauses and I shift so his hand brushes the satin fabric of my bra. Dylan smiles, and circles his thumb over my hardened nipple through the material. I rub my lips together, shifting my focus to his parted lips. I need to taste him, lock in all my senses.

As he claims my lips with his, Dylan's tongue tangles with mine again. Reaching around, he unclasps my bra and touches my freed breast so lightly, the intensity causes me to moan into his mouth.

Dylan pulls away again, and yanks his T-shirt over his head. Oh, my God. He's unreal. Men in real life don't have perfectly sculpted, muscular bodies. *Do not lick him. Do not lick him.* I place a hand on his taut chest, brushing his nipple with a finger. He sucks in a breath and cocks an eyebrow at me. "Your turn?"

I hesitate.

Dylan moistens his lips, and lays his head back on the sofa. "What's wrong?"

"Nothing, I'm just feeling a bit...shy."

"I hope you're not doubting how fucking gorgeous you are, Sky." He runs a finger along the front of my T-shirt, circling around my breast. "I've spent a lot of time the last few days fantasising about your tits."

His sudden, growled honesty arrests me further. "I noticed."

Eyes shining, Dylan puts his hands behind his head. "So…?"

The last time anyone saw me naked in the daylight was around five years ago. Correction – the last time anyone saw me naked in the daylight and was aroused by the sight was five years ago. Grant and I would often get dressed or undressed together, but his reaction was never the same as the one going on inside Dylan's shorts.

The curve and heat of his chest begs my breasts to be squashed against them, the desire to connect skin on skin pushes out the possibility he might not like what he sees. I pull my T-shirt over my head, and let the white, satin bra slip down my arms to the floor.

Dylan's gaze caresses my nakedness, and he cups my breasts again. "You're fucking beautiful," he says as he closes his mouth around my pebbled nipple, and sucks gently.

I swear I'm ready to rip all my clothes off and let him show me the rest of his obvious sexual prowess. Curling my fist into his damp hair, I gasp at the wet heat flooding straight to between my legs. Dylan grips my hips, holding me to him as his mouth continues its attention to my skin.

The ridges of his muscled back are like nothing I've felt before – his skin softer than I imagined. As he switches to my other breast, I dig my nails into his back, convinced I'll fall backwards to the floor if he lets go. Every muscle in my body has lost all strength, my sole focus Dylan. His scent. His touch. His warmth. After three days, this shouldn't feel so natural.

Dylan shifts, twisting and laying me onto the sofa, covering his body with mine. The weight of him smothers me but this is what I want. I think. Crushing his mouth on mine, he runs his hard fingers along my naked leg, to the edge of the fabric of my denim shorts. An embarrassing whimper escapes me as he slides his hand between my legs, the barrier of the material between his fingers and my sex.

"Oh!"

He stops abruptly withdrawing his hand. "What's wrong?"

"No, nothing. It's fine."

Dylan shifts his weight off me, propping himself on one arm. "Sorry. You're right. I don't think we should."

I'm right? When did I indicate I didn't want this? "No, honestly, I'm good…"

Heart hammering against my chest, I extend my hand and place it on his chest, recognising the matching beat. The colourful sleeve of tattoos stops around his shoulder, and I run a finger along the edge.

"No. I said. This isn't good." Dylan moves away completely, face flushed and I stare wide-eyed.

"What's wrong?"

"I said last night." He pulls his T-shirt back over that perfect physique I planned on exploring. "What if this gets spoilt?"

"This? What's this? Two strangers having a holiday romance?"

He blinks. "Yeah, kind of, but this is more, Sky. You're worth more."

"This doesn't have to be more," I say, a sweaty, panting mess in front of him.

He runs fingers through his hair. "I told you what happens when I fuck girls, I don't want to have that with you, I want to…"

Oh, my God. Fucking. Again. "Be friends?" I cross my arms over my naked chest and scrabble around on the floor for my top.

"Yes…no… Fuck, I don't know. The last couple of days with you have been amazing. There're a few more before you need to leave – I don't want to spoil this."

The pink in my face caused by his touch and kisses is replaced with embarrassment from his words. I climb off him, stumbling as I do and pull the top over my head.

"Don't let me down so gently, Dylan. If I'm not the kind of girl you like to *fuck*, fine. Just say."

"Sky, in case you didn't notice, I have a hard-on the size of fucking Florida here, you're sexy as hell. And I wasn't going to *fuck* you. You deserve more."

I need to stop kidding myself. I wanted this. Him. The fantasy.

"It's not as if we'll ever have a relationship, is it? So, we either do this or we don't. I don't think this between us would ever be more than sex, Dylan."

"Maybe."

"Maybe what?"

He huffs and leans back. "Look, sorry I upset you. You have no idea of the self-control it's taking not to drag you upstairs and show you exactly what you do to me."

I scoff. "Show me a good time, you mean? Arrogant much?"

He stiffens. "I don't get complaints usually."

"No, your endless lines of girls are probably grateful that the famous Dylan Morgan lets them into his bed. You know, I think you're probably right." I stand and grab my discarded bra from the floor. "This is a bad idea."

"Sky…" He stands and touches my arm, but I shake him away. "Oh, great; so, even this has fucked things up?"

"Forget it ever happened!" I snap and on my wobbly legs, I stomp upstairs.

In the bedroom, I climb onto the top bunk and curl my knees under my chin. Was I really planning on sex with an almost stranger? Good thing he has more self-control than I have, because awkward would've been an understatement if we'd… I never have sex with people I don't know. Ever. In fact, apart from Grant, I've had sex with two other people. Sexual hedonism doesn't suit me.

Holding my breath, I listen. The house is often noisy – creaks, groans and tapping fill the quiet, as if the place is alive. I don't notice them usually, but when I'm straining to hear Dylan, they magnify.

Footsteps on the stairs halt on the creaking floorboard between the two bedrooms. Panic rises – I don't want to talk to him. A few minutes later, his bedroom door closes and footsteps thunder back downstairs. The front door slams.

We can hide from the reality of our lives, but we can't hide from the reality of who we are. I grab my book from the bottom of the bed, fighting my impulse to google Dylan, because I don't want to know who he is yet.

*****

A few hours of embarrassed sulking later, I stalk downstairs. I've spent a fair bit of the time listening for movement in the house, but since the front door slammed shortly after our encounter, there's been no sound.

Good.

Dylan returns later in the evening and I deliberately don't ask where he's been. Where can he go? He's bedraggled, clothes damp and hair wet beneath his hoodie. The rain stopped a few hours ago and I can only presume he went on a very long walk.

We eye each other warily. If I stare at him any longer, the blushing will start so I turn away, back to my book. Books are useful objects for ignoring people.

"I was going to order pizza if you want something?" he asks.

"I'm fine. Thanks. I ate."

"Okay."

I always have room in my life for pizza, but I don't want to be around him. I'm not Dylan's new toy and each time he kisses then rejects me, the worse I feel. I'm hyperaware of his every move as Dylan gets a drink in the kitchen and makes a phone call to order his meal. Do I leave the room before he comes back and traps me in his orbit again?

"Sky, can I talk to you." Dylan lowers himself in the armchair. He's removed the jacket and rubs his hand along his arm, a sign I'm beginning to notice spells unease.

"No."

He pulls his mouth tight, "No?"

"Correct."

"Right." He hesitates, shifting as if he's about to stand again, then remains seated. "Why?"

"I think we need to take this arrangement back to what it originally was. I'd leave but I haven't got..." I stop. He doesn't need to know I'm basically homeless. "I'll leave in a couple of days, unless *you* want to go now."

"I'm not leaving," he says, tone becoming icy.

"I didn't say you had to. But let's keep out of each other's way?"

Dylan stops the arm rubbing and studies me with tired eyes. "If that's what you want."

"I made a mistake, Dylan. I just came out of a relationship. I'm hurt, and I think that's what caused this...situation. So you playing games with me hasn't helped."

Crap. Didn't I say I wouldn't talk to him? I have to get out of this room before I say anything else.

"I'm not playing games..."

"I'm sorry, Dylan. Please. Let's forget all this. Enjoy your pizza."

Attempting to disguise my trembling hands by tucking them and the book beneath my arms, I do my best at stalking out of the room, and upstairs.

My heart thumps for a long time once I'm cocooned in my bedroom, and away from him, mind and body swirling with contradictions. I'm a confused, hurt girl escaping a broken relationship. I'm not the heroine of some book where a sexy rock star falls for the confused, hurt girl and makes everything better with amazing sex and sweet words of undying love.

Chapter Ten

The next morning, I wash the smell of Dylan from my hair and body and replace it with the familiar scent of my strawberry body wash. I had plans before Dylan interrupted them: find-me-again time in peaceful Cornwall. Today, I'm going to follow my plans. Wrapping a fluffy blue towel around my damp hair and another around my body, I open the bathroom door.

Dylan. He's on the top stair, on his way to his room from downstairs and he freezes. I stop too, caught by his familiar roving look; and tighten the knot on my towel. The world is conspiring against my attempts to resist this man. Dylan grips the handrail with hands that sent shivers across my skin, skin now exposed and heating as I recall the smooth strength of Dylan hidden beneath his T-shirt. His words about how amazing my lips felt on his also leap into my mind as I stare at his mouth. Being this irresistible should be a criminal offence.

"Fuck. Sorry," he mutters.

We're stuck. I need to pass him to get to my room, which faces the top of the stairs, and he needs to pass me to get to his room. And in the small hallway, there's room for little else than the sexually charged space between us. The logical solution? Step back into the bathroom, but I can't move. Water drips down my legs onto the carpeted hallway; and if he doesn't stop the gawking, I'll be a puddle on the floor too.

Dylan climbs the final stair and I step backwards, knocking into the wall. The towel wrapped around my hair falls, revealing wild tangles. I try to grab the towel before it hits the floor. Stupid move, because the action causes the towel around my body to slip, I manage to hook the towel back up before more than the top of my breasts are on show for Dylan.

He squeezes his eyes closed, and I'm convinced he's holding his breath.

"Fuck," he mutters again.

The space between us contracts as Dylan inches past. I attempt to control my telltale breathing difficulty with a cough. He pauses. There's no doubt in my mind he can read exactly what my body wants. The expression in his blue eyes suggests he's one ounce of self-control away from responding.

Dylan doesn't touch me, but his effect on me in this moment is beyond anything Grant could do with a kiss. How's that possible? Dylan engulfs my judgement and if he did kiss me, everything I said last night would evaporate.

Heaving in a breath, Dylan continues by and I tense as his warm, bare arm brushes mine. When he gets to his bedroom door, he rests his head against the wood and expels the breath.

"Sky, please go and get dressed before I do something that will really piss you off." His voice is hoarse, spoken to the white door.

For a split second, I picture myself in a movie, dropping my towel and having a guy crazy for my irresistible body. Then I shake the ridiculous notion from my mind and grapple for the bedroom door handle.

Stepping into my room, I close and rest against the door, heart thumping. I have to get out of this house and away from him; clear my senses of the Dylan Effect.

*****

I drive to a nearby town and wander the tourist shops where I proceed to buy a pile of junk I will never do anything with apart from put in a drawer. Cute pottery figures of dragons, pretty notepads with matching pens, and a snow globe for my collection. When I was six, Gran bought me a snow globe from her visit to Scotland. Half a dozen snow globes later my family decided this unintentional collection was a hobby, and since then snow globes are the gift received from holidaying relatives. This globe has a summer beach scene inside which is plain odd.

I chose this town due to the size of the cream teas at the central cafe. Inside, I sit on a wicker chair at a table covered by a red and white tablecloth and wait for my order. A young girl, with dark hair scraped into a ponytail, brings me a metal pot of tea and a huge scone accompanied by small pots of jam and cream.

Tucking into my scone, I gaze around the small cafe. Tables are crammed together and most of the customers are older than me, and couples. Licking cream from my fingers, I have a pang of loneliness. Last time I came here was with Grant, and he frowned at me for using all the cream on my scone. I picture him - brown hair touching his ears and the sparkling green eyes that drew me to him all those years ago. But I don't miss Grant; the knot in my stomach is because of Dylan. If Dylan were with me, we'd chat and laugh. He'd tease me and I'd retort until we reached stalemate. Then he'd kiss me.

Whoever this man is, I'm caught in a gravitational pull to him I've never had before. As if a part of me and part of him knew each other before and are reconnecting. Which is bullshit, according to my non-romantic brain, but perfectly logical to characters in the books I read.

Dylan stays in my thoughts as I drive back to Broadbeach as I wonder what he's spent the day doing, and feeling sad that he's basically stuck where he is. How can he be so famous, people around here would recognise him? He's being too cautious, it's not as if he's royalty.

A trip back to Asda on the way home is required (Sorry again, Mrs Hughes). This time, I buy a sensible mix of all food groups, although some are better represented than others (crisps equals vegetables, right?). I'm happy with the fact I have ingredients to make actual meals, rather than pre-packed rubbish, although, those curries in the refrigerated section do look good...

Curries. Dylan. I should've left the night I dropped the curry on the floor. That was a sign, right? A waste of good curry, but I think, even then, something imperceptible linked us. So who am I kidding? I couldn't leave then, I couldn't go yesterday, and I'm returning to Dylan now.

The magazine section taunts me. I could casually flick through a couple of the magazines I never touch, to see if I can find Dylan's name or face. Or if he's famous enough, he may even be on the cover with a lurid headline - or a lurid woman.

I ignore the magazines, pay, and leave.

As I lug carrier bags from my car to the house in the drizzling rain, I mutter under my breath about the lack of Dylan who could help. When I get inside, the sound of water running in the bathroom upstairs flashes images of a naked Dylan across my vision. I dump the bags on the table and return to the cold drizzle.

The cupboards in the kitchen are narrow and full of plates, so there's little room for my purchases. I squat on the floor attempting to fit rice and pasta into the cupboard and don't notice Dylan come into the room.

"I'll help you unpack," he says.

In response, I bang my head on the cupboard I'm leaning inside, and shoot him a look while rubbing my head. "Thanks."

He's wearing a remorseful expression, but no shirt and his hair is damp. Exactly like the first time I saw him in the house. But without my knickers in his hands.

"Sorry about earlier," he says, "you have a weird effect on me."

I ignore the comment. "Is the semi-nakedness to try and distract me?"

He smirks. "Possibly."

I make a 'humph' noise and return to my unpacking.

Dylan pulls items from one of the bags and inspects them. "I should give you some money. I'm eating your stuff."

"Maybe go and buy your own then!" He makes no response. I straighten and take a jar of sauce from the table.

"I can't. Can I?" he asks.

"You can't hide forever."

The old, tired look reappears and he runs his tongue along his teeth. "I know."

Obviously, he's not elaborating or leaving to go shopping soon, so I carry on, ignoring the shaking hands and queasy feeling in my stomach.

"So I take it from all this food that you're staying then?" he asks.

"Of course, why would I go?"

"Because you said you're uncomfortable with...this."

"There's room here for both of us. You can pay me for food if you want." Sod the healthy food. I need biscuits. I tear open a packet of chocolate digestives with my teeth.

A small smirk appears on Dylan's face. "Sky..."

"What?"

"You, you're so natural and wonderful and downright fucking funny."

"Don't start the games again!" I shove a biscuit into my mouth and flick the switch on the kettle.

Grinning, he grabs a biscuit and imitates me.

"Not used to girls who eat?" I snap. "Prefer the skinny ones who starve themselves?"

"This is about yesterday still? I don't prefer skinny girls." He places a hand over mine.

I want to pull my fingers away, but his touch and his closeness is annoyingly soothing.

"Please don't," I say quietly.

"Hmm." Dylan rubs a biscuit crumb from the corner of my mouth and I tense. "Okay, I'll cook something, to say thank you for sharing with me."

"No, it's okay..."

"Do you think I can't cook?"

"I think you don't cook much, Mr Rock God."

Dylan steps back, face darkening. "Don't take the piss."

"Don't behave like one!"

"You're very feisty tonight."

"Some guy pissed me off."

"Then he needs to make things up to you."

I wipe my hands on my shorts. "Okay, cook. I'm cold and I'm getting changed."

After extricating myself from the presence of the man who I resolved was not going to affect me again, I stomp upstairs. I'm annoyed with myself for still wanting his hands and mouth on mine. And for still wanting to know what sex with Dylan would be like. Talk about mood swings, I don't think I know what I want anymore.

Chapter Eleven

Sexual tension. This is what I'm walking into when I go downstairs, and I'm not used to tension. I stare at my reflection as I pull fingers through my damp hair. Brushing would send the blonde waves into a frizz. Grant said girls should wear make-up if they wanted to look pretty and freckles are ugly so I should cover them up. I've not worn a scrap of make-up since I left him.

What does Dylan think when he looks at me?

What does his opinion matter? From now on, I'm me and the world can get knotted if they don't like the Sky I am.

I rummage through the clothes stuffed into my rucksack, and pull out the least creased T-shirt I can find. It's dark blue with a Disney character on the front, my slouching, beach holiday clothes. I groan, but the other items are summer dresses and I feel...exposed in those. The underwear I have to choose from isn't much better. Not all as bad as the pair Dylan had hooked on his fingers the first night, but no matching set. The realisation I'm debating what underwear to put on for eating dinner with Dylan is a shock. He doesn't want sex anyway. Pulling on my denim shorts, I head towards the fragrant smell downstairs.

Disappointingly, Dylan has managed to find himself a T-shirt with a different band picture on the same faded black cotton.

"Is *this* one you?" I ask pointing to the symbol.

"I knew you were going to ask that. No."

I shrug. "What are you cooking?"

Steam rises from the sizzling and spitting pan behind and he turns to stir.

"Stir-fry chicken with some sauce you bought." He holds up the jar. "And noodles." He points to the boiling water in the pan next to it.

"Very impressive."

"Reserve judgement until you've eaten."

"I'll read my book while you finish then," I say, walking away.

"Aren't you going to help? Get plates or something?" he calls after me.

"Nope!" I grin. Maybe I'll help wash up.

The billionaire and his PA are getting hot and heavy in the elevator when Dylan interrupts my reading.

"Put down your smut, and come and eat." He leans over the sofa behind me, his spicy Dylan scent connecting with the words on the page. I'm reading about sex when attempting not to think about it? Smart move... I should've put the book down as soon as the story got as steamy as the boiling noodles.

I snap the book closed. "This isn't smut! If it was smut, there'd be no plot."

He arches an eyebrow; I doubt there's any point discussing my choice in reading material with him.

The small dining table contains two mismatched plates filled with noodles, vegetables and chicken. I sit and inhale the mouth-watering smell rising from the plate.

"Not bad," I say.

"I knew you'd want wine..." He pours a glass.

"Are you having one?" I ask as he pours a second. "I thought you were dry."

Dylan shrugs. "One glass, I can control myself."

The connotation of his words doesn't go unnoticed, so I pick my fork up, and push it into the middle of the mound of food.

"Noodles," I remark, twirling some around my fork.

"Perceptive."

"A tip for you - don't cook a girl something she could spill all over herself on a first date."

"Date?"

I cringe. "I mean, in the future, when you date."

He scoffs. "I don't date."

I bite the noodles so I can't comment.

"I'd date you though," he says quietly.

My stomach shrinks at his comment. Great, I was looking forward to the noodles. Ignoring him, I stab at a piece of chicken.

"Sky?"

"How exactly would you date me, Dylan? When you can't go anywhere in case every teenage girl in the world descends on you?"

"After this."

I place the fork on the table, heart turning rapid fire. "After what?"

"When we go...back, I want to see you again."

"You're delusional." However, his eyes tell a different story. "Are you *serious*?"

"Yes."

"You don't know me."

"Isn't that the idea of dates, to get to know someone?"

The noodles stick as my mouth dries. "I don't think..."

Dylan reaches across the table and touches my hand. "Come on, people do this all the time. They meet, like each other and start dating. I want to try doing that with you."

"I don't think dating is something that would happen between the real Sky and Dylan, do you?"

"Why?"

"Who are you really Dylan Morgan? From what you've hinted, you don't even live in the same country as me, or the same world." I pause. "We're living in an illusion. Where you're Dylan, I'm Sky and the rest of the world doesn't exist. As soon as we step outside of the fantasy, we won't exist anymore."

I wait for an answer as he stares at his plate, but he ignores my question. "I'll take that as no?"

I don't reply.

His face tightens, and I again get the feeling people don't say no to him often. Silently, Dylan continues his meal, the tension between us thick. I gulp down wine and refill my glass. I want Dylan to *want* me, but yesterday he didn't. He's confusing the hell out of me.

"Okay," he says eventually. "Let's talk about something else. Can we carry on with this...arrangement? Will you get to know your Dylan a bit more?"

"My Dylan?"

"The Dylan only you know." The intensity in his eyes pulls at my resolve.

"Who's he?"

"Not the person I left in London three days ago. The guy you're reconnecting me with; giving life to."

"I think you're doing that yourself."

"With the help of a smart-mouthed girl who doesn't take any shit from me, yeah, I am." His eyes shine.

I can't help but smile. "Okay, I can carry on smart-mouthing you for another few days if you love it that much."

"I do," he says quietly and carries on eating.

We clear the plates, returning to the relaxed banter of earlier, ignoring talk of the real world again.

"About yesterday," says Dylan as I empty my third glass of wine.

Oh, nicely played, he starts on me when I'm more 'relaxed'. "Yesterday doesn't matter. Forget it."

"Yesterday matters to me, because I upset you. Can I explain?"

I shrug and top up my glass.

"I'm selfish, spoilt and always get what I want."

"Nice line in self-deprecation, Dylan."

"Can you listen for once, instead of playing word games with me?"

I make a zipping motion across my lips and he gives a tiny shake of his head. "I wanted to prove to myself that I could be different to the selfish, spoilt guy I am; the one who takes what he wants and doesn't give a fuck about someone else's feelings. That's why I stopped."

He pauses and after a few moments I realise he's waiting for a response.

"Oh. Okay. Well, how about I'm not the normal kind of girl you meet and I'd tell you to stop? Or are you telling me you couldn't stop yourself?"

Dylan grips his wine glass, a muscle twitching in his cheek. "No," he says darkly. "Never."

"This is funny; you're talking as if you want to protect my honour or something. I'm not a virgin, I'm perfectly aware of what I'm doing and what I want."

I blush at his slow smile. "What you want?"

"I didn't mean..." But the shallow breathing has started again.

Reaching a hand across the table, Dylan rubs his thumb across the back, shooting familiar sensations up my arm. "You do weird things to me, and I want to get to know you to figure out why."

I run my finger around the rim of the glass, defences pierced so soon. "Fine, take me on a date then."

The grin that lights up Dylan's face and my world appears. "Awesome, thank you."

I slip my hand from under his and return to my meal.

Several more glasses of wine later, I pay a visit to the bathroom and come downstairs to the humorous sight of the rock god and the washing up.

"I said I'd do that. You cooked."

The sink is practically overflowing and the soapsuds spilling out. Several of Dylan's rings rest next to the sink. His arms are covered in soapsuds up to his elbows, his face a mix of confusion and amusement. "I think I put too much soap in?" I giggle at him and he frowns. "So I don't wash up often. I have a dishwasher."

"I bet you don't load the plates."

"Sometimes."

I raise an 'I doubt it' eyebrow.

"Okay, no."

The childish Dylan glint enters his eyes, one I'm becoming all too familiar with.

"Twenty-four years old and you don't know how to wash-up? You'll never make anyone a good wife," I tell him.

Scooping up a handful of bubbles, he wipes them down my face. "You'll have to teach me."

"Hey!" I wipe them off and scoop a handful of my own.

"Don't you dare!" Dylan steps back, fighting a smile.

Grinning back, I wipe the bubbles down his freshly shaved face. Dylan growls and grabs my wrist dragging me to his chest. Holding both wrists with one hand, he scoops a handful and rubs them into my hair. Shrieking, I wriggle from his grip, ducking away from him. Before I can move two steps, he grabs me from behind, powerful arms holding my waist. I lean away from him, dragging at his fingers.

"Keep still!"

"No more bubbles! Sorry!" I gasp.

I'm not sorry he wants to touch me again. Definitely not sorry to be held against his hard, muscled torso, and have his hands touching my skin where my T-shirt has ridden up.

Dylan pushes me towards the sink. We're both facing the bubbled water but I can't reach them because my arms are trapped. I tense, waiting for the soaking.

"No, please!" I'm gasping with laughter, giving the wrong impression.

"What if I don't want to let you go?" he whispers, and then nips my earlobe. Dylan releases my waist and runs both hands beneath my T-shirt, palms across my stomach. "What if I want to apologise for before?"

I can't move, his hips pinning me to the kitchen bench. "I don't know..."

He kisses my neck, running his tongue along my shoulder before nipping my collarbone. I hitch a breath as he pulls my hips towards him, his arousal against my back surprising me.

"Oh..."

Dylan turns me around and pushes aside the items left on the kitchen bench. "I stopped because the selfish, spoilt Dylan wanted you." He holds me around the waist and lifts me onto the bench. "But if I make this about you instead, that's not selfish, right?"

"Oh..." *Jeez,* where's my power of speech gone?

"Can I kiss you again?"

"I think you're right; you do need to find a new way to relate to women," I say breathlessly.

Pressing himself between my legs, hard muscled thigh against mine, Dylan pulls my hair into a ponytail and wraps it around his hand. "Currently, this is the only way I know how." Placing his mouth softly on mine, he runs his tongue lightly across my lips, setting a soft buzz across my face.

"Okay, the meal and chat was a good start, maybe next we can…" I begin, clinging to rational thought.

"Tell me what you like," he interrupts, resting his forehead on mine.

Dylan's sudden change of pace disarms me; two minutes ago we were playing like kids. Now we're back to adult territory. With a capital A. I wrap my arms around his neck, tracing the short hair at the nape. His eyes darken, reflecting my desire and rewinding us back to the 'snuggling'.

"Dylan, I am stupidly and incredibly attracted to you to the point of needing an asthma inhaler when you're close but..."

"But I put you off with talk of fucking. How about we don't fuck? There're plenty of other things we could do..." The suggestion in his low tone reconnects the physical us. "All I can think about is you; I'm obsessed by your mouth." I allow Dylan to place his lips on mine, a tentative touch as he waits for my response. I answer him with a mouth-mashing kiss, parting my lips, allowing his tongue to play with mine. The want from yesterday courses through my veins with the alcohol, and as soon as I taste him, I want more. I want all of him. We kiss fiercely, gripping hair, biting lips, giving in to everything we're hiding.

Maybe he's using clever words as a way to get into the not-small-enough knickers I'm wearing, but I don't care. Who am I kidding saying I don't want him?

I make a soft noise of disappointment as he pulls away. "So? Tell me. What do you want me to do?" he asks.

"Kiss me again."

"Is that all?"

I grab his head and pull him to me, losing myself in the taste and scent of him, his skilful kisses unravelling me further. He pulls away and slides his mouth down my neck, licking and sucking until I wriggle against the sensation.

Dylan slowly slides a hand beneath my shirt, and I arch towards him so his palm reaches my breast. Through the satin fabric, he rubs a nipple with his thumb, placing his other hand next to me as he leans in, tracing more kisses along my neck. He's hard beneath his jeans, and his comment about erections and Florida makes sudden sense.

"Anything else?" he asks, breathing shallow. The fact I'm affecting his breathing too is a huge turn on. *Me*. I do this to him. He continues his attention to my breast, teasing my nipple with his fingers. "Tell me what else."

Alcohol paving the road ahead, I wave goodbye to modesty and drag my top over my head. I unhook my bra, pushing the straps from my arms and fix Dylan with a challenging expression. He pulls off his T-shirt and adds it to the growing pile of clothes on the floor. I place a hand on the smooth muscles, dragging my fingernails down to the curve of his abs.

Dylan moistens his lips as his gaze moves to my breasts, tracing a finger from my neck towards my breasts before cupping one with his long fingers. "You are so fucking gorgeous."

His mouth closes around my nipple, sensation jolting to my core as he sucks. I press myself against his thigh, shamelessly rubbing against him and he pushes his hand underneath my backside, squeezing me closer. Dylan spends the next few delirious minutes exploring every inch of my exposed skin with his tongue and lips. The warmth from his mouth evaporates when he shifts his attentions, cooling my hot skin as he licks and sucks at my nipples. I groan and lock my legs around Dylan's hips, attempting to hold him as close as I can.

I'm a shaking, panting mess when he lifts his head, and I wriggle towards him, not wanting him to stop. Dylan puts his palms on my back and squashes my breasts against his chest. A gasp escapes as my hardened nipples touch his smooth, warm skin; a connection that's only the start of what my body wants from him. We collide mouths again, his heart hammering against mine in unison. Holding each other's heads, as if not wanting to let go, we kiss fiercely as if this is the end when it's only the beginning.

Now, he's unbuttoning my shorts.

I freeze and Dylan stops. "I want to touch you," he says, pulling on the zip. "Is that okay?"

Ohmygod, is this ever okay? This is okay. Yes? Stop thinking. "Please…"

Dylan slips a finger in the front of my shorts, struggling to reach me through the tight denim. Watching for my reaction with darkened blue eyes, he tugs at the shorts and I move to allow him to remove them. My hands go to the button of his jeans and he shifts.

"No. Just you," he says. "Mine are staying on."

My underwear pulls down with the shorts and they hit the floor. He slowly runs his hand up my inner thigh, and I moan anticipating his fingers reaching my sex. As Dylan reaches my wet heat, he sucks air between his teeth before closing his mouth over mine again. I groan as he pushes a finger inside, teasing my clit with his thumb as he moves his hand. Waves of pleasure pulse into every nerve ending; and I dig my fingers into the sinews of his back, holding on so I don't collapse. I close my eyes, focused purely on the sensation, unable to believe this is happening to me.

"You're so fucking wet," he growls against my mouth.

I struggle against the gathering bliss, not wanting this to end, moving my hips to match the movement of his fingers. "What are you doing to me?"

Dylan nips at my neck and ear lobe, short, heavy breaths in my ear. "Whatever you want me to do. Or do you want me to stop?" There's a teasing tone to his voice; this isn't about asking permission.

This is torture. I fumble with the button to his jeans but he swats my hand away. "No, I said you."

"But I want..." His mouth crushes mine again, the rhythm of his fingers inside me crashing through my body. I'm on the brink of losing control when he stops and steps back.

I want to protest, but instead a whimper escapes my throat. Dylan licks his fingers, hooded eyes on mine. "I want to taste you," he murmurs.

Oh, holy crap.

Dylan doesn't wait for a response. He kneels on the floor in front of me, the warmth of his breath against my sex, and pulls my legs towards him, setting them on his shoulders. The shaking intensifies as he presses his mouth to me, tongue gliding along my wetness and teasing the sensitive bud. I grip the edge of the kitchen bench and stifle a cry.

"Fuck, you're wet and hot and *fuck...*" The vibration of his voice against me intensifies the engulfing sensation.

"Oh, God!" I cry out as he slides a finger inside, continuing to explore me with his hot mouth.

Then Dylan demonstrates what an expert he is at this, and I suspect his shift in direction isn't only for me. Licking, sucking, thrusting with his fingers, he brings me to the brink over and over. Then each time he stops, prolonging things to the point I'm ready to scream at him.

When the blinding orgasm hits, and the stars dance in front of my eyes, he drags me to the floor, across his lap and holds me until I return from his galaxy to the world. Dylan buries his face in my neck, and strokes my hair swearing repeatedly under his breath. The thud of his heart against mine, and lust in his hooded eyes when our eyes meet again has me grasping at his jean's button for a third time.

"No," he says breathlessly, "Just no."

I run a finger below his hair where strands stick to his face. "Please, Dylan, you said what I wanted?"

He smiles. "Nice try."

"You're being unfair," I pant.

"I know, and to myself." Dylan squeezes his eyes closed, shifting beneath me. "Fuck, this is hard."

I nudge my nose against his ear. "I'm aware of how hard. You could..."

Drawing a ragged breath, Dylan places his forehead on mine. "No. Fuck, Sky, I want to so fucking much but no." His arms tighten around my waist, fingers tickling the sensitive spot at the base of my spine, "How about some more snuggling?"

"Snuggling...?" I can barely hide the disappointment in my voice.

Dylan stands, still holding me around the waist and I wrap my legs around his. The sensation of his erection beneath the rough denim against my sensitive sex as he walks upstairs sends new shockwaves through my body. I want *him*, not snuggling.

In his bedroom, Dylan pushes back the covers and sits, the pair of us falling into bed. Hope flares he might have changed his mind, but he pulls me to his chest, wrapping me in his arms. Dylan's heart thumps against my naked breasts, rapid heartbeat gradually slowing as he strokes my hair. He soothes me as easily as he sent me crazy and I fight the urge to push him to finish what we've started. I think he's as aware as I am what will happen if we start kissing again, and here because all he does is hold me.

A silent understanding holds us in the moment, the weird link to the man I hardly know fusing me to him. The moon shines through the open curtains, casting a blue glow across the room. I turn onto my side and snuggle into him.

Dylan squeezes me tight and kisses my neck. "I haven't slept with someone else for years." He whispers, "Don't leave my bed tonight."

"I don't want to." I kiss the arm wound around my chest.

As I drift to sleep, he rubs his nose against my cheek. "I love the world we're in, where you'll always be my summer Sky. I could live here forever."

Chapter Twelve

The sun streams through the room, the brightness waking me. I squint at the seashell curtains, delving my sleepy mind for where I am. Beach house. Bed. With... *Ohmygod*, Dylan lies with his arms wrapped around my waist in a tight grip, as if I might disappear if he lets go.

I loosen his hand, and shift away. I'm naked and he's slept in his jeans, which can't be comfortable for him and makes me uncomfortable. I want to cover up; however great he made me feel last night, being naked in the bright summer's day is odd. Searching the room, I spot one of his black T-shirts near the edge of the bed. Bending, I reach for it and pull it over my head. Dylan's scent covers my skin, the way he covered my body last night. Did that really happen? I know I was drunk, but what he did sent me spiralling higher. A familiar tingling and tightening takes hold at the memory of his mouth, hands, tongue... and the thought of what he denied me.

I sneak to the bathroom.

When I return, Dylan is awake. I tense, okay so we didn't have full sex but came pretty, damn, close. What now? Dylan runs his tongue along his lower lip as he regards me with the old look from last night.

"You look sexy as fuck in my clothes," he says, "especially the way that T-shirt doesn't quite cover your ass far enough."

The intensity of his gaze fires pink into my cheeks and I tug on the material.

Dylan frowns. "What's wrong?"

I hesitate, not sure if he wants me here or gone. "I'm practically naked and you've still got your jeans on."

He looks down at himself. "Yeah, that was needed. It's pretty hard to control myself around you."

I tip my head and give him a doubtful look. Propping himself on one elbow, shoulder muscles tensing, he frowns back. "Don't you believe me?" Unsure how to respond, I perch on the bed. Dylan shuffles towards me, and places a hand on my thigh. "Sky?"

I rub my lips together, taking in the sight of his impossibly toned chest and shoulders. And the biceps - the ones I wanted to lick in the first day. Still do. Licking... I colour again.

"Come back to bed," he says. "I want to snuggle more."

I fix his darkening eyes with mine. "Snuggle?"

Dylan sits and pushes my hair behind my ears, before kissing my forehead. "Snuggling, waking in bed with someone and not..."

"Fucking them and leaving?"

He pulls a face. "Don't start that, Sky... Never with you; I told you that the first night I kissed you."

"We didn't get that far anyway, so I'll believe you after we do...that."

Dylan strokes my cheek. "After we do?"

"If we do, I mean." His ability to match me in clever comebacks is annoying.

"So you're not sure you want to? That's cool…," he says.

I take his right arm and study the mash up of tattoos, eager for a subject change. "Do any of these mean anything?"

From his wrist to his shoulder, yellow stars and a swirling black pattern meld with bright flames. A blue bird covers most of the skin on his arm, tail feathers stretching towards his wrist. The head of the bird pushes through blue fire, colour exploding to the edge of Dylan's shoulder. I run my finger along the picture.

He gives a short laugh. "That one's fairly significant, yeah."

I follow the outline with my finger. "You're an ornithologist?"

He meets my smirk with a shake of the head. "No, Sky. It's not a bird."

"Isn't it an eagle?"

"There're flames?"

"Roast eagle?"

Dylan clamps his hands either side of my face and kisses me hard on the top of my head.

"Oh, fuck, you're the funniest, most genuine chick I've met. Ever. I like you so fucking much."

"So you *are* an ornithologist." I pull my head away and meet his confused eyes, "If you like chicks."

"So sharp, I'm going to cut myself on you one day." He nips my shoulder.

"What is it then, your tattoo?"

"A phoenix."

"Oh, nice; I mean, it's a good picture."

"You thought the tattoo was an eagle though, so the picture can't be that good."

What is with the barely contained amusement on his face?

"Big tattoos aren't that nice." I pull a face.

"So you don't want to inspect the rest of my tattoos?"

"No thanks."

"Come back to bed then, summer Sky who hates tattoos."

"Take your jeans off," I say boldly.

A sharp sound of air sucked through Dylan's teeth is the response I get. "You're telling me what to do?"

"Might be."

"Hmm." Dylan lies on his back, and stretches his arms over his head then twists his head to mine. "Do you want to leave this room today?"

His words are a challenge. I have one too. "Yes, because you're taking me on a date."

The laugh bubbling from his chest prompts a smile of my own and he rubs his large palm across his face. "I'd better get a shower then..."

I relax.

"In a minute..." Before I have a chance to react, Dylan lunges at me; then he pulls me backwards onto him, burying his face into my hair. "You're naked...," he whispers.

"Apart from your T-shirt."

"That can be fixed."

Following a small struggle (and not much resistance on my part), Dylan pulls his T-shirt over my head. Then before I have a chance to protest, his mouth is back on my breasts and hand sliding along my backside.

*****

Something changed. We move from uneasy edging around the unspoken truth about the lust we share for each other to a comfort in each other's skin.

But he still hasn't taken his jeans off and by now I'm embarrassing myself with the obsessive need to see him without jeans. Touch and feel... I blink. No.

There was a suggestion he might follow me into the shower, but following a lot of grumbling at himself, Dylan declined. As I washed myself, and brushed the extra sensitivity lingering from our night and morning together, I fought the desire to go back and drag him in with me.

As I dress, I hear his shower running and if I had more brazen hussy and less cautious girl inside, I might have snuck in.

Instead, I tramp downstairs and pour cornflakes.

The Dylan who appears downstairs, freshly shaven and smelling of spices from his shower, is a man I could spend all day in bed with. This is a relaxed, happy and open guy. The tiredness in his features has ebbed, and this morning it's as if the worry has flowed away completely. The loosened shoulders and bright face take some of the age away from Dylan.

He crosses the room and slides long fingers beneath my chin, kissing me softly. "Mmm. Cornflakes, I'll have some."

I push the packet towards him, spooning another mouthful because I'm lost at what to say.

He takes the box in his ringed fingers, and the everyday sound of cereal hitting the bowl enters the not-so-everyday world we've pulled ourselves further into.

"So you want me take you out somewhere?" he asks.

I choke on my cereal. "I was joking about the date. I thought you were in hiding."

"I'm going to prove to you I want to date you. We need to go in your car though, if it's still drivable?"

"You mean since that arrogant dickhead ploughed into the back? I drove off remember?"

The one remaining cloud clears from his face. "Yeah. Why did you drive off?"

"I thought you had a gun."
Dylan snorts. "Really?"
"Really. Now where are we going?"

Chapter Thirteen

We climb into my car, Dylan looking completely out of place scrunched up on my tattered passenger seat. He pokes around in the footwell with his toe.

"You have a lot of books here."

"I always forget to take them out of the car."

"I can't remember the last time I read a book. I should." He picks one up and stares at the man on the cover whose physique matches his, "Maybe not one of these."

"No, these are probably not your thing."

He flicks the pages, thankfully not opening to read one. "Or are there some tips for me in here?"

Last night... "I doubt you need sex tips."

His eyes widen. "Oh! So they are porn?"

"No!" *Much.*

"I meant tips on how men should behave," he teases. "I could learn how to treat you nicely?"

The contradiction in this situation is the guys like him in my books are more on the 'bad' end of the scale - and that's what I like about them. But no way am I telling Dylan this fact.

"So where are you taking me?" he asks.

"Where do you want to go?"

Dylan pauses and taps the dashboard. "Somewhere I wouldn't usually go."

"And away from the general public I suppose?"

"Yeah and that too." He taps the dashboards. "Where did you go yesterday?"

"Only as far as the next town - Sandchurch, wandered around the shops, ate scones..."

"We can go there?"

"I'm still not asking who you are, but do you think you're safe to go there? You seem a bit paranoid about being spotted."

Dylan runs his tongue along his teeth. "Was the town busy yesterday?"

"Not really - mostly a few older couples, and most of those were in the cafes."

Dylan wriggles his nose like a kid. "What do you reckon? I'm bored of the beach now. Plus I want to explore some more of you." He puts his hand over his mouth. "Sorry, I mean explore more *with* you - other places from the past."

I ignore my body's reaction to his teasing. "Okay..." I turn the key in the ignition. "But are you sure?"

"I brought this." Dylan holds up a baseball cap. Grinning, he shoves it onto his head and pulls the peak down. "No hair and a hat, I'll be harder to recognise."

I point at his arm and say, "Tattoos?"

"Good point, I'll get my hoodie." His tall figure slips out of the car, emptying the space of the presence I don't want to admit gives me goose bumps on my arms - and makes me wish he hadn't stopped last night.

*****

We park the car beneath an oak tree, at the edge of the car park furthest from town. Dylan walks besides me, hunched downward with his cap pulled down. After a few steps, he slides his hand into mine, the gesture arresting me. He flashes me a smile and I roll my eyes at him.

"We're on a date; I get to hold your hand."

My chest tightens at his words. Date. With Dylan Morgan the Mysterious?

Dylan isn't content with handholding. He slides his fingers along my arm, or hugs me close, breathes the scent of my hair, as if he needs to be in constant contact with me. As we enter the town, Dylan tenses, his hand gripping mine harder. Few people walk the paved streets, and fewer cars pass. Older couples weave in and out of the small shops, or sit on plastic chairs outside cafes in the quiet, narrow streets. As we continue, his shoulders relax, although his focus remains on the floor.

"What should we do?" he whispers.

I smirk at him. "I like shopping…"

Dylan wrinkles his nose. "Okay, then." He follows me as I tug his hand and walk through the quite, cobbled streets.

Crammed in an antique shop, Dylan wraps his arms around my waist with his chin on my shoulder. The tiny shop has shelves running to the back of the building on each wall, and one running centrally. If there were more than three people in this shop at once, there'd be a fire risk. With Dylan, we take up the whole width of one side.

"What are you looking for?" he asks, as I flick through a cardboard box of paperback books, hoping to find a treasure amongst the dog-eared collection.

"Is that a philosophical question?" I ask.

He jabs a finger into the sensitive spot at the side of my waist. "Snarky... I only asked a question."

The sensation of Dylan's body against mine prevents my ability to exist in the real world. The weirdest thing is that this is completely natural. I can't explain to myself how being in the presence of a man who I hardly know (but have been a little *too* intimate with) soothes me. His hips resting against mine; the way our bodies fit together - how is this more natural than Grant?

"I like odd things," I reply.

"Odd things?"

I give up on the books and head further into the shop, Dylan still attached. "Yes. Why else would I like you?"

"I can think of a few reasons," he says in a low tone.

I'm glad I'm facing away from him, because the annoying heat fills my face again and travels back *down*. Just a few words and he turns me on...

On the pine shelves in front is a bizarre assortment of items, like a crazy person's mantelpiece. Jammed into every inch of space are colourful glass bottles, old teacups, badly painted pottery animals, spoons; hand drawn labels with prices on dangle off some items. I pick up a strangely misshapen vase, the orange glass not fused properly at the top.

"Shit, that's ugly," remarks Dylan.

I giggle. "I like it."

"Seriously?"

Setting the vase back down, I head towards the back of the shop. Dylan releases his grip on my waist but instantly slides his hand into mine. I pull it away.

"I'm not going anywhere, Dylan. I can't move for one thing. And I need both hands for inspecting ugly vases."

Dylan pushes my hair to one side and kisses my neck. "I like touching you and being around you."

The intense blue eyes meet mine, and I wait for a teasing comment about our antics last night and this morning. He doesn't say anything, a relaxed happiness shines at me instead.

Pushing the arousing images from my mind, I nod. "I kind of like being around you."

I get another poke in the waist as he says, "Gee, thanks. *Kind of...*"

I bite the corner of my lip and Dylan's look drops to my mouth. *Oh, God, please don't try making out with me in an antique shop.* The confined space holds the same charge between us as yesterday outside the bathroom. Some of the 'what if?' sexual tension from then has gone, replaced by 'we could do that again and more' tension that hovers between us with every brief kiss and touch today.

I inspect my hands, closing down my senses as much as possible, but when the man who did wickedly wonderful things to my body last night is so close that's difficult. Dylan's sandalwood scent and the warmth of his body, so close to mine, fog the world, and if I meet his eyes and see desire too I'll have no choice. I'll have to kiss him.

"Oh, hey, look at this! Did you ever have one of these?" Dylan reaches over my head, not helping my attempts to disengage my senses. "Look."

In the palm of his hand, Dylan holds a figure made from seashells set on a small wooden plinth. 'Made from' is a loose definition; several shells are glued together and googly eyes attached to create a barely human-looking statue about fifteen centimetres tall.

"Oh, my god, that is awful," I whisper, "What the hell is it?"

Dylan inspects the monstrosity. "I think it's supposed to be a souvenir gift for a lucky friend or family member. Did you ever have one?"

"If I did, I think I'd remember."

"I've got one at home somewhere." He catches my confused expression. "I like odd things too." I roll my eyes at him, and then he bends towards me, his mouth uncomfortably close to mine. "Although that's not the only reason I like you, Sky."

Sucking in a breath, I edge around him back to the front of the shop before I lose sight of the world.

Dylan follows, slipping his hand back into mine, still carrying the godawful shell figure.

*****

The slatted wooden bench we sit on overlooks the rugged landscape below, the sea bluer beneath the summer sky. The fluffy, white clouds burn away as the day progresses, and we choose to sit beneath a tree for shade from the strong sun. Dylan unzips the blue hoodie, huffing at the heat.

"Maybe you should take the jacket off?" I suggest.

He shifts his baseball hat forward, pulling the peak lower. "I don't know..."

"I think people will stare at you more for wearing a jacket on a hot summer's day."

"Maybe." Dylan holds my hand, stroking my arm with his other hand. I'm unused to someone being so touchy-feely, and normally I'd be irritated after several hours of this but I crave to be in contact with him too.

An older couple passes by holding hands. They're a similar age to my parents, although mine would never hold hands since they divorced a couple of years ago. The woman wears knee-length beige shorts and a loose brown T-shirt, greying hair is stylishly cut into a bob, her body touching the man as they walk in a natural, years' old rhythm. The carrier bag he's holding suggests they've been buying junk at souvenir shops, like Dylan's shell monster.

"Most people here are that age," I say, indicating the couple. "Not your audience, I suspect."

Dylan watches them silently for a few moments. "I hope one day that's me," he says eventually.

"A balding man at the seaside carrying his wife's bag?"

"Yeah, living in a house by the sea with my dribbling wife asleep on the sofa," he says and laughs, placing his other hand over mine, trapping my fingers between his warm palm.

His words arrest me as I remember my night asleep on the sofa the day we met. Is there something behind them? I side glance at him and he's staring at the ground, arms resting on his knees. "I'm sure you have the money to do what you want when you get old?"

"I have the money to do what I want now, but I can't do what I want."

"That's an odd thing to say."

He laughs softly. "I'm odd remember?"

I rest my head on Dylan's shoulder and he wraps an arm around me. After a few minutes Dylan shifts. "Okay, you're right, I'm too fucking hot."

I chomp hard on my lip against making a comment about how 'fucking hot' I think he is as he removes his jacket. The tattooed arms stand out against the muted greys of the seaside town and I lean across and kiss his bicep.

Dylan raises an eyebrow. "I thought you didn't like tattoos."

"I don't, but I like your arms." I raise an eyebrow in return.

He wraps the muscled arms around and pulls me close. "Sky?"

"What?"

"I'm the happiest I've been forever," he says, and rubs his nose into my hair.

"I think you're exaggerating, Sandchurch isn't that exciting."

"Here, with you, is the happiest I've ever been."

A seagull nearby pokes around at a discarded wrapper, and the sound of the breaking waves on the beach below fill me with the happiness of past summers here.

"Because we're caught in our childhood memories?" I ask him, turning my head to meet his eyes.

"No, because I'm here with you. I've never wanted to be around someone as much as I crave to be around you. Weird, huh?"

"Odd." I know what he means, but surely he knows this is an illusion too.

"Odd…" He captures my face in his hands, soft mouth on mine. We lose ourselves in a magical kiss to match the spellbinding world we're living in, a kiss and a place I want to go on forever.

I don't know who Dylan Morgan is, but my heart hurts at the thought of how this will end. Famous or not, I'm leaving this man behind in a couple of days and trailing back to Bristol.

I crave Dylan too, but I can't tell him. We enmesh more as each hour passes and I'm dreading the pain when our lives are pulled apart again.

Chapter Fourteen

We head home to Broadbeach, and I tell Dylan I need to stop at the supermarket and pick up some snacks. He looks at me as if I'm speaking a foreign language.

"Snacks? You just went shopping yesterday. How much do you eat?"

I slap his shoulder. "Cheeky... I forgot to buy chocolate yesterday. And you drank half of my cans of coke."

"Right. Sorry, I'm not used to buying my own food. I'll give you some money."

"Seriously? No, I don't want your money."

Dylan pulls his wallet from his shorts pocket. "How much is chocolate or whatever? I haven't shopped recently."

"Seriously?" I repeat.

The more time passes, the greater my suspicion this guy is more famous than I realise. He chews his lip, and I get he doesn't want me to comment.

"I presume you're not getting out of the car. Do you want anything?"

"Not at the moment. Maybe later." He raises a suggestive eyebrow and I tut at him and open the door.

We've chosen to stop at the out of town supermarket again, a trip here will be quicker and the car park is bigger for hiding in. With a basket full of high fat and high sugar snacks, I pick up some apples too. For balance.

Following a trip through the self-serve checkout, I stroll across the car park. Dylan is slouched in his seat, sunglasses and cap on. I dump the bags on the back seat and smirk at him.

"What's funny?" he asks.

"You. In this car. Not quite your style is it?"

"I like being in your car; because I'm with you."

Again, Dylan's simple words fill my stomach with a warm fuzziness, partly because I feel exactly the same. Following our weird date to Sandchurch, a tiny part of me believes there could be more to this than a holiday romance.

Holding the thought, I turn the ignition, the car doesn't start. Several attempts later and things aren't looking good. Grinding and spluttering from the engine indicates we won't be moving anywhere soon. As I repeatedly attempt to start the car, Dylan shifts in his seat, stiffening.

"What's wrong with the car?" he snaps.

"How the hell should I know? I'm not a mechanic."

An elderly couple pass the car, the man struggling with a piled trolley and Dylan slumps in his seat, holding his forehead. "Fuck."

"What?"

"We have to get out of here? There's a lot more people around than Sandchurch."

"I'm trying!" To reinforce this, I grind the ignition again.

At a loss of what to do, I pop the bonnet and climb out. Propping it open I stare in confusion at the greasy engine. What am I looking for? There's plenty of petrol and I know how to check the oil and water but that's the limit of my expertise. Tears of frustration prick my eyes as I slam the bonnet shut again. Through the windscreen, I see Dylan sitting arms crossed tightly over his chest.

Today is another unusually hot summer's day and the sun adds to the perspiration on my forehead. I climb back in the car and Dylan looks expectantly at me.

"What? I haven't fixed anything."

"Shit!" He lowers his window. "It's fucking hot in here."

"Calm down. I'll call the breakdown people and get them to take a look. Maybe it's the battery."

Dylan squeezes his eyes closed, and sucks in a breath. "No. You can't call people."

"What? Do you want to sit here all day? Or walk back to the house?"

We're at least ten miles from the town, and further to the beach house.

"They'll recognise me. Tell someone."

"I don't think everyone in Britain is looking for you. Don't be ridiculous!"

"Wait." He pulls his phone from his pocket and stares at it. Putting the phone on the dashboard, he taps his cheeks with his fingers, retreating into his thoughts. I cross my arms and watch him. His eyes glaze.

"What are you doing? Trying to fix the car with Zen?"

"I should've fucking stayed at the house," he mutters.

"This isn't exactly my idea of a great end to a day out either," I retort.

The happy glow from our date dissipates as the stress-head Dylan reappears.

"Fuck this!" He climbs out of the car and sits on the bonnet, long legs splayed out in front of him.

As he talks to someone on the phone, a young mother with a trolley containing a toddler and what looks like half the shop wheels past him. Her eyes grow to saucers as she looks at Dylan. For a moment, I think she's going to stop and I flick my gaze between her and Dylan. She pauses. *Shit.*

I spring out of the door and grab his arm. He looks around in alarm.

"Get in the car!"

"What?"

"Jamie! Get in the car - the kids are waiting for us to pick them up!"

Dylan's eyes narrow. "What the fuck are you on about?"

"I don't have time to hang around in the middle of a supermarket car park." I emphasise the part about the car park and tug his hand.

The supermarket car park isn't Dylan's natural environment, and I'm pretty sure any fan of his would still recognise him, even without his hair; but he doesn't move.

"I'm talking to someone about moving the car."

Is this guy insane? I move closer and wind my arms around his neck, tiptoeing and holding my face close to his ear. "I think someone recognised you."

Dylan's hands roam around to my backside, pulling my hips into his. He slides his face towards my ear. "Who?"

I hunch my shoulders as his cool breath tickles. "Some woman with a trolley."

Sliding hands up my back, he pulls his head away and holds my face, crushes his mouth on mine. Annoyed he's gone from swearing at me to presuming I want to kiss him, I nip his bottom lip. He nips mine in return and loosens his grip, laughing. Wobbling slightly, I steady myself on the car, touching my mouth. I swear I'm about to fall on the floor in a dizzy heap.

"Has she gone?" he whispers.

What? My addled brain tries to catch up. "Who?"

"The person who was looking."

"Probably, why?"

"I thought that might throw her off the scent."

"So Dylan Morgan kissing a woman is more inconspicuous than hanging out in a supermarket car park?"

Dylan lightly touches my face; small zaps of electricity seem to flow from his fingers. "Don't take this the wrong way..."

Oh, right. As soon as people say something like that, you know you will. I tense. "What?"

"You called me Jamie so I carried on the charade." As if the word charade isn't enough of a punch in the guts, his next words follow this up with stab in the heart. "And you're not the sort of girl Dylan Morgan would be seen kissing."

I smack my hands into his chest, hurt firing straight to the insecure centre of my brain, triggering immediate anger. "What the hell? You dickhead!"

He steps back, alarmed, and tries to catch my arm but misses. "No, listen, that's not what I meant."

Head whirling from the desire replaced by anger, I go to the other side of the car and grab my handbag from the footwell. "Stay here and find someone else to help you. I'll get the bus and bloody walk home!"

Tears of humiliation press behind my eyes, blurring my vision. I know he won't follow me, expose himself more and even if he does, I don't care. I storm across the car park towards the bus stop I saw near the other side of the store.

"Sky!" he calls. "Really, you got this all wrong. I'm not saying that's what I think." I keep walking as Dylan's heavy strides catch up behind. "Sky!"

Dylan grabs my arm and spins me around, causing a tear to fall from my eye. Great.

He stares at it in alarm. "Sorry, you're right, I'm a dickhead, I didn't mean for you to take what I said this way."

"Let me go."

Strong hands cup my face, and I twist my head trying to get away from the intensity of his look. "Listen to me, Sky. I'd swap you for a hundred of the girls the press and public expect me to be with. You're genuine, funny and real. You've touched a part of my soul I thought died years ago."

"Cut the crap, Dylan."

"No, I'm not just saying this - it's true. I know we don't know each other very well but something about you fills a space inside that's been empty for so long. Don't let me fuck this up before we've started."

I yank his hands from my face, before his words break through my defences. "Maybe you should write a song about it."

"That's unfair, Sky."

"I wish I'd left the day I first met you, the games don't stop, do they?" I snap. "Don't follow me."

He doesn't.

*****

I sit on a metal bench at the bus stop controlling my ragged breaths. How stupid am I? Letting this guy play with me; indulge in his fantasy for ordinary girls. I chew the inside of my mouth, willing the stupid tears to stay unspilt.

To get to the house, I need to take two buses and walk a couple of miles. Sweat sticks the summer dress to my back and legs, by the time I reach the door my calves sore from walking in crappy summer sandals. All the way back, my chest stayed tight, his words replaying; not the lies about touching his soul and that crap, the ones about him not being seen with someone like me.

I step into the shower, washing off the day and him. What was I doing? Living a fantasy with a mysterious rock star? The type in books who profess undying love before the story ends? My story isn't ending this way. If I listen to my head and not my heart, mine is about to end on a train back to Bristol, car dead in a supermarket car park.

One of Dylan's T-shirts lies on the floor by the sink and I stare at it. If I were a worse person, I'd take the item as a souvenir. But of what? What was this? And if I were a complete bitch, I'd call a newspaper to see if I can bargain for information of his whereabouts. Find out what his real worth is, because it'll be more than I'm worth to him.

Chapter Fifteen

The obsessing about Dylan Morgan doesn't abate as I make myself a snack and debate whether to leave or not. The old desire to not know anything is replaced with a consuming need to find out who he is. So when I pick my phone up to search train timetables, the control I've held onto disappears.

I punch his name into Google. I don't have to type his full name in the search box before the box fills for me. Immediately a page appears with a link to Wikipedia, images and stories.

The man in the picture doesn't look anything like Dylan, apart from his eyes. His hair is longer - half way to his shoulders, dark brown with a slight curl. This changes his face shape completely. The possibility Dylan's lying crosses my mind but his eyes are the clincher. They're different shades of blue in different pictures, colour changing with his mood like those rings I wore as a teen.

Wikipedia feels too intrusive (ha ha) so I scroll to the stories. Then I see the band name.

Blue Phoenix.
Holy shit.
No way.

The tattoo. Dylan was practically telling me and I didn't click. Evidently, his semi-naked presence switches my brain onto standby.

I'm clueless and boring when it comes to music, but everybody knows who Blue Phoenix is. Calling them 'big' is an understatement, they're huge. So how did I not know? I trawl my mind but can't find any memories of pictures of the band members; couldn't even tell you how many people are in the band.

But I've heard friends talk about them - I think Tara went to their stadium gig last year. I know she raves on about them sometimes, but I have an enviable capacity for only pretending to listen to anything that bores me, so I have no idea.

And Blue Phoenix aren't sanitised like the famous boy bands. These guys have a reputation and a lot of internet fan sites. I mean, *a lot*. I click on one. More pictures of Dylan, and other band members. In a lot of them they're shirtless or turning smouldering looks to the camera. There's also pictures of Dylan with girls, a lot of different girls. Beautiful women dressed up for awards nights or dressed down in bikinis at exotic locations. Tall, willowy, silicone enhanced and glamorous. Girls who don't exist in my world.

Who look nothing like me.

Dazed, I click back and read the first news story.

'Fans furious as star disappears – Blue Phoenix forced to postpone tour'

The mysterious disappearance of international bad boy rock star, Dylan Morgan, has teenage girls around the country venting their anger on the venues who are powerless to do anything. The band's manager, Steve Bennett, claims to have no details of his whereabouts. Rumours of a split, and fake death notices on Twitter and Facebook have sent the fandom into a tailspin.'

I speed read the rest of the article, staccato heartbeat accompanying me. Background I'd rather not know about Dylan follows including a list of his demeanours. The article is accompanied by him with a model I've vaguely heard of. Again, tall, skinny with silky black hair and perfect everything. His girlfriend?

I want to throw up. This guy? What the hell is he doing here? And with me? What an amusing game I must've been - clueless but falling for his spin. I might not be a groupie but I've been caught in his full beam and dazzled into believing he wanted me. This is my fault for not investigating who he is before now - I fooled myself into a fantasy worthy of a best-seller. Why didn't I know who Dylan was when he told me his name? I'm vaguely aware of boy band names because they're plastered on the TV 24/7, but I know little about rock bands. Blue Phoenix is one of a few I've heard of, just not well enough to recognise them. *Stupid, stupid girl.*

Afternoon melds with the evening and I'm locked in the world of the internet, spinning in circles as I learn everything about Dylan I can. Like an addiction, one taste of insight into his life and I need more. Everything. Some articles will be lies and others exaggerated, but the essence of who Dylan Morgan is runs through. This is reality, and one I won't be part of.

The bang of the front door pulls me out of the internet world and I rub my eyes, glancing at the time: almost nine pm. That's a lot of time dizzying myself with the life and times of Dylan Morgan. Footsteps ascend the stairs again, but the floorboards don't creak and he returns back down. Where did he go when I left him in the supermarket car park? And is that my business anyway?

I pick up the paper where I've scrawled train times; if I go soon I can be on my way to Bristol in an hour. The decision to leave was made when I discovered the truth about Dylan. The overwhelming shift in our day blew apart our new world. I pile clothes into my rucksack and head downstairs with my full bag, Dylan stands as I walk into the lounge, the old weary look from the lane outside Broadbeach back on his face. We lock gazes for a moment, and then I stalk past him into the kitchen. Gathering stray books and sunglasses and pushing them into my handbag, I panic about getting past Dylan without speaking to him.

"Can I talk to you?" he asks softly.

I turn. Dylan leans in the doorway, the exact way he has every one of our days in this house. But this isn't my Dylan anymore; I've replaced him with stories and images from the internet.

"How did you get back here?" I ask.

"The same way you did. I walked."

I blink. "What if someone saw you pursuing some girl you wouldn't be seen dead with?"

Dylan moves into the room. "Don't. Say. That," he says through clenched teeth

I stand my ground. "How else am I supposed to take it?"

"You completely overreacted. Haven't you listened to anything I said - how I feel about you. About us."

"Us? There isn't an us!"

"Of course there fucking is! Otherwise you wouldn't be so pissed off with me!"

I glare. *Touche.*

He pushes his hand through his hair. "I called someone to come and get us. If you'd waited..."

"Who?"

"It doesn't matter." Does this mean people know where he is now? This gets worse... "I've asked them to take your car and fix the engine too."

"I don't need anything from you!"

As I attempt to push past him, Dylan steps in the doorway. "Please, Sky. I meant what I said. Don't go."

"I have to go!"

He extends a hand as if about to touch me and I step away. Dylan's shoulders slump. "Can't we talk about this? Until I said what I did, everything was going so well. Don't leave yet, not because of one dickhead comment."

"Things are different," I say quietly, hardly able to meet his eyes.

"Why? Because of the sex?"

"I know who you are now," I blurt.

A transformation comes over Dylan. Muscles rigid, face hardening he looks at me with eyes retreating back to his soul. "How?"

"I googled you." This sounds funny, apart from he's not laughing.

"Why?"

"Because my curiosity took over, and I needed to know who you were."

He runs his tongue across his teeth. "And?"

"I think I should leave. I don't want to get caught up in...whatever."

Whatever existed has shattered into pieces, because when I meet his eyes, Dylan has gone. "I wish you hadn't done that."

"I was going to find out eventually. You should've told me."

"We said no to the real world, so I didn't. Just like you didn't tell me who you are. It's not fair you've done this, I can't fucking google you."

"I'm an accountant-receptionist-dogsbody and I live in Bristol. I just spilt up with my boyfriend of five years, whose family I unfortunately work for. So I'm probably jobless now too."

"That's not much compared to what you know about me. Or think you know."

"There's nothing much to know. I've not had the most eventful of lives."

Dylan slumps against the doorframe. "Do you know how fucking hard it is to be owned by everyone around you? What that does to a person? Coming here freed me – meeting you, the first person who treated me the way I deserve, both good and bad. You showed me who I could be. And now you know who I am, I'm their Dylan Morgan again, not your Dylan Morgan."

"Mine?"

"I mean the one you know. The one you freed by not knowing the other one." He rakes a hand through his hair. "Too fucking good to be true."

"But this was always temporary. We would both go back to our old lives and everything would be over. Playing out fantasies about returning to the world of our childhood where nothing can touch us is an illusion."

"I wanted to live in that illusion for longer." He turns his head, hands still in his hair. "You let me breathe, Sky. You connect me to something long gone, and now that's lost again."

The tattoos, face and physique are the rock star Dylan Morgan - the man whose life I spent the last few hours dissecting. But the man in front of me isn't the Dylan Morgan from the internet. He's the guy who made me laugh, touched my aching heart and pulled me into our new world.

"Leave then. Go further than Broadbeach. You have the money, disappear and make a new life.

"Where? How? Are you listening to me?"

"Okay, if you can't run then face things. If someone is trying to control your life, take the control back."

"That's hypocritical - you ran away from your problems!"

"To get my head together after things ended with Grant. But even in the first day of being apart, some of how I felt was relief. Grant was trying to change me and I'm never going to be anything but myself from now on. I control my life, no one else. You should do the same."

"You're telling me to go back?" His tone is incredulous.

"Not if you don't want to. Dylan, do what you want. If you need time out to get your head together, fine, but face them - whoever - and tell them."

"It's not that fucking simple!"

"Why?"

"I've done this since I was seventeen, Sky. How can I stand up for who I am when I haven't got a fucking clue who that is?"

Suddenly everything makes sense, the reason why he's behaving like a boy holidaying on the beach. His life has been crazy, privileged and unreal. Dylan is a shell of the seventeen-year-old kid who gave up control to others, so he could get the life he wanted. Dylan got everything he wanted, but has nothing.

"I don't know what to say to you. I don't understand your life or the world you live in." My head hurts from the intensity of the conversation; of him revealing so much I have no right to hear.

I tense as he approaches. Searching my eyes with his lost ones, Dylan rubs my cheek with the back of his hand. "Say that you'll stay with me a little longer."

His touch reconnects the strange 'us'. "Why?"

"Because I want you here. With me. Telling me home truths and making me face shit."

"I can't," I say hoarsely. "I don't want to be here when the press or whoever tracks you down. They're looking for you and I'm not getting dragged into your life."

When he grabs my face by both cheeks, I'm startled. "Sky, please, I want you. I want to get to know you, all of you. I don't know why but we were meant to meet and we did, exactly when I needed you. You walked into my world and showed me a glimmer of a different life I could have."

I push his hands away. "What if they're out there now? The person who saw you? And now, you've told people where you are? No, Dylan. I can't do this. I'm about to start a new life, one I can control."

We face each other, I'm shaking with the realisation of who he is and the fantasy world crashing around our ears.

"Tomorrow. Wait until tomorrow?" he asks, eyes wide.

"What's the point?"

"The point is you don't have your car and it's getting late. I'm leaving tomorrow too; I'll have someone take you home."

I pull a face. "You'll have someone take me home? I don't want anyone taking me anywhere! I want my car back!"

"Then you'll have to stay here, won't you? Until your car's fixed - they said tomorrow."

Perspiration covers my back again; I'm backed into a corner and this is what life would be like if I dated Dylan. Dated. *Ha.* He was more delusional than I realised.

Dylan's phone rings and he answers it immediately. His face darkens. "What? Where? Fucking deal with it!"

I chew on my lip, the world around imploding.

"How? Okay, well I'll have to fucking leave then." He pauses. "Who gave them the fucking address?"

My pulse rate spikes as Dylan walks out of the door, continuing his conversation out of earshot. He can't hide what's happening; I can guess. Scanning the room for any remaining items, I push them into my bulging rucksack. I can't think straight. Things have gone from days out at souvenir shops to life with someone who people are *looking for*. How do I leave? Where do I go?

I stomp to the front of the house. "What's going on?"

Hand in his short hair, Dylan shakes his head at me as he continues the conversation. "Half an hour? Who contacted you? No, you get on fucking Twitter or whatever and tell them I'm somewhere else. I don't know - the fucking moon!"

Dylan launches his phone across the garden and I flinch as he slams a palm into the side of the house. For a minute, he rests his head against the bricks, chest falling and rising rapidly.

"Did someone find out where you are?" I say as calmly as possible.

"Yes." His tone is bitter, defeated.

"The supermarket?"

"Sandchurch."

"But I didn't see anyone...?"

Dylan turns, rests against the wall and stares up at the evening sky. "Someone always sees."

And that's why we could never co-exist in each other's lives.

"So I guess we're not waiting until the morning?"

He doesn't take his eyes away from the stars. "No, we have to go."

"Someone's coming to take you home?"

"Yeah." He looks at me. "Will you come with me?"

"What? No, no way. I'm going to my friend's place and picking up the pieces of my life."

"Sky..." Dylan steps towards me, touching my cheek. "Come back with me, at least until we know you're safe."

"Safe? From what?"

"Whether the press knows who you are - they have pictures."

My stomach turns over. "What pictures? Who?"

Rubbing my cheek with his thumb, Dylan studies my face. "You said your life is a mess - that you might not have a job, stay with me while you sort things out?"

"I can't." My voice is hoarse, barely a whisper.

"Why?"

How can I say because going with him drags me further into this? Can't he see? Tears well, frustrated my bubble burst and the world is pouring in. Annoyingly, a tear slips from my eye and Dylan's face fills with alarm. He kisses my cheek, kissing away the tear.

"Don't worry, you'll be fine. They'll forget about you."

And you'll forget about me if I leave now. I inhale deeply. One last time, I place my mouth on his; lose myself in Dylan, and the intensity of the kiss. As his lips meet mine, I know this is a mistake as I'm reforging a connection I'm trying to break. Fate brought me to this incredible man and then handed over a part of my heart and soul to him. But the new knowledge of who he is, what that means and how this has to end, catches hold and pulls me back to reality. He can never be mine because he belongs to so many others, and I'm not the person to help him lose those people.

I withdraw; touch his cheek. "Go and pack. How long until they're here?"

"Maybe fifteen minutes. Are you coming?"

My heart tears in two, as I'm torn in half. "Yes."

"Thank you." Dylan grabs my face, kisses my mouth hard and disappears inside.

Pulling my phone from my jacket pocket, fingers trembling, I dial a taxi. Light shines through the doorway of the sanctuary I came to four days ago, the time it took the get pulled under and drowned by the man from the sea. I know I have to go to keep my head above the water.

My rucksack rests on the floor in the kitchen, and I pull the bag onto my shoulder. I don't know how long Dylan will take to pack, I need to decide now.

The half-moon in the cloudless sky illuminates the lane leading away from the house, as if guiding me in the direction I need to go. Chest tight and pressure building in my head, I glance back at the door. Dylan could reappear anytime, and make this harder. I walk along the lane towards the road above the house, pushing through the remaining walls that surround my fantasy world.

Part Two

Chapter Sixteen

Dylan

Two weeks since I saw Sky; since we left behind our fantasy world of sand and sunshine. Fourteen days since she walked out of my fucking life, and hit me harder than our cars collided.

I haul my ass out of bed, feeling like crap. The empty bottle on the table mocks me. Months since I last drank heavily and here I am again, back into my old way of coping. Empty bottles, empty head. Now everything is worse because I caught a glimpse of how life should be: with Sky.

Do I not learn? This is what feeling something real does. Every. Fucking. Time.

Sky, the infuriating girl who I tried to keep my hands off and failed. The moment I touched her skin, I left reality and moved into our illusion by the sea. In this Sky and Dylan world, I was free; freer than I thought I'd be the day I decided to run from this shit.

Impossible Sky, the girl who knows me because she never knew me. She gave breath to a new Dylan, the man I want to be, and without her, he'll suffocate again. Every morning I wake aching to hold Sky again, to cocoon us in our fragile world we created, and every night I crave the soft warmth of her in my arms. *Fuck, listen to me...pathetic.* She's right; I should write a fucking song.

Sky won't give us a chance, refuses to see me. I'm shut out as if I never existed. She says I'm chasing something we could never be, that everything was an illusion. But the connection we made was more than an illusion.

Our Sky and Dylan could exist in the real world too; Sky just needs time to realise.

*****

Sky

Twenty-two, homeless and jobless; not what I planned when I hung around in Bristol to be with my childhood sweetheart. At least we never got married or had kids although not through lack of trying on my part - my subtlety was brick-like on that topic for years. Then I gave up, deciding we'd be one of those co-habiting couples. Grant said marriage was "just a piece of paper." Wrong. I put money into the mortgage for his house, paying "rent" and allowing him to keep my name off the titles. I paid for the upkeep. And what am I entitled to now? Nothing. Look up naivety in the dictionary and beside the word, you'll see me.

My job. I turned my back on the chance of university and worked for his family firm as the 'office manager'. This entails accounts, sales, admin, coffee maker and occasional cleaner. I am an expert on finance contracts and a complete fail on life.

Naturally, my break-up with Grant and subsequent disappearance ends my employment. I'm sure I could fight back for unfair dismissal, but I haven't the desire to communicate with a single one of Grant's family.

I move in with Tara, into her spare room, where I fight with her plethora of cuddly toys and clothes for space. A bed and a roof over my head are a start in my move forward in life. With my office skills, I can take temporary contracts until I find a proper job. If I'm brave, I'll switch towns too and get as far away as possible from the dickhead and his stupid family.

Dylan haunts my thoughts and dreams. And my mobile phone. He has guilted me over walking out on him. I thought he'd be over me in a couple of days but he calls daily. We have the same conversation over, and over, he wants to see me; I don't want to see him. The glow of the holiday romance stays, and if I allow the other Dylan I never knew in, those memories will be destroyed.

Social media exploded when Dylan reappeared, news of his holiday with the mystery girl speculated on. The palpitations caused every time I open the internet, expecting to see my picture, lessen each day. Two weeks on, and my name and face remain unknown. That's the way I want to keep things and another reason to steer clear of Dylan. My life is already upside down, with Dylan my life would spin out of control.

Following a morning registering at employment agencies, I meet Tara for coffee in our favourite cafe. She's seated in our regular spot, in a wooden booth on the vintage-look cushioned seats. The expensive fixtures add to the effect, I think they're going for a Gatsby art deco theme. I'm pretty sure us customers pay for this fit out through overpriced coffee.

Tara's immaculately dressed in her understated, natural way. Next to her, I always feel like a scarecrow – her sleek brown hair versus my unruly straw-blonde waves and her expensive, coordinated blue skirt suit versus my cobbled together interview outfit of a short black skirt and white shirt. Tara offered something of hers for the interviews, but she's several inches taller and a size eight to my size twelve.

On the stone table, next to her cup of mocha, is a glossy magazine. When I approach with my latte, she studies me, red-painted mouth quirking at the corner.

"What?" I ask her smirking face.

"You never discussed your holiday with me. How was it?"

I open a sachet of sugar and tip the contents into my drink. Then another. "Fine."

"Fine? Anything else? Meet anyone nice?"

The fake innocence to her voice raises a red flag so high the whole of Bristol could see. "In Cornwall? Not likely."

"Mmm." With delicate fingers, Tara flicks through the magazine, stops on a page and turns it to me. "Is that you?"

Perspiration not from the summer warmth grows; the situation I've dreaded in front of me. I'm looking at a grainy photo of Dylan and me, several grainy photos. In the one where we're kissing I'm hard to identify, but someone has managed to get closer to my face in on one of the other pictures. The photo is blurry, but not blurry enough to fool my best friend.

The beautiful cafe lurches. "Oh."

"Oh, my God!" shrieks Tara and I shush her. "What the hell? No way! This is you?"

At this point, I'm not sure if her incredulity or the fact she knows pisses me off most.

"Keep your voice down. Yes. I was stupid. It's over." I glance furtively around but nobody pays any attention, the lunching city dwellers focused on sandwiches and phones.

She leans across the table, long hair almost dipping into her coffee. "Did you…you know?"

Why reply when my bright pink face does for me?

"Sky! You dark horse! How was he?"

I hold a hand up. "Stop there. I'm not talking about Dylan."

"Why? Did he pay you to keep quiet?" she whispers.

"Do you think I'm a whore?" I snap "Or gold-digger?"

Tara frowns. "Okay. Sorry, I didn't mean... What happened?"

"It's a long story. It happened and the whole situation is over and done with."

Who am I kidding? I don't want everything over and done with, but I'm too old to live in a fantasy world where rock stars date Miss Average.

Sipping her coffee, Tara watches me over her cup. "You know what's funny?

"In my current life, not much."

"You don't even like Blue Phoenix!" She giggles. "Did you tell him that?"

"I didn't know who he was! Not until the last day."

She splutters. "Right…"

I ignore her and read the article. There was a 'no comment' from Dylan and his manager, and nobody knows who the mystery girl is. There are a few not so pleasant comments about why he's with me, which I expected; and a line from his girlfriend about how they'll split up now. Girlfriend. That's the part that hurts the most - confirming my suspicion about the model I saw in the internet story I read at Broadbeach.

"Do you think anyone else will recognise me?" I ask.

"If they want to find you, they will," Tara says nonchalantly. "They probably want the scoop on why he disappeared in the first place – did he leave because of you?"

"No. I met him there. Tell me, do you think they'll look for me?" I press.

"Who knows – if he's done with you and you're not interested in selling your story, I'm sure they'll forget about you. Once he moves onto the next girl." She pulls an apologetic face. "No offence."

Done with me. Nice. I don't tell her how Dylan called Gran; and sweet-talked her into giving him my number, in the pretence of returning my car. Or his daily phone calls, ending in a drunken one last night. At least he sent someone else to drop my car off instead of driving over. A guy built like the proverbial brick house, wearing a suit and a curious look delivered my freshly washed and freshly functioning car the day after I returned. I wonder how much he's paid to keep quiet about me.

So all I have to do is keep my head down for a few days, and forget about the man who exploded my world.

*****

I step out of the fourth interview of the day, jaw aching from false smiling and head aching from yet another mind-numbing "computer skills" test. The situation I'm in depresses me as I wander towards the car park. Three years ago, I could've left and gone to university in a new city, I had the grades but I stayed with Grant instead. I couldn't see the point in studying another three years when his family had a job for me, so I chose to stay with my security blanket. I mean my boyfriend.

Now things with Grant are over, I have the opportunity to start again. I'm sick of the treadmill life of nine to five. But, what do I want to do? Who the hell knows? I don't.

This worry is on the back burner following my meeting with Tara. I scrutinise every person I pass - middle-aged lady with small white dog; mum with screaming baby; group of teens sat side by side texting on their phones and not communicating. I'm paranoid they'll jump up and run through the car park shouting "It's her!" but no one pays any attention.

I drive home in a daze, the images from the magazine flipping my mind and stomach. Nobody knows who I am; everything will go away. I repeat the words repeatedly as my car crawls through the traffic towards Tara's home.

Parking on Tara's street is a military manoeuvre at the best of times. Finding a space isn't the issue - the problem is the politics surrounding which rectangle of tarmac belongs to who. The first day I parked in what I presumed was a free space, and then endured the wrath of a middle-aged man in a brown suit with an interesting comb-over hairstyle. He lives five doors down but claims the spot is his.

Now I park around the corner so if I do accidentally invade someone's territory, they won't know where I live.

Pissed off that the July weather equals rain clouds and not sunshine, I tramp along the street, skilfully weaving around the dog crap on the pavement - sometimes avoiding people's eyes helps in life.

Tara's home is a Victorian house converted into several flats. She says she's saving for one of the new apartments near the river. I nodded and saved my question about when a 'flat' becomes an 'apartment'? I suspect there's a pound sign and a few zeros involved.

As I approach the house, I spot a figure in a familiar blue hoodie perched on the low brick wall bordering the pavement and overgrown front garden.

Dylan.

I freeze, heart stuttering. What the hell is he doing? His head is down, hair covered by his hood, but if hardcore fans recognise him from the streets of a sleepy, seaside town, I doubt this'll be much of a disguise.

"Dylan?"

He looks over and in his face, I recognise the Dylan from the day we collided. Beneath his hoodie, Dylan's dull eyes brighten when he notices me. He straightens and gives a lopsided apologetic smile.

"Are you mad? Sitting in the middle of a busy street?" I hiss.

An elderly lady trundles by with a wheeled shopping bag.

Dylan doesn't take his pale blue eyes off mine. "Not exactly a hive of activity? Besides, I'm hiding in plain sight. No one's looked twice at me."

I take in his appearance. He's unshaven, in scruffy clothes with black circled eyes - exactly as when I first met him. I recognise the blue hoodie covering his tattoos as the one I wore in Broadbeach.

"I said I didn't want to see you," I say quietly.

"I said I had to see you. I need to talk to you," he replies in a low tone. "I tried to stay away but I think I deserve an explanation. You just walked away and that was unfair."

"I had to."

"Why?"

"Because I wanted to avoid this. I thought you'd forget me as soon as I went, I didn't expect you to want to see me."

Confusion lines Dylan's face and he stands. "I told you I wanted us to be more, why would you think I'd forget you? I'll never forget you."

Already his words are piercing my resolve, and I pull myself back to the reality sitting in my bag. "Have you seen this?" I pull the magazine out, still folded at the offending page, and show the article to him.

"Yeah," he says without looking at the magazine.

"Can you make sure I don't get dragged into anything? Get your people or whoever to pay someone?"

He moves closer, too close. My thoughts scatter, the scent of him pulling me back to the incredible things he did to me.

"My people?" He laughs. "Sure. If you come with me and talk to me."

"No."

"Why?"

"I don't want anything else to do with you and your life, Dylan," I say, even though my body is begging me to reconsider.

I edge past him towards the steps leading up to the flats.

"Sky. Please." He folds a hand around my sleeve before I can get by.

Tears prick my eyes, in frustration with him and the situation. "What do you want from me?"

"You." The sincerity in his face knocks the breath from me. "Sky, I want you to give us a chance. Things were going well until..."

"... I discovered who you really were and our fantasy world imploded."

"I was going to tell you, once I realised I wanted more than the Sky in our fantasy world."

"Holiday romances are great while they last, but they always end." I smile weakly.

Dylan sits back on the wall and buries his hands into his pockets. "I have so many things I want to say to you, Sky. I don't know how to make you understand that I currently don't give a fuck about anything but trying to make things work with you."

"How? How would we work? In Broadbeach, we had fun because everything was different. This is reality."

"And I want you to be part of my reality," he says, turning the eyes I could drown in back to mine. My Dylan Morgan's eyes.

Exasperated, I throw the magazine at him. "This. This is your reality. You can't exactly pop round to watch a movie with a takeaway, or meet me at the pub for a quick drink after work, can you? And I can't be part of your insane reality."

"Don't I fucking know it," he growls, picking up the pages as they fall on the floor. "And I want to protect you from this bullshit."

"Then leave me alone."

Dylan's face hardens, and he stares at the concrete path. "If you hadn't found out about this Dylan Morgan, would you have given your Dylan Morgan a chance?"

I wince as the realisation hits. He gave part of himself to me and I'm rejecting more than rock star Dylan Morgan.

"Dylan, I'm asking you again. Leave me alone, you're making things hard for me by being here. If anyone finds out who I am…"

Dylan jumps to his feet, and I stagger back as he approaches and takes my face in his hands. "Why won't you see me again? What did I do?"

"Nothing...you didn't do anything wrong. We had a holiday thing which is over now." My traitorous body reacts to his touch, skin heating beneath his palms and desire to be in his arms again.

"And that's all our time was to you? A holiday thing?" His scrutiny doesn't waver, and I summon the courage to meet his eyes and lie. Lie to the man who filled my world with more colour and happiness than I've had in my life for years.

"Yes, that's all." A sinking in the pit of my stomach contradicts my words.

The anger I expect doesn't come; instead, his mouth pulls into sadness. He rearranges his features and drops his hands. "Okay."

"Sorry."

"I guess I just needed to look at you and hear you say the words to accept I don't mean anything to you," he says.

This guy is hurting; hurting more than before he met me. However, this isn't my fault, I can't feel guilted into doing something I don't want.

"Sorry," I repeat.

As we face each other, vivid memories of our time together tumble into my mind on replay, stirring the powerful emotions this man elicits from me. Days spent rationalising the situation, of locking my Dylan Morgan in a box in my head seem pointless in this moment. My heart has been broken once and too recently, my ability to trust scratched away. I want to preserve the memories of the happiness I had with Dylan, and not risk revisiting the pain of loss and rejection I know will follow. However much he believes what he's saying, reality will treat us unkindly.

But I want him so much. The contradiction keeps me awake at night; the emptiness left by someone I hardly know confusing. Swapping one man who tried to control my life, for another whose life is so out of control is frightening, isn't what I need right now.

I want Dylan and I know I can never have him. He belongs to so many other people who won't share him with me. Fighting the urge to stay with

Dylan, and talk about the possibility of future us, I hesitate.

Dylan touches my cheek, and I'm sure he can see the doubt in my eyes. "At least let me say goodbye this time." I swallow down the lump in my throat, praying the tears don't start as he strokes my face. "You have my number, call me if you change your mind. I'll wait."

"Please, Dylan…" My eyes tear as he leans in and places his lips softly on mine and I know if I close them, I'm lost again. I back off, before the kiss reconnects us.

Dylan delves his hands into the pocket of his hoodie, sadness and understanding etched on his features. "Bye, summer Sky."

I nod because I know if I speak, my voice will crack. Scared he'll try to hug me, I cross my arms over my chest. Dylan inhales deeply, shakes his head then walks down the dirty path towards the road. His hunched figure disappears around a corner. As I head into Tara's ordinary flat, away from the extraordinary man, I know this isn't the end.

Chapter Seventeen

Sky

Thanks to Tara's friend of a friend's brother (or someone equally vague); I find somewhere new to live without having to fork out a huge deposit.

I'm pissed off about moving from the modern house in the safe suburb I shared with Grant and into a tiny place in the arse end of town, even though I should be grateful. The musty smell in the lounge is only surpassed by the disgusting state of the kitchen. The cooker looks in dire need of cleaning product, and the cupboards are full of crumbs and goodness knows what from the previous occupants. As the place comes furnished, I don't have much opportunity to make the place my own and resolve to buy some pictures to cover the ugly brown marks on the bedroom walls.

Two days later and I'm settling in. If that's what cleaning the kitchen and steam cleaning the furniture means. Something sadistic inside me decides to buy a picture of a coastal scene and hang it over the dent in the lounge wall.

The flat is close to a bus stop, so I don't bother with my car for work, leaving it parked outside my new home. If I drive anywhere, I again have to battle for a space within a fifty mile radius of the flat when I return. Okay, what feels like a fifty-mile radius, especially in the rain.

I haven't heard from Dylan. He never appeared outside Tara's again, and I hope he doesn't track me down to here. I replay the last meeting in my mind constantly, and when I'm half-asleep the conversation ends differently. In this version, I allow myself to connect and he holds me while we kiss. One thing is certain, if Dylan Morgan ever kisses me again, I know the fantasy of Broadbeach will become reality because I won't want to let him go.

Tara comes around with a "house warming" present which is odd on two accounts. Firstly, she's not the sort to waste time and money on frivolities unless they pertain to her. And secondly, she brought me a houseplant, a small Yucca in a brown pot she holds out to me as if she's carrying a stick of dynamite about to explode. With my horticultural skills, the thing won't last a week.

I know the real reason Tara is here – she wants the lowdown on Dylan's and my sexual exploits, which I've so far refused to give her. A part of me worries she may 'out' me to the tabloids but she's a better person than that, thank God. Some people would sell me out for the money, so I'm glad our twelve-year friendship stands for something.

However, I don't tell her any more details just in case.

I spend a couple of evenings torturing myself searching Dylan on Google, which is ironic - I don't want to see him but I'm spending my evenings with him anyway. Dylan has quite a history: the sex, drugs and rock and roll cliché at its very best. Many of the worst stories are a few years old, these days the media are more interested in who he's having a relationship with rather than catching him with illegal substances or getting arrested fighting journalists.

There are some bloody sexy pictures of him though, which does nothing to dampen down whatever remains racing around my body since the night at the beach house.

Did I do the right thing by rejecting something that felt so real, because I won't acknowledge how he shifted my world off its axis?

Chapter Eighteen

Dylan

"If this chick doesn't want to see you, why are you wasting your time?"

Lost in memories of lying in bed with Sky, using the peace and happiness from those quiet moments to calm me, I don't notice Liam come into the gym. I hit the off button on the treadmill and jump down, wiping my face with a towel. Every one of the band have tried talking to me about Sky. I won't discuss her; I'm respecting her decision that she doesn't want to be dragged into my world.

Liam doesn't work out; he's one of those perpetually scrawny people, so I give him a 'what are you doing here?' look. His wavy, dark ginger hair is pulled into a long ponytail today and his green eyes are bright. I guess he didn't spend the night drinking as I did, or needs to punish himself for this on the treadmill.

Liam's the one band member trying to hold down a steady girlfriend. They're engaged, though they've known each other less than six months. We call her the limpet because she's permanently stuck to him.

"Where's Honey?" I ask.

No one but Liam believes this is her real name, but he insists it is. I guess if they ever sign the marriage certificate he'll find out. I bet she's called Tracey or something less exotic.

"Hey, Dylan…" Honey's cutesy voice follows Liam into the room and I cringe. Nobody over the age of five should sound like her.

"Honey."

Miss Plastic Fantastic reattaches herself to Liam, who automatically wraps a tattooed arm around her skinny shoulders. The name Honey suggests sweet and natural, but there's little natural about her platinum blonde hair extensions or the fake nails, tits and attitude. Sweet isn't a word I'd apply to this walking Barbie doll in her tiny clothes either. Liam always falls for the fakes, which is sad because he's such a genuine, nice guy.

Despite the fact her betrothed is here, Honey sweeps an appreciative look over my sweaty body. What is it, exactly, that girls like about guys covered in stinking sweat? Her gaze lingers on my chest and she bites her lip coyly.

There was a time, very early on when we first made it big, when we'd share girls. I'm ashamed about this now, but I was eighteen, high and had girls crawling all over me. More than once, I woke in bed with several girls, not entirely clear how I got there. Man, I was fucking stupid. How I avoided any major diseases, I don't know. Maybe some guardian angel watched over me - one prepared to accept my lack of morality.

I'm a one girl at a time guy now - in my life and my bed. I'm definitely no saint, I have my needs, but I can't stick with a girl. I try but the only chicks I meet are through the industry - groupies and journalists mostly. They already think they know Dylan Morgan, they expect nothing of me so I give them nothing. Sure, I let them in my bed; but I send them away straight after sex, and I'm left with a hollow emptiness. Yeah, I had a few short relationships in the last few years but gave up - the fall out is too hard. Only once, did I let someone close, and she tore my heart into tiny pieces. There's zero desire to try a real relationship again.

Or there was, until Sky. I'm beginning to think she's my punishment.

Sometimes, I consider if Honey is hoping to get to me through Liam; which sounds bigheaded but isn't beyond possibility. Chicks often prefer the lead singer to the bass player in my experience. If she tries, I'll have her out of here on her backside so quick she won't know what's hit her. Liam's the nicest of the four of us – he's had his heart broken more than once, and he deserves better.

"Whatcha doing, babe?" she asks Liam, sliding a hand down his arm. Her huge diamond ring glints in the sun streaming through the window.

"Came to see Dylan, he missed studio time this morning," he replies.

"You guys didn't need me, not for what you were putting down." I swig from my water bottle, why the fuck did I down another bottle of bourbon last night? Honey and Liam exchange glances. "What?"

"Man, you gotta pull this together. What the hell happened to make you like this? Not just the chick – the disappearing, the attitude…" retorts Liam.

"That's your idea of helping is it?" I snap

"He hasn't come to help; he's here to ask you to come out tonight." Honey smiles, and I feel like I'm being sized up for something.

"Out?" I ask Liam

"VIP lounge? Viper Room?" he asks.

"Some of my friends are coming," interjects Honey. "I got some plain ones too if that's your taste these days."

I stiffen. Bitch. "Did you know honey is technically bee puke?"

Leaving her open-mouthed, I stalk out of the room.

I'm a lucky bastard. I own a huge mansion in the country, surrounded by state of the art security. Tennis courts, pools, the whole fucking cliché. I prefer my LA place; God, how up myself do I sound? My bedroom alone is probably the size of the entirety of Sky's crappy flat, the one I know she lives in now. My freshly made bed should be unmade with Sky beneath the covers; I should be smiling and laughing with her, not feeling miserable as fuck.

I sit barefoot on the daybed beneath the bay window and pick up my guitar. The last few days I've attempted to finish the song I started writing in Broadbeach, and working some chords out on the acoustic. I end each session frustrated, and then the drinking starts. But I'm almost there.

The song for my summer Sky.

*****

I swear Honey chooses to drag Liam to the Viper Room because of the guaranteed paparazzi. She loves the attention; checks herself out on the internet every day. The more she's in the limelight; the more fashion houses throw clothes at her to wear when she steps into the public arena. I'm itching for her to suffer a wardrobe malfunction and flash her tits - or worse - to the world. Not nice, yeah, but neither is she. I saw her hitting on Bryn a couple of weeks ago, and she knows I did.

Wearing a miniscule fire engine red dress and heels any normal girl would face-plant in, Honey feigns annoyance at being photographed but ensures they get a picture of her best side. And round, shapely backside.

Head down, I pretend I'm not here. The media scrutiny has dropped off the last few months, but intensified following my Broadbeach escapade. Constant questions about Sky's identity are yelled by media and fans alike, and now the photos Sky showed me are out there. I toy with the idea of making a statement, telling people who she is so she'll have to talk to me. Any chance of Sky changing her mind about us would be blown out of the water by that action. So, I stay quiet.

The Viper Room in Mayfair is a guaranteed Blue Phoenix haunt; one of us is here most nights when we're in England. Of course we're VIP, but for a price, and if they pre-book weeks in advance, the everyday clubbers can get entrance. Early evening, and the place is half-empty so I head through the purple-lit bar area towards our cordoned off section. The white leather seats are arranged in an L-shape around round metal tables. An ice bucket and champagne is propped against one, a couple of empty bottles already lined up.

Jem is playing the rock cliché, each arm across a girl's shoulders. He appears to have a thing for Asian girls currently; a few months ago, all his conquests were blondes. When I approach, he pulls away, grabs his drink and watches me through narrowed eyes. In the past, we were like brothers - he practically was with the amount of time he spent at my house as a kid escaping his fucked up family. Then shit happened, our clashing personalities switched to animosity and we don't talk much anymore. In the purple hued room, his true state is difficult to make out. He's skinnier recently, dark curls tumbling over gaunter cheekbones. His presence is the same - not only because he's the Blue Phoenix lead guitarist. Years of girl's falling over him inevitably adds to his confidence that every girl thinks he's hot as fuck.

The music fades as I approach, our space darker and quieter than the rest of the venue. Besides Jem's appendages, several other girls recline on the seats. A girl with Barbie hair shrieks a greeting to Honey and they embrace with false cheek kisses. Honey pushes the girl towards me.

"This is Jewel."

Jewel smiles seductively and I groan inwardly. I need a fucking drink.

Several hours and an uncountable number of drinks later, Jewel has found her way onto my lap. The row of violet spotlights above us spin as I stare upwards - I'm not used to this much alcohol in public after all those months dry. I remain motionless, as she strokes my leg, fingers playing across the exposed part of my chest. Her tits are at my eye level - awesome tits if you like a mouthful of silicone. Nothing stirs - no reaction from my dick and not because of the alcohol. She's not Sky. So what the fuck am I doing letting this random girl touch me?

Jem's hand is up one of his conquests short black dress, the couple devouring each other. Me and Jem didn't speak - he's high again so there's no point. Jem's hardly said two words to me since I returned from Broadbeach. Suits me. He's a fucking mess - I thought I was bad but he's going to end up the ultimate rock and roll cliché and dead before he's twenty-five. Two stints in rehab and he's no better than he was.

Seated the other side of me, Liam stares at the ceiling; 'the limpet' and friends are absent. Realisation hits: they're all fucking high.

This is why I left. I can't be this or do this anymore. I want to be on the beach eating fish and chips with Sky. I could be snuggling and covering her beautiful, warm body with mine and connecting to something real.

Without a word, I head towards the front doors. The dancers part as I take a shortcut across the dance floor, squinting at the lights strobing across the writhing bodies. I catch a glimpse of Honey gyrating with another guy, his hands holding her backside close to his crotch. She doesn't notice and if I said anything to Liam, he'd tell me to fuck off.

This is fucked up, all of this life.

I leave by the front door, not giving a flying fuck who sees me. I giggle drunkenly to myself: 'come at me, paparazzi, do your worst'. The world shimmers in and out of view as I adjust my eyes to the light, and familiar camera flashes light my way as I head for the car where Dave waits to take us home. I'm not going home. I have to see Sky, cleanse the filth from my night with the clarity of her.

Chapter Nineteen

Sky

Dylan knows where I live.

The first clue is indicated by the housewarming gift from him - a beautiful oil painting of the Cornish coast with a house looking a lot like Gran's in the background. My reaction: I have to move. Can I take out injunctions against world famous rock stars for stalking? Is this stalking yet? I have a low threshold for hassle.

The second clue is the incessant ringing of my doorbell at 3am. I'm particularly pissed off about this because I'm not sleeping well since I got back from Broadbeach.

Aware the doorbell won't stop ringing anytime soon, I crawl out of bed and peer out of a chink in the curtains. The streetlight casts a glow over the road and front garden, but the visitor is too close to the house to see.

I tie my pink, towelling robe and press the intercom button. "What?"

"Sky..."

Dylan. *Quelle surprise.*

"I repeat: what?" Waking me up is a big mistake. Always.

"Can I talk to you?"

"It's three o'clock in the bloody morning, Dylan! Do you think I'm going to change my mind if you turn up on my doorstep in the middle of the night?"

"Sorry. I had a bad night and you're the only person who can make things better."

It's difficult to tell over the intercom crackle, but I suspect he's been drinking.

"Will you go away if I ignore you?"

"No."

"Will you go away if I say I'm going to call the police?"

"No."

I knock my forehead against the wood chip wall above the intercom. "If I talk to you, will you go away and never come back?"

There's a long pause before the crackling voice replies. "If that's what you want."

Pressing the button to open the main door to the building, I run two hands across my hair. The sleepy-eyed girl in the mirror has creases up one side of her face where I've been lying on scrunched up sheets. I definitely have the scarecrow thing perfected here.

The entrance door below closes and butterflies swarm to escape through my navel as footsteps climb the carpeted stairs. I don't want to see Dylan because I want to see him so bloody much. I'm a huge contradiction and my head aches with the confusing thoughts circling. Each day that passes, I'm hopeful Dylan will fade from my short memories of our time but he doesn't. I feel as if a chemical reaction happened when we kissed, and I absorbed part of him into my psyche. I waver every day in my desire to keep away, my heart and mind in a constant battle over whether to contact him.

The footsteps halt outside my flat and I take a deep breath before unlatching the door. 'Must be mad at him. don't be nice. And definitely don't listen to my body.'

Dylan hovers outside the door, an apologetic look on his tired face. An unsure smile flickers across his full, all–too-kissable lips and I squeeze my eyes closed against his immediate effect on me. Denying how I feel when I see him in pictures on the internet is easy, in the flesh this denial is impossible.

"Hey," he says.

"Hey?" I open my eyes and step to one side so he can come in.

Closing the door behind, I stand against it and face Dylan who immediately sits on my sofa. "Make yourself at home!"

"Thanks."

Something is different about him. His eyes are less focused and his muscles looser as he reclines on the sofa and my sarcasm sailed over his head.

"I thought you didn't drink?" I say.

"Some chick drove me back to the bottle." He sticks his bottom lip out.

Dylan not very subtlety scans my night-time ensemble of striped flannel pyjamas beneath my robe. Typical. I make an exasperated noise before I stalk past him into the shoebox kitchen, hoping he doesn't follow. Wrong. Over the noise of the kettle, I hear the rustle of movement and turn to see him in the doorway. He's dressed differently - an expensive looking black woven shirt over his distractingly tight jeans has a couple of buttons undone, allowing a glimpse of the taut muscle beneath. I'm as bad as he is, I decide, as I appreciatively take in how his jeans shape his long legs.

"Why are you doing this?" I demand.

I had a long day in a new temp contract and a visit from rock god Dylan Morgan in the middle of the night wasn't part of my day's plan.

"Because I want you," he says. Not seductively, not arrogantly, but quietly, accompanied by a sadness drawing his features.

I'm disarmed by the simplicity but tell him what I tell myself every time I'm tempted. "This wouldn't work."

"Why?"

I cock an eyebrow. "Do you really need to ask me that question?"

"Sky…" He moves towards me and in the limited space, I can't move away. The lingering effect from the night in the kitchen hovers between us; the desire to reconnect with the passion of that night is hard to escape from.

Where did the air go in this room? "Dylan…"

"Please don't be angry, I'm sorry I came here tonight, but I can't get you out of my head or heart. You're killing me." He lifts a hand and strokes my hair, setting electrical charges across my scalp.

"You're drunk."

"Kind of. Went out with some of the band and had a shit time. So I came to see you."

"You went clubbing in Bristol?" I ask incredulously.

"London."

London's over a two-hour drive. I hope he didn't drive himself.

"I preferred you when you didn't drink," I retort. The smell of alcohol on his breath detracts from my arousal. I'm sure he smells of perfume too, unless he's changed to a floral aftershave. I cross my arms tightly over my chest.

His shoulders slump as he backs off. "Yeah, me too."

"I don't know what you want me to say to you."

He ignores me again. "Do you want to go to the States?"

I blink. Why does he always change the subject if he doesn't like what he's hearing? "What?"

"I'm touring next month. Going on tour is part of what I ran away from but I have to go. You can come - if you were with me I could cope..."

"I can't drop everything and run off to the States, even if I wanted to."

"Why not? If you haven't found a job yet take time out with me?"

I yank open the kitchen cupboard to retrieve a jar of coffee, and a glimmer of temptation appears as the door handle comes off in my hand. Swap a crappy flat and non-job for a summer in the States? Am I mad not to?

I turn back, study the semi-inebriated guy who came to my flat in the middle of the night. Dylan stalked me here and that's not normal. Nothing about him is normal.

"Do you often do this?"

"What?"

"Stalk girls because they say no to you?"

He stands straight in alarm. "No. I'm not stalking you!"

"How can you stand there and say that? Look at this situation. How was this behaviour going to change my mind? You're being creepy! How many normal people travel over a hundred miles to visit someone who refuses to see them?"

The confusion on his face surprises me. Does he not see anything wrong here?

"Okay. I'm sorry. I did the wrong thing. I didn't think." Dylan runs a hand through his hair, drunken eyes fixed on mine. "What should I have done? What do I have to do?"

"Do? Go home maybe?"

"No, to change your mind."

I shake my head. "Not be who you are, which will never happen."

He catches me off-guard, moving forwards and placing his large palm on my face before I can react. "I love you."

Insulted tears fight their way into my eyes and I push his hand away. "Don't say that! Stop trying to manipulate me!"

"It's true. Shit, Sky, I've not felt anything close to how I feel about you for years. This is what you've done to me."

"Don't you dare accuse me of doing this to you! You're drunk and talking bullshit. Leave." I push him in the chest, to push the surge of agreement in my mind away.

"Why won't you believe me?"

I flick my fingers at him. "Because you're a drunk mess. Nobody falls in love after less than a week!"

"Love isn't something predictable, Sky, and doesn't follow rules. You can't decide who to fall in love with, or when. Love and logic don't go together, but when I'm with you, everything makes sense."

Why is he doing this to me? My heart is caged after Grant broke it, mending and fragile. Dylan will forget me, get bored, move on and my life will be upside down. This isn't love; this is power play.

"I think you should leave now," I say softly, scared he may get agitated if I won't accept what he's telling me.

"Something happened though. I can't believe you didn't notice. I feel like I found my missing piece and together we clicked into place. With you, I'm whole. We created something stronger because we're meant to be together. That's what I mean when I say I love you."

"This isn't love. I think you're in love with the idea of us being in love."

Dylan screws his eyes up and mouths the words. The words didn't make much sense to me either.

"I'm in love with the idea of us, yeah." He approaches me and I tense. The metal of his rings are cool against my cheek as he cups my face. Dylan's face is so close; the tiny spark between our mouths I felt the night on the beach is there. His warm breath against my lips, so close I could lose myself in his orbit again.

"So am I, but only the idea," I say hoarsely, fighting the inner screaming to place my mouth on his.

"We could be so good for each other, this is meant to be," he murmurs.

"And so bad, too." With monumental self-control, I pull my face away from his hand. "Please, can we just forget each other?"

Dylan's eyes regain their lost confusion. "Forget? Never going to happen. You're here, forever." He holds a hand over his heart. Sensible Sky would laugh at him, but he's earnest.

"And I'll always carry a piece of you, Dylan. You touched my life and I'll never forget, but I can't let you take over."

"Why do you say that? Why would I? Fuck, Sky, I know better than to try and mess with you."

"Well, you're trying..."

"I would never tell you what to do or ask you to do or be anything apart from yourself. Why would I want to change who I fell in love with into someone else?"

The late hour and onslaught of emotion from Dylan does nothing to help me hold things together. He has to leave before I cry; before I listen to what he's saying and know his words make sense if I want them to. But the Sky standing here has only recently pushed her way out of someone else's control. This Sky has to change, not replace Grant with someone else.

Even if he is a six foot, hot as hell rock star who makes a mean bacon sandwich.

"I don't know, because I don't know you." Summoning my remaining courage, I weave past him and open the front door.

"You do. You're the only one who does."

I tense as he steps towards me again. Dylan shakes his head at my reaction.

"Dylan, please go."

He steadies himself on the doorframe. "I won't give up on you," he says. "I'll wait until you change your mind."

My scalp prickles. "You may be used to getting what you want, but you can't make someone feel what you want them to."

"Sky, if I thought you didn't feel the same underneath your protective walls, I wouldn't be here."

He stumbles and leaves the flat without looking back. Closing the door, I rest against it and stare at the stained ceiling. Why can't he be a normal guy living an everyday life so I could act on how I feel?

Chapter Twenty

Sky

After the restless night, I sleep in and don't have time to shower before work. I hate not showering every morning, but I'm on a new contract and tardiness could end the job. Finding temporary work is easy enough but swapping around different companies is a pain in the backside. So I tie my hair back, use extra deodorant and attempt to make up my face so I look closer to human than zombie.

The summer sunshine warms the day, the cloudless sky brightening my mood. I wish the days in Broadbeach had been sunnier, and then chastise myself for allowing my memories to wander back there again. As I leave the flat, I join the conveyor belt world. Kids wander past the gate towards school; cars drive by and queue at the end of the road and people stack at the bus stop.

A young guy from the downstairs flat I see every morning, but never speak to, leaves at the same time. Today he's wearing a Blue Phoenix T-shirt over scruffy blue jeans, unkempt brown hair hanging in his eyes. I stare in disbelief - as if a part of Dylan has to be in my world all the time. The guy watches me curiously from under his fringe. I rub my face, hoping I haven't left toast hanging out of my hair or something. He mutters a greeting and I resolve to speak to him soon, giving him a breezy hello for now.

A man sits on the low wall outside the Victorian house. He's middle-aged, dressed in slacks and a zipped green combat jacket. He stands as I walk along the path, but I don't register him.

"Are you Sky Davis?" he asks.

I halt unable to control my wide-eyed response to him. "Why?"

Oh, shit. Why did I not notice the camera he's holding in his hand, partly obscured behind his back. My look of realisation meets his and he grins. "I've been looking for you. I wanted to talk to you about Dylan Morgan."

"I don't know what you mean."

He smirks. "Come on, sweetheart. I saw him here last night."

Fuck. Not only does Dylan wake me up to profess his drunken love for me, but also he leads people to my front door. "No, I don't think you did."

I step to one side as the guy from my flats passes. He has earbuds in – hopefully, he didn't hear what the photographer said.

"See, most people think this thing Dylan Morgan had with the strange girl is nothing. But I get there's more to this, especially now I've discovered the girl's name is Sky and he's visiting her here. You can talk to us about everything, Sky."

Perspiration breaks out across my back, the day I've dreaded is here. I don't respond, mind whirling as I walk by.

"Sky."

I turn back to him, and his grin reveals yellowing teeth. *Shit.* I confirmed what he needed to know by reacting to my name. Nice job, Sky.

When he points the camera at me, I know being late for work is the least of my problems today.

*****

I'm no fan of social media. I have Facebook but rarely use it – all my friends from school post pictures of their babies or their holidays and (bizarrely) their dinner but I can't see the point in wasting my time. Twitter is a mysterious universe I haven't touched.

And social media works at lightning speed.

Mid-morning, I'm sitting in the lunchroom, dunking Rich Tea biscuits into my instant coffee, when a text comes through from Tara.

<You're still seeing him!!!!!>

<No>

<Umm. He was at your house. Twitter.>

A picture of Dylan walking away from my flat in the dark is attached. The bastard didn't try to disguise himself.

My hand shakes as I type a response. 'Not what it looks'

<Check this link> A website link is added to her message.

I don't think I want to, but I do. A Blue Phoenix fan blog has posted a series of pictures – several of Dylan last night and one of me looking worse than I thought I did this morning, with added 'wtf?' expression for good measure. Both sets of pictures are clearly taken outside my flat – one in the dark, one in the morning but by the same gate.

Fuck.

Shit.

Already a thread decrying Dylan's choice of woman has begun beneath. A discussion speculating where the picture was taken and how to find me has started.

How to find me?

Holy crap.

<U ok?> Text from Tara.

<Are you home?>

Tara works from home some days, although 'work' normally vies with TV chat shows for her attention.

<Come over>

My pale face and shaking is enough to convince my supervisor I have gastro and need to go home. Head down, heart beating in time with my rapid footsteps, I head for the bus. Dazed, I sit on the bus stop bench. The metal is cool against my legs, and grounds me. I stare at my shoes, mind reeling at what might be about to happen.

All because Dylan can't take no for an answer.

*****

I perch on Tara's expensive sofa in her immaculate flat. I always feel as if I'm walking into a show home when I visit. Unlike mine, there're never empty mugs, half-empty biscuit wrappers or clothes strewn around her flat.

Chewing a nail, I stare at the photographs of Tara and friends - nights out, on holiday, at birthday parties. I absentmindedly wonder why I'm not in any; I'm sure I was at some of the occasions I can see on there. An ironic reaction, since appearing in pictures when I don't want to is why I'm here.

Tara crosses towards me, dressed in yoga pants and a loose black top, hair pulled into a ponytail but somehow making her ensemble appear classy. She hands me a mug of tea.

"Will you tell me what's going on with Dylan?" she asks gently.

"Nothing. Honestly."

"Then why was he seen leaving your flat?"

I wipe my face with my hand. "I didn't ask him to come. He won't leave me alone."

"And you want him to?" she asks, and her disbelief is clear in her tone.

I look at Tara as if she's sprouted an extra, equally pretty head.

"Do you honestly think I could have a relationship with this guy and not end up with my heart torn out and my life a screwed up mess again? He's only doing this because I'm saying no."

"Sky, you already said yes. If he wants sex, he got that, didn't he?" I don't respond so she takes this as a yes. "Maybe there's more? Maybe he really does like you?"

But he didn't get sex, not entirely. God, all I have to do is recall one tiny memory of that night and my lady parts react. I pull a magazine from her table and point at the cover.

"Do I look like her?" I flick through until I find a section comparing models and actresses at awards nights. "Or her?"

My jab becomes more vehement with each person I point to, because this is something bothering me. This is what stopped me; each time I was tempted to reply to him in the first few days after I left Broadbeach.

I left a relationship with someone who tried to change me into the image of how he thought I should be, and I began to mould myself to Grant's image. Dylan Morgan's world's idea of women isn't mine.

Tara interrupts with the same words the other voice in my head uses. "But he already knows you don't look like these girls. He's seen you naked, right?"

"I'm not talking about being more than a size minus 20, I wouldn't want to be. I'm comfortable with who I am. Look at how manufactured they are. What if he wants to manufacture me so I'll fit his world?"

Like Grant did. And I did for Grant.

Tara doesn't respond, sipping her drink. "Hell, so many women would give their right arm to swap with you. You're crazy."

She is never going to understand, she follows the celebrities lives soaking up every detail from her magazines and TV shows. Tara drools over the clothes and the houses - and the men. Is she talking about herself? Would she swap places with me?

"All this doesn't matter because he's going away soon anyway. Then he'll forget about me."

My words hurt, and I wonder what the hell is wrong with me. All the time the words that come out are denial – not wanting to be used or changed. But every time I think about him with someone else my stomach twists into knots.

"So, did you check out the website I linked?" asks Tara.

"Briefly." I clamp up, blanking the not-so-pleasant things written about me. "Do you think they'll look for me?'

"Yes."

"Gee, thanks. Some kind of 'maybe not' encouragement would've been good."

Tara shrugs. "You need to be realistic about this. I guess things will die down."

"If he keeps away…"

Something in Tara's expression concerns me, as if she doesn't want him staying away either.

Tara places her mug on the coffee table. "How about we drive past your flat and see if there's anyone there?"

As we drive across the city, my head spins. Even if they have discovered who I am and where I live, how the hell could they get there so quickly? I only left four hours ago. Tara pulls into my street, her Nissan Micra crawling towards my flat.

"Advance guard," says Tara.

I follow her line of vision. Three girls sit on the wall next to the gate, chatting to the man who accosted me earlier. Tara keeps driving, and I glance at them hoping they don't look up. They're late teens, which is strange – you'd think they'd know better than to behave like the tweens who follow boy bands around. Two of them are bleached blondes in tiny shorts and tops, the third has sleek black hair. All three are beautiful.

"You think they're waiting for me?" I ask when I turn my head back to Tara.

"No, him. But if they see you they might not be too friendly."

Groaning, I slump down in the seat and put my face in my hands. "I should've said no to sharing his pizza and left the house that night."

The look Tara gives me is stranger than before. "You can stay at mine until you figure out what to do."

*****

"I'm not doing this – I refuse to stay at your place."

I spend the afternoon at Tara's mulling things over as she works in her office. There's only so much daytime TV one girl can take. Tara periodically shouts out Twitter and Facebook updates to me. By early evening, this grates on my ears so much I'm ready to start a Twitter account and lash back. Apparently, the fact Dylan has been spotted leaving his country house, and going into some exclusive London club has perked up the fandom. Which I hope means they've left the front of my house.

Tara's reluctance to let me go home and her eagerness to have me stay in the first place raises suspicion. I'd lay bets on her hoping Dylan comes to see me again. When I remind her the press might appear here too she changes her mind.

So at seven pm I walk along my street, heart thumping in my ears. I hold my breath as I get closer. The streetlight illuminates the pavement near the gate, and there's no longer anyone outside. The held breath rushes out, as I pull my keys from my black handbag with shaking fingers.

Chapter Twenty-One

Sky

My phone buzzes dragging me out of dreams about stalkers breaking into my flat. In my dream, I escaped with Dylan, and we sat outside the beach house reading until the house was struck by a tsunami. Bizarre. Tsunamis aren't a feature of the English climate.

Opening an eye, I pull the phone into the bed. A text from Tara.

<Call. Now>

Still lying down, I hit the screen to dial her number. "What? It's Saturday and early?"

"He stepped things up a notch."

My half-asleep brain struggles to catch up. "Who? What? Tara, I'm tired. I didn't sleep well last night."

"I'm texting you a picture. You really need to start watching social media and looking out for yourself."

"At this rate I'm pissing off back to Cornwall, or emigrating. What now?"

I put the call on hold and wait for the beep of Tara's text message, a screenshot from Twitter, time stamped around 3am this morning. More drunken Dylan antics?

Beneath the Twitter profile of @Real_DylanM:
<In love with the summer sky >

Underneath, a long list of tweets profess love for him, other responses bitching about me.

The phone beeps again. Another picture. Another tweet. This is a picture of Dylan uploaded by someone else. This isn't a paparazzi picture because the shot of Dylan and the band looks staged. They're conversing, heads together but Dylan is staring into space with the lost look of a love-struck teen. A tweet attached from profile @DMfanforever:
<Says no tour needs time out b/c of her>

Again a list of replies, some questioning why he's so cut up about me, when I'm clearly not worth his love, while others suggest they should come and talk to me.

Panic seizes my chest. *Talk to me*. Does Dylan know what he's doing? Of course he does. Bastard. I climb out of bed and throw on my robe, dragging fingers through my mess of hair. My bedroom window overlooks the street and with trepidation, I open the curtains a tiny amount and peek out.

Then wish I hadn't. There are at least twenty people hanging around the garden, sitting on the wall or doorstep, waiting. Holding the windowsill, I stare in dizzy disbelief at the unreal scene below.

Me. They're waiting for me. Tears prick my eyes and I sit on the floor, back to the wall.

I startle as my phone rings again.

"I hope your Facebook profile is private," says Tara, my social media guru, "because the media will dig up any dirt on you they can now. He's confirmed you're in his life now, whether you like it or not."

"He can't do this," I say hoarsely, "why is he doing this to me?"

"Because he's in love with you?"

No. Because he's used to people doing what he says, being with who he wants. Instead of letting go, he's trying to trap me. This is fucked up.

"You don't do this to people you love. He's trying to manipulate me."

Tara doesn't respond.

"There's a crowd of people outside my flat. How do I get out? He's got me trapped!"

"Really?" The excitement in her voice pisses me off.

"This isn't a game, Tara. This is my life. Fuck." In anger, I hang up and throw the phone across the room. I hate him.

Awesome start to the weekend. I've no idea whether the fans outside are friendly or not, but I sure as hell don't want to be photographed. As I shower, I mull over my options. Run? Stay? Talk to him and tell him what a fucktard he is - a term I reserve for those who are above and beyond dickheads, one he's joined the ranks of.

The texts start.

Why I'm surprised I don't know, because if they can find out where I live, tracking my mobile number isn't hard. The messages match those on social media. No sympathy for me, apparently I should revel in the fact he's prepared to ruin my life because he loves me.

I switch my phone off before anybody calls. Verbal abuse has to be next.

Banging my head against the wall behind, I inhale and hold the breath, fighting down the tears. I almost gave this guy a chance, but this is who he really is.

Someone knocks on my door and I want to crawl into a hole and hide. Will they kick the door down?

"Sky?" A man's voice.

I hold my breath again and close my eyes. Like monsters under the bed, maybe they'll all leave if I pretend they're not there.

"Sky. This is Steve Bennett. I'm Dylan's manager. I'm trying to sort out the mess the fucker has landed you in." He sounds as if his weekend shares the same super-fun start as mine.

"How?" I shout back through the door. "Put me in witness protection?"

"I've got a car. Will you come with me somewhere the public can't find you while things cool down?"

"You're telling me I need to hide?" I call.

"Sky, sweetheart, just open the door. Here. This is my card." A business card slips beneath the door.

I pull myself up, and then walk on shaking legs towards the card:

Steve Bennett
Phoenix Promotions

And a phone number. I squint through the peephole; a middle-aged man in a business suit, shifts from foot to foot outside. Satisfied he's alone, and who he says he is, I open the door. My eyes tear and he can't hide his surprise as he takes in my appearance. I'm sure I look awesome in my towelling robe with my tangled hair and red-rimmed eyes.

"Take me where?" I ask.

"Somewhere that's quieter."

Steve scowls and his eyes are tired; but he also has one of those faces that have lines from scowling a lot. I wonder how much of the grey around his temples was caused by Blue Phoenix antics? I think Dylan's actions are causing him as big a headache as me.

"Maybe get dressed? They're going to see you when you leave." I stare unblinkingly at him, proverbial rabbit in headlights. "I have a car. They saw me come in and they're waiting for you to come out."

"I can't!"

I walk back into my flat and he follows me.

"Sweetheart, they're not going anywhere soon. Believe me - I've done this before, way too many times to fucking count."

I slump onto a dining chair, picking at the fast food wrapper I forgot to bin last night. "Fucking fuck."

Steve laughs a short bitter noise. "Maybe if you'd let this run its course instead of shutting him out, we'd have avoided this."

"You mean wait until he got bored of me?"

Steve's look shifts to his shoes; I don't think he expected me to read his mind.

Would a broken heart when Dylan used and dumped me have been better than the hell outside my window? I'm gripping onto a life spiralling out of control facing an unknown future; the exact feeling I had the day I found Grant with whoever she is. Living in Dylan's surreal world and ending up broken-hearted would've been easier than being dragged into his life against my will, and dissected by everyone around.

I'm about to become public property and I hate him.

*****

The journey to "somewhere quiet" takes a couple of hours, time in which I gulp air and attempt to claw back normality. The trip from my front door to the car was bad enough. I've seen stars dealing with paparazzi before; and I wonder if they shared the sheer terror of the first time, they were accosted, too. The cameras in my lowered face were bad enough, but when some of the girls shouted at me, I blocked my ears and my mind in an attempt to drown out this strange world I'm unwillingly part of.

The winding country lane passes through a small village before the driver turns sharply into a wooded area off the main roads. The willow trees form a canopy above, filtering the sun into an eerie green light as they spread together across the country lane. The green tunnel this forms feels as if I'm transported to another world, and when I see where we're going I decide I am. From nowhere, and in direct contrast to the natural surroundings, a heavy metal security gate and fence appear. The black, wrought iron gate is attached to a wire fence worthy of a high security prison. Behind the gate, a gravel driveway bordered by manicured trees stretches towards a country house. Is this a mansion or a hotel? I don't know, but judging by the security, I'd go with mansion.

The gates swing open and the car crunches along the driveway towards the huge grey-bricked building and stops close to the entrance.

The Regency building could be the set for a Jane Austen novel, the golden brick cleaned and restored. Smooth lawn borders the front of the house, lined with flowerbeds blooming for the summer. The driveway is clear of other cars. Behind two pillars, the glossy double wooden doors are ajar. I jump as someone opens the car door, pulled out of my silent gawking.

"Grab your bag," Steve says gruffly.

I grab my handbag and stumble out of the car, into the English sunshine. My brain stayed in my flat in Bristol because my powers of speech and movement are minimal.

"This way."

I follow Steve towards the entrance doors, which open into an entrance hall the size of the entirety of my flat. The marbled floor is gleaming white – like those ads for floor cleaner – but in contrast, the walls are grey and black. Stairs sweep upwards from either side, supported on shining black marble columns, and meeting in the middle to form a balcony. Behind the balcony, a huge window floods the room with light.

My common sense catches up. "Where are we?"

Steve doesn't answer, but leads me across the hall, our footsteps echoing through the quiet house.

A kitchen as big as the entrance greets me as we walk through a second set of white painted doors. Everywhere is so clean and sterile looking. The spotless kitchen could be a show home - granite benches span the expansive room and state of the art stainless steel appliances are set into the oak cupboards. A beautiful house, but void of life.

"Jan! We've got a guest – fix her a drink?"

A woman tidies plates into a dishwasher and she looks around. She's around the same age as my mum - late forties - and she looks a little like my mum with her blonde ponytail and kind face. Jan regards me for a moment then her eyes widen in recognition.

"Oh! You're Sky?" She glances behind me to Steve.

"Sky – Jan. Jan – Sky. Jan's the housekeeper officially, but don't treat her like staff," he says brusquely as his phone rings.

Staff? Where in my world does anyone have staff? "Hi."

Jan smiles. "You look tired and hungry. Let me fix you something to eat?"

"Yeah, I'll be back in a bit." Steve walks off, answering his ringing phone.

Floor to ceiling windows brighten the kitchen and to the right of the room, glass doors lead out of the house onto a terrace. On the spacious terrace, a modern wooden table and chairs fill the space, facing onto a view of the nearby hills.

"Where am I?" I repeat, hoping Jan won't tell me I've fallen down a rabbit hole.

"Dylan's place."

Chapter Twenty-Two

Dylan

My favourite place to be when I'm in England is the old barn I had converted into a studio. Blue Phoenix never record here - this is my place – a time capsule of my journey. Posters decorate the exposed brickwork – small A4 print outs from early gigs to huge posters from festivals. Follow the posters around the room and you'll see Blue Phoenix go from being tiny print at the bottom, up to second support and finally to headlining. Glastonbury. Summerfest. Rock in Rio. We've done them all, worldwide, over and over.

Now this life is killing me.

In the photo on the middle shelf, four teenage boys pull moody faces for the camera. Jem has his hands extended into the devil horns salute, brown curls obscuring his eyes, arm across my shoulders. Liam's face is barely visible under his long red hair and Bryn is the nervous looking one, clutching his drumsticks. The last boy in the picture is me - tall and skinny with curls like Jem's. Jem's belief in us was fierce, pushing us into every opportunity to play and sending demo tapes the world over. Like

Jem, I believed we'd make it big and a year after this picture was taken, we did. I changed from the strange kid who sat at the back of the classroom, ignored, to someone everyone wanted a piece of. Suddenly I was the hot lead singer of a world-famous band and the guy the chicks wanted. Man, I fucking loved it.

The shot was taken shortly before our first ever real gig - supporting Chain Saw Babies, a new up-and-coming band. We were seventeen year old, long-haired boys with no clue what would hit them in a few months time. That night, the four friends from St David's were noticed by Steve Bennett.

Blue Phoenix rose and the world turned upside down.

Everything happened so fucking fast - one album later we hit the festival circuit and then toured our backsides off for three years. I saw half the world but was never part of it. By the end of that time I wasn't Dylan Morgan anymore, I was part of the Blue Phoenix brand and played my role. Would I rewind and do things differently? No. I've made some huge mistakes, some that haunt me still, but living for music, fame and money is what I wanted. The problem is, I don't want this anymore.

The soundproofing helps hide where I am, and the distance from the house acts as a warning to others who know to find me here. If Dylan's in his cave, keep the fuck away.

The song I'm writing is killing me as much as the girl the song is about. I'm unsure what bothers me more – the fact she's making me feel like this, or the fact she doesn't feel the same way.

Strumming chords on my acoustic, I piece together the lyrics and sounds. The songwriting pulls me back to the beaches and away from the life, I dragged myself back to. I wish I could say writing this song is cathartic, but the emotions released are raw.

This afternoon I'm in hiding from Steve. Drunken tweets at 3am after fending off Honey's slutty friends again did not make for a happy Steve. He tore a strip off me about the amount of damage control he's had to do recently, from the day I cut my hair and fucked off, and now this. I shut down, told him to fuck off but Steve had a careful line of attack.

His words eat at me several hours later: 'You ruin her life; she'll never want to be in yours.'

Those words hit harder than when my car and life collided with Sky's, the exact consequences of my actions crystal clear. I held Sky out to the world and said 'here she is, come and get her'. I didn't mean to. Now I've monumentally fucked up any chance with her.

Headphones on, drowning in the music, I turn back to the laptop. Something's missing; I can't make this track work. The caller name flashing on my mobile phone catches my eye.

Steve.

Fucking great.

I can ignore him, but the mood Steve's in today, he'll likely come and haul my ass out of here.

"Yeah?" I snap as I answer, "I'm busy."

"So am I, sorting out your shit. She's here." His words are staccato, fed up.

"Who?" Not his PA as well, I hope, anything but that stuck-up bitch.

"Sky, you dick."

Excitement and apprehension vie for space in my head. "Here? As in she's at the house? You're at the house?"

"Yes. Here. Now fucking sort this out. I don't have time for your lovelorn bullshit, we're already behind on the album deadline and the tour kicks off in two weeks. Sort it." He hangs up.

Why did she agree to see Steve, but not me?

*****

The sight of Sky standing and gazing out of the kitchen window kick starts my heart. Her back is to me, small figure rigid in her jeans and dark blue shirt. The denim hugs her gorgeous backside, and I blink away images of her naked and in my arms. The colour contrasts her dark blonde hair, the thick waves pulled into a ponytail. Sky. Here.

I fight my body's screaming need to stride over and hold her, the need to run my hands along the curves of Sky's body, remember how her skin feels beneath my hands. I could bury my face in her strawberry scented hair and close my eyes to imagine we're in Cornwall again. But I don't want to scare her so I hesitate before moving over. She senses me and turns before I reach her.

The Sky looking at me now is nothing like my Sky. Her eyes are stony, face hard and a mask of hurt. Arms crossed tightly over her chest, she challenges me to dare approach. Not the reunion I hoped for.

"Why?" she asks.

I know why Sky has her arms crossed; I can see her hands trembling. I don't know what she's asking about - she could be referring to any one of my stupid, drunken acts. So I do what I guess is expected. "Sorry."

"Sorry?" Her voice is low. "You out me to the world then you say 'sorry'? You bastard!"

The pink creeping across her pale cheeks reminds me of the colour I put in her face when we were in bed. Then my mind travels back there, joined by my gaze wandering along her body. Sky spots what I'm doing and makes a sound of disgust.

"I miss you." As I step towards her, she backs off.

"Why did you expose me? Why couldn't you just leave me alone?"

"Because I can't let you go. I'm trying but I can't. I don't even want to be here. I don't want anything but you right now."

"Have you listened to yourself?" She hisses. "This is stalking! But a thousand times worse."

What the fuck? "No!"

"Yes. You couldn't get what you wanted from me, so you used the means you had to manipulate me! Trap me…"

Fuck. Shit. No. I wipe my palms across my face, through my hair then stand with my elbows at right angles to my head. "No, fuck, no, that's not what happened…"

"Then what? A woman says she doesn't want you and you don't back off? You get your fans to do the stalking instead? You came to my flat for fuck's sake – you knew what you were doing. Then the bullshit on Twitter."

The booze. Again, the fucking booze turning my life to shit. "I was drunk when I did those things…"

Dropping my arms, I step towards her again, and she backs into the window. I stop short. The expression in her eyes isn't fear but anger. This is the girl whose car I rear-ended, but a million times more pissed off.

"Well, now you're sober, do something. Get them off me." She pauses and inhales. "Go back to your model girlfriend!"

"What model girlfriend?"

"The one all betrayed and weeping because Dylan Morgan cheated on her with some girl no one would look twice at." I hate it when she puts herself down and open my mouth to respond. "Her words, not mine. I have no issues with the way I look."

I can't help myself. "Neither do I."

The angry colour reaches her ears. "Fuck you!"

Wow, Sky has a mouth on her when she wants. "She's not my girlfriend. Not anymore, our so-called relationship ended six months ago."

"Then why did she say she was?"

"When we split, we kept up the pretence because I wanted her to. That way no one else made a play for me, I could tell other girls I came across who wanted to fuck me I was taken."

The arms around her chest loosen a little. "So you didn't cheat on someone with me?"

"Ask anyone in the inner circle. They'll tell you. I let her stay in a London flat I don't use, threw her some money now and again and she joined in. It's convenient for us both."

Dropping her steely blue eyes for the first time, Sky rubs her lips together, and her shoulders relax a tiny bit.

"Is this why you didn't want me? Because you thought I was with someone else?" I ask.

"That's one of many reasons. The major one just happened. The small issue I had with the world and his dog knowing who I am?"

"I could've kept you out of all this. We could carry on…"

Her head snaps back up. "You *are* delusional."

"Maybe, but I've never been great at coping with reality, have I?"

In her face, there's a flicker of connection to the beach house us, and for a moment the gulf between us contracts. Until she spots someone behind me, then her eyes widen before she rewraps her arms around herself and turns away. Angry at being interrupted, I spin around.

Steve stands, arms crossed to match Sky's. "Okay both of you. You're going to have to help me with this."

Sky watches Steve warily.

"Damage control. I don't give a shit about whatever the hell this is, I need you to make a joint decision on how we go from here."

*****

Sky

Steve crosses to Dylan, the older man is a good few inches shorter than his rock star charge, but Dylan's body language surprises me. His shoulders slump a little, as if he's being reprimanded. For the first time, I get a glimpse of Dylan's lack of control over his world and a twinge of sympathy pulls at the edge of my heart.

"Kim is on her way over. We sit down, come up with a story and go from there."

"What do you mean? Who's Kim?" I ask.

Steve doesn't look at me. "Kim deals with the media on behalf of Blue Phoenix and we need to give them a story that suits you both. She'll have some suggestions – you might want to talk through your own ideas first. Then you can go."

Neither of us speaks. Then Steve knocks Dylan on the head. "Wake up."

The exchange confuses me. The power balance is off in their relationship, and in a weird way. Steve isn't Dylan's dad, but he talks to him as if he is.

Steve fixes his brown eyes on me instead. "Listen, love, sit down with dumbass here and tell him what you want. Agree on a price or whatever the hell. Kim said she'll be here by three…" He shakes his expensive gold watch around and reads the time. "Three hours. Go."

Dylan doesn't respond and Steve tips his head. "I am not having another Lily situation here, am I?"

"Fuck, no!" says Dylan.

"I bloody hope not," says Steve. "I can only make so many things go away..."

Something unspoken passes between the two men, there's a tension with hidden meaning.

"You don't need to make me go away," I say, "I'm quite happy to do that myself as soon as Mr Rock Star leaves me alone."

Steve laughs and claps Dylan on the shoulder. "I can tell she doesn't take shit from you. I bet that would've been funny to watch."

I bristle at the patronising tone he uses on Dylan. Next, he'll be ruffling Dylan's hair and asking him to fetch his slippers.

"I don't take crap from people," I retort.

Dylan chokes back a laugh, as Steve is rendered speechless for a few seconds.

"You might need that skill, if it's true," says Steve before leaving the room.

The mood in the room shifts, some of the tension leaves as Steve walks out. Dylan crosses to the fridge, a vast double-door monstrosity. "Are you hungry?"

Am I? I haven't eaten today. "A little."

Bread, butter and bacon appear on the kitchen bench and Dylan ducks his head from behind the fridge door. "Bacon sandwich?"

My mind flashes back to Dylan's naked back, as he cooked breakfast on the first day. A teasing smile pulls the corner of his mouth and I'm off-guard. Steve's treatment of Dylan peels away some of the anger layers and exposes the stupid Sky who wants Dylan despite his selfish behaviour.

"Toast, thanks."

He pouts. "Was my cooking that bad?"

"No comment."

A tiny smile escapes me as the tug back to our banter disarms me further.

*****

The view from the terrace outside the kitchen stretches across Dylan's property. Broad stone steps sweep down the back of the house, neatly maintained lawn stretching out beneath the terrace. The burr of a lawnmower fills the silence around and I close my eyes, the smell of mown grass calms my mind.

Dylan fiddles awkwardly with his glass of orange juice. Is he nervous? At least this is a step back from the constant nagging about our relationship.

"Steve. Does he always talk to you like that?"

"Sometimes, we need pulling into line when we do stupid things."

"But you're twenty-four and successful. Not a naughty teenager."

Dylan sits back in his chair. "He's been with us since I was; I guess I'm used to his ways."

I don't voice my true opinion of Steve. I'm grateful for his rescue mission this morning, but he has an agenda.

"Why's Kim getting involved?"

"The band's PR manager. When crap like this happens, we come up with a story for the press. We need something to give them so they'll leave you alone." Dylan doesn't look at me, and he rubs his arm in a way I've seen before, fingers playing slowly over his phoenix tattoo.

"Isn't this easy? You tell him you made a mistake and we're over. Get photographed with someone else? Maybe your model um... whatever she is."

Dylan blows air into his cheeks, gazing across his fields. "Apart from the fact Cressida has moved on. This situation is her chance to wriggle out of things and she's about to go public with her boyfriend, Dean Ryder the football player. Heard of him?" I pull a blank face and he laughs. "No, probably not."

I sip the orange juice, the refreshing iced drink perfect for my dry mouth. Now I'm with Dylan, in another place removed from the everyday, I'm slipping back towards him. As soon as we're together, the Dylan Morgan gravity pulls us closer.

Dylan reaches a hand across the table, curls his long fingers around mine. My first reaction is to snatch my hand away, but he turns my hand over, tracing calloused fingertips across the back before lacing his fingers through mine. A small, intimate touch that fires unexpected arousal low in my body. I ready myself to admonish the smug smile I expect, but his blue eyes remain focused on my hand, rubbing my knuckles.

"So you won't give this a chance?" he asks quietly.

"Nice job. That was at least fifteen minutes without mentioning our situation," I sigh. "We're stuck on an endless loop here, Dylan, and your behaviour hasn't helped. We had a holiday… thing. End of."

"Why end of?"

I pull my hand away and bury my face in them both. He's like a child who can't be told no. "I've told you, repeatedly, this will end badly for me - can't you see?"

"How do you know? Are you psychic? Why not take a chance? Every relationship has a chance of ending badly."

"I don't think I'll be having a relationship for a while, Dylan. As I tried to explain, part of this is because I'm trying to find my way into a new life. Things are scary enough, everything turned upside down after five years of thinking my life was mapped out for me. Until I sort myself out, I can't give myself to anyone else."

"I don't want your life; I just want to be in it. For fuck's sake, Sky, I'm asking you to date me not fucking marry me!"

Whenever he uses the word 'date', it amuses me. "Dylan, look at your life, at your history…"

Dylan pushes his chair back and stands, walking to the edge of the terrace. His sudden reaction alarms me.

"Lucky for the next guy then," he says, resting against the wall. "He might be the biggest dickhead around with a dodgy past but you won't have the benefit of the internet to check him out. The next guy will have a chance and I fucking don't!"

Am I being unreasonable? So much in my life terrifies me at the moment, and Dylan intensifies the fact I have so little in my control.

"I don't know what to say to you. Can we sort out this story?"

Funny how I hardly know him, but already know him so well. Well enough to see in his eyes he's shutting down.

"Whatever, Sky." He stalks back into the kitchen leaving me shaking and on the edge of tears. If only I knew what I wanted to do because now I'm with Dylan, I feel safe. Ironically, because he caused the very thing threatening my safety.

Chapter Twenty-Three

Sky

The blonde woman in the black skirt suit and too tight white silk blouse spends a lot of the meeting with her eyes on Dylan, allowing me a disdainful glance or two through the conversation. Steve sits next to her, drumming fingers on the table and intermittently checking his phone for messages.

The boardroom seems out of place in the mansion-like house, reinforcing my conclusion this place is the central hub for Blue Phoenix as well as being Dylan's house. Dylan and me sit in body-moulding leather chairs, across the long, smooth table from the manager and PA.

The relaxed surroundings aren't reflected in the atmosphere in the room. Since Dylan's childish reaction before, we haven't spoken and now sit apart. Does Dylan not realise this kind of behaviour does nothing to help his cause?

Kim is what I expected – young, beautiful and straight to the point. She pulls out an iPad and taps the screen with long, pink painted nails matching her lipstick.

"So, what did you come up with?" asks Kim.

Silence.

She sinks back in her chair. "Dylan?"

"She wants a 'we're over' story," he says in a low monotone.

The heavily made up eyes turn to me. "Sky?"

"Um, yes." Why do I feel like I'm in the headmistress's office at school?

"I don't think anyone will believe us. Not so suddenly after your oh, so clever, social media barrage, Dylan," she retorts.

I stiffen. "What?"

"Dylan Morgan, suddenly saying everything is over between you the day after his declaration of love. If you were one of his fans, would you think this was true? Or would you smell a story to get people to leave you alone?"

She's right. If I walk back to my flat tonight, nothing will change. Not in my life and not in Dylan's.

"What about if he's seen with another girl? And I can do some story about how he's broken my heart and he can say he's moved on?" I ask.

A low noise escapes Dylan's throat. "No. Don't drag someone else in. I'm not doing that."

I narrow my eyes at him. "I'm the person getting abuse from the fans."

"Abuse?" He looks genuinely confused.

"Don't be naive, Dylan," says Kim. "These girls are on your side and if they can't have you, they won't let anyone hurt you."

"So what do we do?" I ask Miss Perfect, annoyed at the jealous prickle as she smiles at Dylan.

"I said the whole situation would've been better if she'd let things run their course," says Steve.

"Yeah, he wanted me to get heartbroken and dumped," I mutter.

Kim's eyes widen and pink lips part in a light bulb moment. "Not such a bad idea."

"What?" I ask, incredulous that Dylan's not the only one choosing to manipulate me.

"So Sky's here, giving into the inevitable pull to Dylan Morgan, unable to say no any longer." I snort derisively and she glares at me. "After a few days together, everything turns to shit. Dylan Morgan realises Sky's not worth the hassle and they split. Then we get the story out for the right price. Shortly after, Blue Phoenix goes on tour and everyone moves on. End of story."

"I'm not staying here!" I protest.

"Don't worry; you don't have to spend time together. Treat your stay as a holiday – this place is so big you don't need to cross paths with Dylan if you don't want. And at the end of this, you might even make some cash out of selling the story we give you." Evidently, the decision is made, because Kim begins typing furiously on her iPad.

"I don't want money! I have a life and I'm trying to hold down a job. I need to go home."

"Yeah, off you go sweetheart. Back to what I brought you away from," says Steve.

"Dylan?" Kim asks.

For most of the exchange, he's leant back in his chair, hands locked behind his head ignoring me. His childish sulking infuriates me. "Yeah, okay. For how long?"

"That's up to Sky."

All eyes apart from Dylan's turn to me. I scrunch my shirt in my hands, biting inside my cheek to stop retorting to them all. They're right, I can't walk away from the situation now and this is a solution. Despite the fact I blame Dylan for all this, the predicament was inevitable the day I allowed myself to get close to him in Cornwall. If you tangle with the famous, you have to expect consequences. Dylan wasn't the only delusional one.

*****

Lying on a king size bed, I stare at the celling, unable to comprehend why I let myself get into all this in the first place. Falling for a guy on the rebound isn't uncommon, I just chose the wrong one.

The guest room they've accommodated me in is more of a guest apartment. The bathroom alone is twice the size of the kitchen in my poky flat and contains a huge white bath on bronze claw feet. A giddy sense of holiday takes over as I inspect the bathroom, delighted to see the bath is a jacuzzi. I could pour in one of the bottles of amazing smelling gels and lie in there with a book, maybe a glass of wine...

I reluctantly gave my flat key to Steve, who's sent someone to collect some clothes. Great, another stranger looking at my underwear. Dylan offers to buy me new things but I refuse. I also give Steve a long list of books – I intend to treat this as a couple of days avoiding Dylan and pretending I'm at a health spa in the country. Then life can move on.

Really? Am I misleading myself as much as Dylan does?

A knock on the door pulls me out of bath time fantasies. Are my belongings or books here? Hopefully the person outside is bringing both.

Dylan. He holds the same rucksack I used for my holiday to Broadbeach; his strong arms that once wrapped around me are wrapped around the bag. He holds the same closed off expression and stiffened stance as earlier, so why is he here?

"I brought your stuff."

"Thanks."

He walks across the plush cream carpet, into the room and puts the bag on the bed. Awkward about him in here, I hover by the door.

"Did they get you everything you needed?" he asks gruffly.

This is different, businesslike. Either he's changed tack or he's finally accepted the truth.

"I think. Thanks."

When Dylan reaches the doorway, he ensures he gets close enough to brush my chest with his arm on the way past.

I inhale sharply, and he places his mouth next to my ear. "Feel free to throw your underwear around the room."

I hold my breath. Grant never had the same subtle mix of scents as Dylan, and definitely didn't trigger memories of amazing sex. I never realised until Dylan how evocative the sense of smell is – and in this situation, my mind blanks. Harder blue eyes than earlier today meet mine, the eyes of someone who's opened up and been kicked closed again.

"I'll bear that in mind." I cringe at my husky voice and clear my throat. His mouth tips into a knowing smile.

"Jan said she'd make you some dinner. I won't be there, don't worry."

As he leaves, I manage to prevent myself asking him to stay. I think my mood swings are as bad as his are.

*****

The walk from my room to the kitchen takes several minutes, and after a few wrong turns through half-empty rooms, I find the place. The sparseness of the house strikes me, as if this is a show-home. There's no lived in, comfortable feel to the environment and some rooms still smell of fresh paint. Dylan must have a number of properties, especially if he lives in the States part of the time. Either that or his half-empty house is a reflection on his life.

I pull my flannel shirtsleeves over my hands, and hover in the doorway. Jan busies herself setting out plates on the large oak table, and doesn't look up until I'm brave enough to approach.

"Sky! How are you?" She gestures to a matching oak chair across the room and I obediently sit.

"I feel weird."

Bringing a large, steaming bowl over to the table, Jan smiles sympathetically. "Weird situation."

That's putting things mildly. I peer into the bowl. Fresh pasta in a tomato sauce, mixed with vegetables and a strong smell of herbs. She adds a second bowl containing salad. My stomach rumbles appreciatively.

"What would you like to drink?"

Wine. "Water, please."

Jan sets a plate, cutlery and large glass of sparkling water in front of me then sits in the chair nearby. The vast table fills the room, but doesn't change the emptiness.

"Does Dylan live alone?" I ask.

"Sometimes, but often the band stays here. The house is large enough for all their egos." She smiles to herself. "There's a recording studio – well, two but one's Dylan's private place."

My stomach twists. The band. "Are the others here now?"

"Liam and Honey are staying. The others are back tomorrow I think – they've things to finish before the tour."

Honey? I had a friend at school who had a guinea pig called Honey. It wasn't the brightest of animals.

"I bet they all keep you busy."

"Hmm. Well, I don't clear their mess up on my own or cater to their parties. I'm here in the day, and then I go home."

Spooning pasta into my bowl, I take in the surroundings. Every minute I'm here, I'm on high alert. Fish out of water doesn't even come close to how I feel. Small talk; I have to do small talk.

"Have you worked here long?" I ask.

"Three years. I considered leaving after the first year, but Dylan persuaded me to stay. I saw some stuff I wasn't happy to see."

The middle-aged woman pulls her lips tight; and whether she wants to tell me or not, I don't want to hear.

"Life here is different now though; they've mellowed. Well, some of them." She fixes me with a loaded look. "Like Dylan."

I shift in my seat and focus on the pasta, twirling some around my fork. If I eat, I don't have to talk.

"Did you know him before?" she asks.

"Before what?"

"Before he disappeared. Did he leave because of you?"

The pasta sticks in my throat. "No."

"Hmm."

"Hmm?"

She stands and brushes imaginary crumbs from the table. "He had a different look when he first came back. He was still unhappy but he was brighter."

No, not her too. What is this? Is Dylan getting everyone to guilt me into a relationship?

"Amazing what the summer skies and sea air can do for someone," I say.

Someone behind giggles. "Sure is, summer Sky."

I twist in my seat. The owner of the giggle and American accent can't hide the surprise on her face when she registers me. My expression matches hers. Talk about rock star girlfriend cliché; here she is in glorious Technicolor with perfectly straight, long, blonde hair to match the perfectly white and straight teeth she's flashing at me. Honey is impossibly elegant in tight, hip hugging jeans with silicone breasts straining beneath her tight leopard skin top. Oh, good God.

"I'm Honey." She crosses and holds out a hand with talon-like red nails. "I'm Liam's fiancée.

"Congratulations."

"Thank you, darling."

Darling?

Honey strolls over to the fridge, hips swaying in a way suggesting she was or is a model, or she would like to be one. She pulls out a bottle of water, and delicately places her mouth round to drink.

"So you're his summer Sky?" Is she mocking me? The saccharin sweetness in her tone has gone.

"I'm Sky, yes."

"I think you did the right thing, darling," she says. "You're not his type. He'd get bored. Save yourself heartbreak because Dylan isn't very… accessible."

My scalp prickles at this bimbo telling me what I should or shouldn't do. Is there jealousy from her here? No, she's engaged to someone else.

I keep my game face. "Yeah, I figured that might happen..."

Honey sashays towards me, stopping close enough for me to gag on her heavy perfume. "Still, make the most of your stay here. I doubt you'll experience anything like this again."

Her words irk. No, they piss me off. She's suggesting I'm not worth this luxury and somehow below her; someone like me isn't worth Dylan. Whatever the reasoning is behind her bitchy comments, the words have my back up enough to step into Dylan's life a little. A two fingered salute to Honey. Just for a day or two. No more. Honest.

Chapter Twenty-Four

Sky

Waking the next morning, and refusing to be intimidated, I shower, dress in my non-Honey clothes and seek out breakfast. The adrenaline kicks back in when Jan's friendly face from the normal world is absent. There's milk in the fridge and I don't want to root around in cupboards for cereal so I settle on a glass full and an apple from the bowl on the kitchen bench. Now the excitement of books and baths has worn off, discomfort has pushed in. I want to go home.

I sneak back to my room, snuggle onto the day bed beneath the bay window and read a book about college kids in America - I've avoided all books with rock star heroes since Broadbeach. Several hours later, with a headache coming on, I summon up the courage to leave the room. I'm a guest, I should explore, and I need some fresh air.

Half an hour wandering the grounds and I definitely feel like I've been spirited to a different world. To navigate the whole estate would need a car; the house alone is twice the size of the hotels in Greece I stayed in with Grant and a lot more luxurious. The outside of the house contradicts the interior with the preserved brick facade and carefully restored windows. I pass a huge, sparkling pool overlooked by several wrought iron balconies, steps leading upwards. Why would someone have a pool in the English climate? Oh, yeah, status.

The lawned gardens stretch in every direction, the woods bordering the property in the distance. There's other buildings further from the house - one looks like the old estate cottage and another a converted barn or stables.

I sit on a wall near the entrance to the house, attempting to take everything in. The quiet and lack of people around strikes me, something I'm unused to. I haven't seen Dylan since yesterday, even though he's on my mind the whole time. The anger towards him ebbed with the confusion on his face at what he'd done wrong. Then witnessing how Steve treats him added in sympathy. His life truly isn't his own, and he doesn't have many coping strategies in his struggle to step outside.

An expensive red sports car heads down the driveway and pulls up close by. I stand to leave, not wanting to meet the tall guy who climbs out. I back towards the stairs leading to the front door, debating whether to run inside or not.

Rolling his head and stretching out his shoulders, the stocky man snaps something at the driver. He's broader than Dylan, with a mass of auburn curls falling across his face and shoulders. Tight black jeans, a baggy band T-shirt and combat boots finish off his image. Is this Dylan world of Blue Phoenix a collection of clichés? And if it is, what does that make me?

As he has sunglasses on, I'm unable to tell if he notices me hiding in the shadows. He pulls them off and strides over. I tense, waiting for a loaded comment but instead he grabs me in a bear hug, big arms wrapping around me and squeezing out my breath like a hairy boa constrictor. He holds me by the shoulders, chocolate brown eyes studying mine.

"Summer Sky!"

I wish people would stop calling me that.

"Yeah. Hi."

"You changed your mind?" He raises an eyebrow.

"No, she didn't."

I jump at Dylan's voice. His sharp tone reminds me of the Dylan I met when our cars collided, and the closed off expression from earlier remains. He's dressed in his usual jeans and T-shirt combination, but for the first time he's wearing a Blue Phoenix T-shirt. The head of his phoenix tattoo disappears under the sleeve stretching across the biceps I pictured myself licking on the first day. He's in the Dylan Effect proximity and my nervousness doesn't help the heavy breathing.

Dylan strolls down the steps towards the other man. "But you can keep your hands off, Bryn. She doesn't do rock stars." His eyes flick to mine. "Much."

Colouring, I shove my hands in the back pockets of my jeans and examine the ground.

"Bad luck, man." The sound of Bryn clapping Dylan on the back follows, and their voices retreat into the house.

Why am I pissed off I wasn't included?

*****

The rest of the day I float around, like a ghost haunting the place, invisible, hovering at the edge of their life. I make frequent trips to the kitchen in the hope of finding Jan but never do. Occasionally I hear male voices carrying along the hallways from other rooms, raucous laughter and shouting. There are also girls' voices, and I picture a room full of half-naked groupies. Jealousy isn't something I'm permitted when I've rejected him.

This isn't for me. The lifestyle of the rich and famous equals boredom. Bird in a gilded cage, I traipse from room to room trying to decide what to do. Clouds roll in outside, the end of the English sunny summer's day, and the rain starts. Running out of options, I make a quick sandwich from the cold meats and salads I find in the fridge before retreating to my room.

One day down, two to go?

I take a wrong turn again; this place is a bloody maze. Dylan's lack of variety in decor doesn't help navigation. Maybe breadcrumbs from the sandwich will help find my way back to the kitchen next time, like Hansel and Gretel lost in the woods. I pick at the edge of the sandwich as I prepare to back out of the opulent sitting room I've stumbled upon.

"Hey, it's the little lady herself." A man's voice carries over the low music coming from the huge speakers across the room.

From my position, I can see long legs in dark denim jeans and bare feet, a tattooed arm resting on the edge of the sofa. His head is behind the white leather cushioned chair and he leans forward, face obscured by long, dark curls. His hair is longer than Bryn's, matching mine for unruliness. Pushing his hair back with one hand, he takes a good look at my figure, slowly and deliberately.

"Sorry," I say and turn to leave.

"What for? Come in! Jacinta's around somewhere, she'll get you a drink."

Something about this man bothers me. Not because he hasn't told me his name, but because along with his over-enthusiastic tone, he appears tightly coiled, like a rubber band ready to fly across the room.

"I'm okay. But thanks."

"You *are* Dylan's Sky?" he asks.

"I'm Sky."

"Where's Dylan?"

"I don't know."

"Oh? Are you his Sky or not?" He drains the contents of the glass he's holding and dangles his arm over the side of the chair. The glass hovers between his long, fingers; fingernails painted black.

A soft click of the door from the opposite end of the room alerts me. A tall girl wearing a short, tight silver top covering very little of her ample chest, and a skirt I'm sure is actually a belt, crosses the room. She only has eyes for the man, and positions herself on his lap.

"I'm Jem. This is Jacinta. All the Js."

Jacinta turns her head as if only noticing I'm in the room. Her eyes are vacant; she's somewhere else. Drugs? I shiver, and my thoughts must be apparent because Jem gives a sardonic grin.

"You can have some of what she's having?" he asks.

"No thanks."

"I meant champagne. Do you like champagne?"

I shake my head, not wanting to stay in this room. Jacinta slides her hand up and down Jem's thigh, and he pulls her sleek black hair to one side and kisses her neck.

"Get Sky a drink, babe," he says and shifts so Jacinta has to move.

She stands and he slaps her backside as she walks away. If I thought Dylan was an arrogant wanker when I met him, he had nothing on this guy.

"I'm okay." I hold up the sandwich. "I'm going to eat this and..."

"Sit down then." He stands and strides over.

His request is more a demand. I'm pissed off with my inability to retort to this guy. He scares me and now he's close, the smell of whisky surrounds him, and his edginess disturbs me further. I'm convinced that if I try to leave the room, he'll follow. Reaching out, he tucks a strand of hair behind my ears, and I jerk at his touch.

"Dylan's summer Sky..."

Run. Get out. Leave the house. This guy's intentions aren't good. Something's wrong - something I don't understand. To evade him, I bump my backside onto the white leather sofa behind. He keeps close, and sits on the glass coffee table opposite.

"Tell me, Sky, was Dylan always your favourite Blue Phoenix guy?"

"I didn't know who you were before a couple of weeks ago."

Jem's glazed eyes widen, and then he frowns. "Oh, really? You too?"

"What?"

The plate is balanced on my knee, and I stare down at the sandwich. I don't know what he's doing or why, but I hope to hell Jacinta comes back soon.

"He believed you?"

"Why wouldn't he?"

Jem shifts closer, knee touching mine, and he places a hand on my thigh. In ordinary circumstances, I'd give him a mouthful and stomp out of the room but my brain has locked my body into fear. Why?

"Do you know we used to share girls?"

"Okay!" I say loudly, and stand. The plate drops to the floor. Reverie broken, I sidestep him. Not wanting to hear what he's telling me is enough to switch my brain back on.

"Sometimes, we'd swap," he continues. "Like, if he met a girl first but I wanted her, we'd trade. We keep tally and he owes me big time." Jem giggles; increasing my fear, he's high.

Jacinta approaches with two glasses of champagne and Jem's mouth curls. "Where the fuck's my drink?"

She blinks at him. "You asked me to get her a drink."

"You got yourself one too but not me!"

The dark edge to his tone frightens me more than Jacinta; she gazes at him blankly.

"Fuck it, I'll have champagne." He grabs the drink and knocks back the contents in two gulps before shoving the glass back at her. "Now get me a fucking bourbon."

Through the whole exchange, he hasn't taken his eyes off me. I shuffle towards the door, away from the broken plate. He remains seated on the coffee table, his coiled muscles and predatory stare terrifying me. My sarcasm and wit fail at the exact moment I need them.

"Enjoy your stay, Sky," he says and snorts softly to himself.

I didn't like Jacinta when I saw her, but I'm certain her interruption wound back whatever he intended to do.

"Thanks," I mumble.

He allows me to leave.

Dazed, I retrace the steps from before, wanting to find my way back to the bedroom as soon as I can. The situation has more than freaked me out - meeting Jem was a slap in the face to the Sky who was considering testing Dylan's world for a few days.

I step through another door, into another situation. The decor of the room matches the entrance hallway with black marble pillars stretching to the ceiling, stairs heading upwards towards the next floor of the house. A swimming pool fills the room, a jacuzzi bubbling quietly at one end.

This house is a dream house but also a place from my nightmares - identical hallways lined by identical doors - and now I'm living a bad dream.

Natural light pours through the windows, over the occupant of the pool. My shoes squeak on the grey marble tiles alerting the swimmer. Dylan. He stops swimming and pushes a hand through his wet hair.

"I g-got lost," I stammer and back off.

"What's wrong?"

"Nothing."

"Sky?" He swims over and pulls himself onto the edge of the pool, water trickling down his sculptured chest the same as the day by the sea. Why do I forget how eye-poppingly sexy this guy is?

He wipes water from his face. "You okay?"

"I've changed my mind. I want to leave," I tell him.

"I thought you said you'd got lost."

"I have. In more ways than one. I think I want to go home..." I hate the way my voice wavers; I hate I let Jem get to me, and most of all, I hate I agreed to stay here.

Dylan pulls himself to his feet while I attempt to avert my eyes from how his blue board shorts cling to his anatomy. Or how when they're wet, they sit that little bit lower on his hips, revealing that little bit more of the 'v' shape Grant never had. I attempt and fail.

"Sky, stop perving and tell me what's wrong?"

His attempt at humour lightens me a little. "I don't feel right here, Dylan. This place - I'm not comfortable here."

"Something's upset you. You're shaking."

"No, I'm not."

Dylan grabs my hand and pulls it towards him. "Yes. Look."

I try to pull my hand away, but he closes his tightly around mine. "Did security not know who you were and get heavy? I told them about you..."

I shake my head. "No. No. Honestly, Dylan, I'm okay."

Water drips down his face. "Okay." Dylan leans over to grab his towel from the floor.

I don't know why, but I'm expecting more, but once I close him out by telling him I'm okay, he returns the favour. "I'll go then..."

He scrutinises me as he dries his hair. "I was going to call you anyway."

"Call me? We're in the same house."

"Technically."

"I suppose this place is the size of a hotel..."

"Yeah." Is he uncomfortable about this? He bought the house...

"What were you going to call me about?" I ask.

"Tonight."

"What about tonight?" I don't do 'tonight', not with Dylan. Tonight, I'm packing.

"There's a party."

"Thanks for the heads up - make sure you turn the music down by 10pm."

He gives me his 'you're funny, Sky' look. "No. You have to come."

"Not my scene." I turn to leave; his near nakedness is addling my brain and could lead to me being persuaded to join in his episode of the Young and the Beautiful.

"Sky, this is for us to make a scene as a backup to our story."

"A scene? What do you mean?"

"We have a fight or something in public for people to spread around social media." He pauses. "So, I'm not using the party as an opportunity to get in your face and talk you around."

"Your idea?"

"No. Kim's."

I bet, and I can imagine her haughty face overseeing the situation. "I'm not sure..." I grasp for and excuse. "I don't have anything to wear."

Dylan laughs. "Nice excuse."

"I mean I don't have anything suitable for a rock star's girlfriend to wear." None of the clothes Steve brought from my flat are what I'd wear out shopping, never mind to a party.

"I can get you something?"

"And you know my response to that!"

He huffs. "Fine. Check the wardrobe in your room?"

"For what?"

"You're in the guest room. People often leave clothes – there's probably something suitable."

Second hand clothes from skinny girls? Those are unlikely to fit me. "No. I'll wear something I have. If I go."

"Suit yourself, but if you want to disconnect yourself from Blue Phoenix, this is the easiest way. Then you won't have to subject yourself to my presence again."

We both wait for the other to speak. The room is humid from the pool and heating, and the atmosphere between us hangs in the claustrophobic air.

"Why were you going to call me? Why not come and talk to me?" I ask.

His distant pale blue eyes connect straight back to the Dylan from Broadbeach, the one looking to escape. "Because seeing you is hard."

Dylan throws the towel across his shoulders and climbs one of the sets of metal spiral stairs leading to a part of the house I haven't been in.

As his figure disappears, Jem re-enters my mind. I hope I don't take a wrong turn on the way back to my room this time.

Chapter Twenty-Five

Sky

Whoever packed my bag was male. The rucksack contains mismatched tops and trousers, a pair of faded jeans, a plain white work shirt, a short red party dress and my favourite blue and white floral summer dress.

I lay the creased dresses on the bed and compare them. The red dress has a wine stain on the front from last year's Christmas party, so I dump it back into my rucksack. This leaves two options- summer dress or jeans. Judging by the expensively dressed people I've watched climb out of cars this evening; jeans would get me escorted off the premises. The summer dress I wore in Broadbeach is my only option.

Creeping down the hallway from my bedroom, towards the sound of the loud guitar music and the hubbub of voices, I reach the curving staircase at the front of the house and peer down. People mill around in the marbled entrance hall, air kissing and admiring each other. Even from a distance, I can see expensive looking, presumably designer, dresses and well-tailored suits. There's no high street fashion down there. I look down at my floral summer dress and flat shoes; I'm no Disney princess ready to make a sweeping entrance at the ball.

I can't walk into the throng of people below; I'll be eaten alive.

I head back along the hallway, past my room, to find the set of stairs leading down to the end of the house with the kitchen. Maybe Jan will be there, and hopefully no one else. I can't imagine this is the sort of party, where people hang out in kitchens. I recognise my streaming thoughts – panic mode bringing on bubbling, burbling nonsense waiting to fall from my mouth.

I walk into the kitchen and Dylan's alone on the terrace outside. My chest tightens and I halt.

The glass door is open and he faces away from me. He's wearing a suit and holds a short tumbler glass in his hand, the light glinting off his rings. My heart stutters, and the confusion between anxiety and attraction hits. I'm turned on by this hot as hell man who turned my world upside down, there's no getting away from that, but how is that enough? Dylan turns and walks towards the kitchen, pausing when he sees me.

"Sky."

"Hey."

He sweeps a gaze across my ensemble. "I like what you're wearing."

His scrutiny makes me uneasy. "Very funny."

"No, I do. You were wearing that the first day I met you." He knocks back the rest of his drink. "I remember how sexy you looked in that dress. How sexy you look in it now."

"This is just a dress from Next, nothing fancy."

Dylan steps forward, on the very edge of acceptable personal space. "The dress shows your curves, and you look natural."

He needs to step back and stop talking about my curves the way he did the night in the beach house, and I dismiss the reaction my body wants to have to Dylan calling me sexy.

I swallow. "I don't think natural fits here."

"You're beautiful, Sky," he says, eyes softening as he lightly rests his fingers on my face.

"I guess your suit isn't high street?" I say, moving my head away from his touch.

"I told you I looked fucking hot in a suit," he says and grins, pulling at his jacket.

A quote I once read springs to mind, about how a well-tailored suit is to women what lingerie is to a man. In front of me is exactly what that quote means. I'd retort about his arrogance but he's a hundred percent correct. The expertly tailored dark grey suit and crisp black shirt beneath covers all the ugly tattoos; the open neck adds a more casual look. With one hand in his pocket, and the other holding his empty glass, he's searing hot, model material again. No wonder this guy is number one on all the Top Ten lists of world's sexiest men. A secret surge of smugness he wants me sneaks in and I slap the reaction down.

Crossing to the kitchen bench, he pours himself another drink from the heavy bottle. "Do you want one?"

God, yes. "Okay." I don't go for spirits much but one glass should help the nerves.

"So you're going to accompany me to the party?" he asks, filling my glass with a dark liquid.

"Accompany you?"

"We should arrive together, even if we leave apart." His words and expression are loaded as he picks up the two glasses and inclines his head towards the next room.

The music and light filter under, and I inhale as he opens the door. I only need to do this once, I tell myself.

"Cheers," he chinks our glasses and drains his in one go.

I copy him, setting my glass on the small table nearby. Dylan chuckles then bows indicating the door. As he opens the door, Dylan slips his arm around my waist in a way so natural the gesture breaks my heart, and almost my resolve.

"Have fun," he whispers, his breath sending tiny shockwaves across my face.

*****

Dylan strides through the open door and his presence fills the room, capturing the attention of everyone around. True stars like Dylan carry something intangible with them that pulls the world towards them. Whether an energy of a different nature to other people, or the sexuality they exude, something causes men like Dylan to shine in this world. I stiffen as the nearest people scrutinise us registering his proprietary arm around me and stealing looks at my ridiculously inappropriate dress.

The party spans several rooms, guests draped across sumptuous black leather sofas in this room, and through the open door I see others spilling out to another terraced garden. I veer around them with Dylan's arm tightly around my waist; my anchor in this sea of brightly coloured fakery. Music blasts from the speakers in the next room we pass through, where bodies move and connect beneath the strobes.

"I didn't expect there to be so many people," I whisper to Dylan, as we step into a quieter room.

I meet the shocked expression of a skinny girl with shining brown hair tumbling across her face, her skin stretched across high cheekbones in her pale mask of a face.

"We need a good audience, so Kim invited half of London's 'it' crowd. Now go with this." He moves his arm to my shoulders, pulling me close as we cross the room towards a small group.

Aware of the scrutiny, I keep my eyes to the marble floor. When I look up, amusement shares confusion in people's expressions, and despite my nerves, I'm glad they don't think I fit.

A guy as tall as Dylan stands against the grey wall, legs crossed at the ankles as he watches us approach. He's chosen the usual Blue Phoenix mix of T-shirt and jeans, and unusually dark red hair pours across his shoulders. After a glance at me, the guy gives a thumbs up to Dylan. Dylan's grip on my shoulders tightens and I wriggle away, nervously brushing the front of my dress.

"Hey, sweetheart," says the guy. "Nice to meet you. Honey told me you were at the house."

Honey. Oh, great. I scan the room but there're a few Honey clones so I have no chance of spotting her.

"This is Liam," says Dylan. "He's the bassist and an all-round nice guy."

Liam pushes Dylan in the shoulder. "Ruining my image, man."

"Hey, one of us has to be the nice guy."

Dylan attempts to take my hand and I cross my arms, tucking my hands away. Liam watches. "I think you have to show everyone here that you're together before you show the world you're not." He winks at Dylan.

"Where're the other guys?" asks Dylan.

"Jem's choosing a victim. No fucking clue where Bryn went." I shiver at the word and Liam smiles. "I don't mean real victim. Girls usually don't see things that way." He pulls himself from the wall. "I'd better find Honey - she's high. Nice to meet you, summer Sky."

As he walks away, I shake my head, hoping to shake some reality back in. "High?"

"Yeah. Want a drink?"

Dylan's nonchalance shocks me, building back up the protective layers he stripped away. If Dylan's drinking again, is he doing anything else?

I study his pupils and he holds my gaze. "I'm not high, Sky. I don't do that shit anymore."

"Just drink?"

He snorts. "Says the girl who downed more than a bottle of wine the night we met."

The pink creeping up my neck is partly the truth of his words, and partly the reminder of the night we met. The evening that changed the course of my life for the second time in the same week.

"Well, I need a drink now," I tell him. "Another one. A big one."

"Sure thing."

I widen my eyes in alarm as Dylan's mouth brushes mine, unprepared for the power of his lips on mine after time apart. The reaction is predictable, a desire to respond engulfing my common sense. Thankfully, Dylan steps away.

"Sorry, just keeping up the pretence." He runs a finger across my lips, smirking.

I touch my lips as if I've just been electrified, as Dylan strides across the room. A girl with black pixie cut hair watches, and then turns empty eyes toward me. She's far enough away I don't need to acknowledge her, and the way she studies me with a disdainful curve to her mouth should embarrass me. Instead, I lift my chin and stare right back.

No one here is any better than I am.

A young waiter, smartly dressed with spiked brown hair passes with a silver tray carrying glasses of champagne, wide-eyed as he takes in the crowds around. Wondering why Dylan left to find a drink when so many are available, I take a glass, and gulp the wine. By the time another waiter dressed in the same uniform but older passes, my glass is empty so I swap it for a new one.

Four glasses later and Dylan hasn't returned. At least my discomfort lessens as my blood alcohol level increases. I giggle because I'm against the wall at a celebrity party trying unsuccessfully to hide behind a fake plant. What a weird night.

If Dylan's decided to abandon me, shouldn't we have a fight first? Then I can go back to my room, pack and wait for freedom? I pull myself from my safe spot and weave through the bodies, thankful that as the party has grown, the interest in me is lost in the crowds. Heading in the direction Dylan went, I fight through a jungle of silicone, suffocated by a deadly poison cloud of perfumes.

Several fruitless minutes of searching later, the dizzying atmosphere heightens my light-headedness and I move towards an open door. Stepping through the doorway into the summer night air cools my face, and I breathe deeply in an attempt to clear my head of the party. An old set of stone steps run down towards the dark; two figures stand at the edge of the lit area and I freeze. Dylan and a girl. My stomach knots tight – her arm is on his, and he strokes her cheek. I can't hear what they're talking about but they appear intimate. She's small and slender with straight, dark hair. Dylan's relaxed with this girl, more so than he was with me earlier. I chastise myself – why be jealous? I told him I didn't want him.

Yet I am. Unbelievably, fluorescent green, Godzilla-size monster jealous. I thought he wanted me, and I'd begun to rationalise wanting him. Is he about to humiliate me at the party by parading another girl in front of everyone?

I stare as the couple talk in low voices. They touch each other's faces and hair as they speak, and then the girl holds Dylan's hand in both of hers. When Dylan kisses the top of the girl's head and turns, so does my stomach.

I stumble backwards, hoping he can't see me illuminated by the light from the room behind. I back inside just in time.

"Hey, little lady, where you going?" A hand catches my elbow and the voice carves fear along my spine. Jem.

"Nowhere much. Drink, I'm looking for a drink."

Jem fixes me with an intrigued expression, and runs his tongue along his teeth, as he looks me up and down. "Nice dress, Sky. You certainly stand out in it." His low voice sends a shiver through.

"Because I own clothing bigger than a handkerchief?"

He smiles. "Funny. Let's get you a drink."

Jem's American drawl is more pronounced than Dylan's, although Dylan's is also stronger since he came back here. Someone bumps me, and a girl stalks past, heels clicking across the tiled floor.

Before I can react, Jem takes my hand and leads me towards a quieter room. A wooden bar spans one side of the room, several metres across, with a drinks selection worthy of a pub. Identical looking platinum blonde girls serve drinks, their large breasts barely covered in the cut off white T-shirts, shorts half way up their backsides. This is Dylan's house; did he choose the staff?

I hang back near the opposite wall as Jem gets a drink. The girls go straight to him, and I compare Jem to those around. He's wearing a grey suit similar to Dylan's and a few eyes in the room are trained on him. He knows this, and holds himself tall, looking aloofly at the matching girls in front. His presence is similar to Dylan's, but not as all encompassing. His star doesn't shine as brightly.

Jem returns to me, holding a glass of champagne. When passing the glass to me, he deliberately rubs a thumb along my hand. I gulp the champagne, shifting my look from him; the guy Liam said was looking for a victim. He takes a long drink of the brown liquor in his glass then licks his lips whilst staring at mine.

My discomfort level grows by the second; is he flirting or threatening? What is it about this man that locks up the snarky, sure-of-herself Sky and throws away the key?

Jem places a hand on the wall and leans forward, breath on my face. As tall and muscular as Dylan, Jem has the strength to match. I've experience of how strong Dylan is when he's touched and held me before, but this never worried me. Jem's scent is different, a similar spice but heavier. Add to this the unfocused eyes and low voice and I'm scared.

"What's the deal?"

"Pardon?"

"You and Dylan, what's the game?"

"No game."

He sneers. "Kind of a big coincidence?"

"What the hell?"

"You staying at the house with him. Planned it, did you? What happened? Is he not the guy you wanted him to be?" His tone hardens.

"That's not what happened..."

He touches my nose with the tip of his finger. "Did you want to try another one of us?"

I pull my head back and scrutinise his face. He's not sober at all; his eyes are those of someone elsewhere.

"Fuck you," I hiss.

His brown eyes widen, and then a grin sneaks across his face. "If you want..."

Nice one, Sky. I side step but he places the other hand against the wall, caging me in. "He won't give you money."

"I don't want his money!"

From the corner of my eye, I'm aware of heads turning to us. A girl in a silver glove of a dress nearby points and looks are thrown my way. Do they think I've started on a new band member?

Dylan appears behind Jem, face hard as he claps him on the shoulder. "What the fuck, dude?"

Jem steps back and holds his hands up in a gesture of surrender. "Just chatting."

The anger on Dylan's face is directed at his friend, not me. "You okay, Sky?"

I nod.

"I'm trying to suss out what her deal is, man. This is all fucking dodgy. Look at her... seriously? You can do better than that."

I grit my teeth and step away, unsure whether to respond. The scene we're causing has more than a few interested onlookers.

"This has fuck all to do with you, Jem. Piss off."

"Yeah? You fuck off without telling anyone then come back ten times fucking worse than when you left." He scrutinises me. "And for her?"

"I didn't go down there for her. I fucking told you. I met her there!"

"Whatever. You're still a mess thanks to this manipulative bitch."

"You arrogant wanker!" I say, too loudly.

"You want to be in his life or not, summer Sky?"

"Don't call me that."

"I got a story to tell you..."

"I'm sure you have a whole bunch of stories," I reply.

"A story about me and Dylan and a girl a bit like you."

"That's nice," I want to get away from this guy; he has nothing to say I want to hear. "Dylan, can we go?"

"Should we tell her our story, Dylan?" presses Jem.

Dylan's face is expressionless, but a muscle twitches in his cheek. Jem raises an eyebrow at Dylan; but whatever he hopes to achieve, Dylan doesn't bite.

"Do what you like," Dylan says.

A grin spreads across his face. "Nah. Maybe Sky can do her own research. Check out Lily Parker."

"I'm sure she can, if she wants," says Dylan in a tone dropping the room temperature.

Despite telling Jem I'm not interested, I make a mental note of the name.

"Yeah, whatever," he says to Dylan, eyes trained on my face. "Little Miss Summer Sky, I got the measure of you." He looks to Dylan. "She'll bring you to your knees, fuck you over and leave. Haven't you learnt anything?"

Dylan shoves Jem. "Stop talking. Now. Not everyone gets involved in the same fucking messes you do."

Jem and Dylan face off, like tomcats ready to tear each other's fur out. I inhale, wishing the hell I'd stayed in my bedroom. Jem makes a final scornful noise, looks at me as if I'm something from the bottom of his shoe, and backs away.

"She's playing a clever game with you, man!" he calls, draining his glass.

Satisfied he's stirred the pot enough, Jem tips his fingers away from his head in a mock salute, and then steps away from us.

Trembling from anger, I shrug off the hand Dylan places on my arm. Jem bumps into a small Asian girl, turns and wraps an arm around her shoulder. She smiles, and looks up at him. He whispers something in her ear then slides a hand to her backside, squeezing. My stomach turns. I guess he found his victim then.

I thrust the glass of champagne at Dylan. "I'm leaving."

"Sorry about him. He has issues..."

"Really? Thanks for pointing that out."

I walk away, back to the throng in the next room. Weaving my way through the suffocating throng of people, I head for the door to the kitchen, the short cut to my end of the house and the edge of the party. Dylan pursues me, trying to grab my arm a couple of time, but I shake him off.

Bursting into the cool of the darkened kitchen, I halt with my back to Dylan. "Now can you see why I don't want to be involved? And that's just the tip of the iceberg."

We're alone in the kitchen, the silence a contrast to the hubbub of the party. The sound fades further as the door behind me shuts.

"Sky." Dylan touches my arm again, carefully turning me around.

Pissed off with the tears fighting their way into my eyes, I hold down the desire to run. Dylan places a palm on my cheek, rubbing a thumb across my cheekbone. The heart-thumping reaction to him intensifies.

"I want to go," I whisper, looking at my hands. "Not just away from the party but away from this house."

"Tomorrow?"

His face is shadowed, the only light from the nearby window.

"It's always tomorrow with you," I say hoarsely.

"Of course. There's always tomorrow. Every day." He smiles. "Hanging on to today is hard, but tomorrow is always in reach."

"Very deep."

He attempts to hug me and I stiffen. "Is she the answer?" I ask.

"Who?"

"The girl you were with." The girl didn't look like the complaining model girlfriend in the magazine. Is she a new girl? Filling the gap he says only I can? "Are you going to humiliate me? Is that the scene? You're going to bring her inside and carry on with…whatever. Dylan, with a more suitable girl?"

"What? No!" He succeeds in placing his fingers back on my face and I recoil. "Who are you talking about? Cressida isn't here - I told you."

"Outside. The dark-haired girl." The jealous pang twinges again, but I have no right to him.

"Sky, her name's Myf. She's a good friend - one of the few people who can keep me grounded. She helped me when things got bad; she dragged me to rehab before I self-destructed. I was talking to her about how fucking hard this is for me."

"Right, sure. I don't know why I agreed to any this!"

I attempt to get to the door and Dylan steps in the way. "Don't leave."

Six-foot-plus of solid muscle stands between me and the way out. Sexy as hell guy, who kick started my heart and I'm no longer a hundred percent sure I want to go.

"Move, Dylan."

"No. Not until you listen to me. I have to tell you some things."

"I don't want to hear them again!"

"Why?" He raises his voice. "Because you're scared you'll believe me or because you'll have to admit you feel something?"

He's right; he knows he's right. I try to get behind him to the door but he puts his hand on the door handle. "Sky! Just fucking listen to me!"

"Don't swear at me!" I lose my temper and shove him.

Dylan catches my arm, and pulls me towards him. I'm caught in his grip, the hard planes of his chest against mine and hyperaware of the thin material as the only barrier between us. The warmth and scent of my beach house Dylan engulfs.

"I had to speak to her because it's pointless talking to the guys about this. Seeing you again tonight is killing me because this hurts. Really fucking hurts, Sky. I feel like the world held something out to me – a chance to be someone else - and then snatched the chance away again."

His words pierce my armour. "Dylan…"

"Why does who I am have to change anything? I've never connected to a person like this before and I know you felt the same connection to me, so I fought for this. I'm sorry if I went about things the wrong way, I wasn't thinking straight. I just wanted the opportunity to show you what that week meant to me."

"It wasn't even a week," I whisper.

The sincerity in his words and his earnest expression strips away another layer of defence. This time when he cups my chin, I don't back away.

"I'm in love with you. Is that strange? Yes, but I am. You fill a gap in my soul, Sky, and I don't want to lose you."

Nobody has ever spoken to me in this way, and he doesn't need to. Dylan has no reason to seduce me with clever words and subtle seduction - he had the chance in Cornwall.

If he weren't Dylan Morgan, he'd have a chance. I waver.

Dylan places his lips on mine, sending a wave of sensation through my body, and the last part of rationality slips away. I'm lost the moment his mouth touches mine, the connection he talks about fusing us. He can't love me; people don't fall in love after a week. Yet if I go with the unspoken ways we understood each other from the first day, and the speed in which we opened up to each other, maybe there is something more. Perhaps not love but the something he's fighting for in his weird, fucked up way.

Hesitantly, he pulls me to him by my hips and slides his hand up my back. The way our bodies shape against each other pulls us into our intense world where only we exist. The moment I respond to his kiss, his mouth claims mine. He runs his tongue along my bottom lip and I part my mouth, allowing him to kiss me deeply. Losing my grasp on anything but the warmth of Dylan and the places our bodies touch, I grip his short hair and tangle my tongue with his. He tastes of the whiskey he drank before, and of the Dylan, I kissed on the beach.

Dylan moves to kiss my neck, his stubble scraping along the skin firing heat to the centre of me. He places his lips gently against the sensitive spot beneath my ear, encircling my waist so the charged gap between our bodies disappears completely. His hair tickles as he moves to planting kisses along my throat, before crushing his mouth against mine again.

Unable to breathe from the intensity, I pull away air pushing from my lungs in short bursts. Convinced my legs are about to collapse, I hang onto his arm, and his grip around my waist tightens. His arousal is evident against my hip, spiking my own in return. Dylan places his forehead on mine, his breath heating my skin.

In the moment with Dylan, we return to our illusory world and I understand at last what he means. With him, where I am doesn't matter because the world we exist in follows us everywhere. We don't need to be in Broadbeach and we were never in a bubble. This is real.

"Let's leave the party. I can't do this. I want them all to go away, and the world be me and you again," he says, running his fingers long my cheek.

"Aren't we supposed to be putting on a show for everyone?" I whisper, sliding a hand along his hard back.

"Fuck that," says Dylan. "I'm stealing you away with a bottle of champagne to somewhere quiet where you'll have to listen to me."

Chapter Twenty-Six

Sky

Drinking several drinks in quick succession at the party has disarmed me, and I allow Dylan to take me by the hand and lead me away from the house. My brain is on standby, my heart and hormones firmly in control. Being dragged across a country estate by Dylan after the kiss he gave me is euphoric; his words in the kitchen intoxicated as much as the alcohol. The buried Sky who wants Dylan has pushed her way through, and I doubt I'll get her to leave again now. The fight is over and the Sky whose heart and soul belongs to Dylan won.

"Where are we going?" I ask.

"Somewhere no one else is allowed but me."

The summer breeze is warm as we cross the lawn, the moon casting a blue light across the perfect summer's evening. I inhale the scent of jasmine and woody earth, enjoying the natural freshness after the artificial scent of the house.

"Come on!" Dylan tugs my hand and we leave the lawn for a path running into the trees.

"Where?"

Dylan halts. A square, brick building stands before us. Disconnected from the main part of the house, the place was once a barn or stables because the building isn't large enough to be a cottage. "Here."

Pulling a key from his back pocket, Dylan unlocks the heavy wooden door and pushes it open. I hesitate outside as he walks in and flicks a switch. When I adjust my eyes to the light, I step inside and rewind to a teenage rock star wannabe's basement.

A beaten up sofa rests against one side of the room, a rough patchwork of mismatching green and brown cushions. Posters paper the walls like in a teen bedroom, although most teens wouldn't have their own band up there. Dark veneer shelving lines one wall and holds a bizarre assortment of items - hats, empty drinks cans and the kind of souvenirs you buy in tacky tourist shops. I smile as the weird shell creature from Sandchurch catches my eye. The place is an eclectic time capsule of the last seven years of Dylan's life.

A laptop is connected to the mixing desk taking up half the room. An acoustic guitar rests on the carpet-tiled floor. Pages, ripped from an A4 pad, are strewn around; words are scrawled and crossed out covering the paper.

This place is more Dylan than the pile of overpriced bricks we walked away from.

"Your cave?" I ask.

"Kind of."

He removes his jacket, throwing it over a chair, and then pushes stray papers from the sofa and sits, holding the two glasses out. I take them while he pops the cork on the champagne and fills the glasses. Bubbles spill over the edge and I shake them from my hand.

"So I'm honoured to be allowed in here?" I ask as I sit.

"Nobody comes in here, seriously."

"Thank you, then."

With his spare hand, Dylan tucks my hair behind my ear and I shiver at his touch. "You're somebody to me, and I can share everything with you."

Desperate to shift the conversation, I search the room. "Oh, look! A lava lamp." I hand him his glass and turn on the lamp. These lamps always fascinated me, the liquid movement hypnotic.

"Sky?"

I rub my not entirely sober head. "Can we not get all talky?"

Dylan's mouth tips in amusement. "Talky?"

"Rebound girl here." I indicate myself with the wine glass.

"I don't think so."

"I spilt up with my boyfriend two days before we met! How is that not rebound?"

Dylan drinks, the curious expression in his eyes indicating he's considering his answer. "Because you stopped loving him months before you split."

His words slap me, and I'm as pissed off as if he actually had. "How the hell do you know?"

"Sorry, presumptuous of me." He takes my glass and shifts closer.

I'm here, hidden from the real world. Slightly drunk and with a guy who only has to brush my arm to make me want all of him.

"Why do you have this place when you have a house full of empty rooms you could use?" I ask.

"Sometimes, I want to leave the world back there alone, as you know. This is disconnected somehow. When I walk in here, I'm away from the fucked up reality that exists back there." He indicates the direction of the house with his head.

I take my glass back from him and drink because he's looking at my mouth again. If he kisses me, I don't think I could be responsible for my actions.

"Do you sleep here too?" I ask, looking around.

The rest of the place is piled with cardboard boxes stacked high against the wall. He indicates another green, wooden door at the back of the room. "I'm a bit of a hoarder. So there's no room for a bed, even though I often stay here all night."

I spy a half-empty bottle of bourbon on the table near the mixing desk. "That would send you to sleep?"

"Yeah, I've been known to sleep on the sofa." Dylan shifts, taking my glass again, the light touch charging through me. "We need to get a little bit talky though,? And not this small talky."

"Do we?"

"Yes, otherwise I'm going to kiss you again."

Dylan has me caught in his blue-eyed scrutiny, the suggestion of where the kiss leads made clear by the brief glance at my breasts. Darkened eyes meet mine as he chews on the edge of his lip.

"Okay, talk," I squeak.

"Funny, Sky." He brushes my face with the back of his hand.

Maybe I should kiss him before I explode.

"What really puts you off a relationship with me? The fame? Me? My world?" he asks, watching me warily.

"All of them."

"I think you're scared I'm going to try and change you like Grant did?"

"He didn't change me, I changed myself."

"Because of what he wanted."

"Because I didn't know any different, I thought if we were in love, we needed to make sacrifices."

Dylan strokes my cheek. "Sounds like you were the one who made all the sacrifices, these things work both ways. He sounds selfish and a fucking idiot to throw you away. I'd never ask you to do anything or be anything. Why would I when to me you're perfect as the Sky you are?"

I snort. "Perfect? No one is perfect."

"I meant you're perfectly Sky, and I love that Sky."

Love. Again. I down my champagne while staring at the floor. "Stop saying the word."

"Okay, you have an overwhelming effect on me which triggers feel good chemicals in my brain and I crave being with you so I can keep feeling this way." He smirks and I pull a face at him.

"You're having a chemical reaction? Very logical."

"Too logical, Sky..." He brushes a thumb on my lips. "Fuck the chemistry, we were meant to meet. I never believed in destiny or soul mates or any of that bullshit but then you came along. I always knew I was lost, but I didn't realise how much until I met you."

Dylan covers my mouth with his, a gentle kiss I don't expect. The craving he spoke about overwhelms me too. I have a confusing need for this man to hold and complete me, even though I'm fighting to stand on my own in the world.

Giving in to the longing, I wind a hand around his neck, stroking the short hair at the nape. Dylan makes a soft noise in his throat, and shifts closer. I run my tongue along his bottom lip and he responds with a fierce kiss, teeth almost colliding as our tongues push against each other. Our hearts thump in rhythm, matching the way our lives have joined in a shared direction.

However much I tell myself this isn't what I want, I know life has other ideas. Dylan's stubbled face scratches at mine, my lips sore from the intensity of our harsh kisses in the kitchen and now. I tremble and the heat we're creating is going to combust if we don't stop soon. I pull away, and touch my mouth as I meet the eyes of the man who has stolen my soul and given me part of his in return.

"Be with me, Sky," he says softly. "Not now or tonight. Be in my life."

I'm distracted by the smell of him; the sandalwood scent mingled with the heat from our desire tearing me away from anything but us.

"You're already in my heart and head. I've spent two weeks trying to prise you out and you won't leave," I whisper.

"Because part of me is part of you, I believe that. This isn't fate, or chemistry but deeper." He holds my face in both hands, tone earnest and I know he truly believes his words.

"Don't get talky again."

Laughing, Dylan pulls me onto his lap the way he did when we snuggled at the beach house. He grips me around the waist, thumbs rubbing the sensitive spot on my back through my dress.

"I can't out talk you and your smart mouth, but I think I'll always know how to shut you up," he says, looking up at me with an unmistakable intensity.

My breath hitches, because I know he's right. I have no smart comebacks to the silencing kisses and touches. "Shut me up, then," I say.

A knowing smile hovers on his lips and he looks at my breasts, which are at his eye level. "One of the reasons I like this dress? Buttons." He undoes the top button. "Buttons all the way down."

He kisses the skin he exposes, lips cool against the heat, as he slowly unbuttons the rest. The soft touch lights the fuse paper on the repressed desperation for his hands on my body. I run trembling hands along his back, dragging my fingers across the ridges of muscle hidden beneath his shirt. Dylan leaves the buttons and grips my hips, pulling me close. I drown in Dylan, his touch transporting me back to the night at the beach house. He runs his nose along the sensitive spot at the base of my neck, his breathing heavy to match mine.

"Tell me to stop if this isn't what you want," he says against my neck, the heat of his mouth burning my skin.

The shaking mass of arousal I've become could never refuse. I've stepped away from my opportunity to step out of his life and I know why - because Dylan's filled a gap in my soul too. I don't know why, or how, or what's next, apart from I'm giving my mind a sabbatical and going wherever Dylan is taking me.

Slipping the floral dress from my shoulders, he nips my shoulder then plants soft kisses towards the top of my breasts, palming the soft mounds through my cotton bra.

I fumble with the buttons of his shirt, and once I've undone the minimum to fit over his head, I pull the shirt upwards. Dylan helps, exposing the smooth lines of his chest. I run my fingers along his chest; hands across his shoulders then trace his tattooed arms. This man's hard, muscled body never left my fantasies.

In a swift movement, Dylan unclasps and dispenses with my bra, tongue teasing my nipple before I have a chance to react. The sudden intensity pools hot desire between my legs. I moan and grip his broad shoulders, digging my nails into his smooth flesh.

He stops and looks up at me. "Good job those aren't as sharp as your tongue."

"Oh, very clever," I say, "Now who has a smart mouth?"

Not listening, Dylan rests his head against the back of the sofa, rubbing my exposed thighs. "I have a lot of difficulty controlling myself around you. So I apologise now for what I'm about to do."

A million scenarios crash into my head; the inevitability of the chain reaction we caused when we kissed in the house is finally here.

"What are you about to do?"

Dylan skims a hand across my belly, fingers hovering at the edge of my panties. "Remember when I said I'd never fuck you?" he whispers. "Do you remember what I said?"

I want to speak but my brain is mush, waiting for those fingers to explore, so I shake my head.

"I told you, you're worth so much more than that; the things I could do to you..."

I groan; he's teasing me and his arousal straining his trousers pushes against my thin underwear makes his delay a hundred times worse.

"I dreamt about touching your curves and enjoying the softness of your skin from the very first night in Broadbeach. Every single minute your mouth was close enough, I obsessed about kissing you."

As if making up for lost time, he runs his fingers along my back, stroking gently before moving his hands and cupping my breasts. As he circles his thumb around my hard nipples, I shuffle backwards on his knee so I can reach the button of his trousers. This time he allows me to unfasten them with my shaking fingers.

For a heart-stopping moment, I think he's going to change his mind again. Dylan lifts me from his lap then sets me in the sofa. Oh, God, please don't say no again... Instead, he stands and shuffles out of his trousers, the expensive suit pants landing on the floor next to his shirt.

At last, I get to see Dylan in his underwear in real life - I've seen a couple of pictures on the internet but in those photos his black briefs didn't include a barely restrained erection.

Oh, holy fuck. This is the definition of a killer body - dangerous and threatening to any girl's self-respect. And he wants me. I hungrily drag my gaze across his smooth chest, taking in the sight of his rock hard abs and the lines disappearing into his briefs. Dylan doesn't stand for long; he pushes me backwards onto the sofa and when his naked chest meets mine, the contrast of the softness of his skin over the unyielding strength of his muscles undoes me further.

I arch my back as he slides a hand beneath my bottom, my hardened nipples brushing against him. Dylan groans; his rigid length presses against my increasingly sensitive sex. He pulls my leg around his waist and nibbles on my lip as I gasp for breath, drowning in the moment with Dylan.

"Oh, fuck!" Dylan stops and sits back, raking his hand through his hair.

"What?" A trembling mess, I'm alarmed at his sudden halt to proceedings. "Is it me?"

"No, Fuck. Shit." He stands, staring down at me and I sit up, unable to keep my eyes off his arousal.

"What, Dylan?" I sit.

"This is my place. No one comes here. So I haven't got any fucking condoms!"

I giggle in relief and at his frustration, ignoring my own, and he smiles in return. "I'm so wound up, right now. I could hold you down and tease you until you come but I'm too selfish." He sits next to me, winding both hands into my hair and gripping possessively. "I want you. I want to be inside you, with you surrounding me, together completely like we should be."

His words flood more arousal through me, the image of what he's suggesting has entered my head on a number of occasions and isn't far away now. I lean in for another mouth-mashing kiss, unsure what happens next. I won't have sex with Dylan without protection; leaving my heart unprotected is enough for tonight. But I ache to do what he says.

"What do we do?" I gasp, as his mouth encloses my nipples again.

Dylan runs hand up my inner thigh, fingers playing at the edge of my underwear. "I don't know, but I've fucking waited long enough!"

I gasp and slap his shoulder playfully. "Dylan Morgan! You presumptuous, jumped up rock star. How do you know I'm interested?"

He slips a finger into my panties and I gasp as he glides over my sex. "I don't think this shows lack of interest, Sky."

I grip my thighs around his hand before he has a chance to tease me. "Dylan, don't start…"

Dylan removes his hand, darkened eyes searching mine. "I'm taking you to bed." He throws my dress at me and smirks. "But no streaking naked across the lawn."

We dress quickly, laughing, natural with each other. More fierce kisses and touches later, we sprint across the grass holding hands. The summer breeze cools my cheeks but no other part of me, the awareness of this amazing man searing desire through me.

"This way," he whispers and opens the door in the darkness at the back of the house, pulling me through. I laugh, heart bursting with joy then exploding with sensation as he pins me to the wall in the darkened hallway, sliding his hands beneath my dress and up my thighs.

I pull him in for another kiss. He laughs softly against my mouth then scoops me over his shoulder, the way he did at the beach. I shriek, and hit his backside and he responds with a slap on mine.

I don't notice anything about Dylan's expansive bedroom apart from the huge bed in the centre, and he flops me onto the plush, white bedding. Tearing his shirt over his head, he disappears through a door at the other end of the large room. I unbutton my dress and shimmy out of it, removing my bra too. I hesitate, deciding to leave on my panties and sit on the edge of the bed - I'm not quite brazen enough to remove everything.

Dylan returns with foil wrappers, which he places on the bed.

"I needed to make sure you haven't changed your mind," he whispers, "but the fact you're almost naked suggests you haven't."

"Almost."

Dylan grins. "I can fix that." He kneels on the bed and runs a finger along my stomach. I wriggle at the sensation. His touch skims my hips as he hooks two thumbs through my underwear and slides them down, then drops the thin material to the floor.

He hungrily takes in the sight of my nakedness and for the first time in my life, I don't feel exposed under a man's scrutiny.

"Fuck, you're beautiful, Sky," he growls then presses me into the bed.

My heart hammers as our mouths meet, teeth clashing with the raw intensity of the kiss. Dylan takes my wrists in one broad hand, and holds my arms above my head. I make a breathless sound as Dylan's rough kisses shift towards my breasts, before he closes his mouth around my pebbled nipple. He pushes my legs apart with his knee, fingers travelling up my inner thigh until he discovers my wet centre.

I buck against him as he slips a finger inside, moving his mouth back to mine. His tongue thrusts into my mouth, matching the movement of his finger and I move against him, pushing myself against the palm of his hand.

For what feels like eternity, I drown in the sensation of his attention to my body; his expert kisses and touch bringing me to the brink and then letting me go again, over and over, until I can't take the building pressure anymore.

"Dylan, stop..." I jerk against his grip on my hands.

Dylan releases my hands and kneels back. "Too much?"

"Not enough," I say, hands going towards his trousers. I unbutton his trousers as he watches me through heavy-lidded eyes.

"But this is okay?" he asks with a smile, stepping out of his trousers and briefs.

I hitch my breath at the size of him compared to Grant and shift forward to run my fingertips along his shaft.

Dylan sucks air between his teeth and shakes his head at me. "Don't Sky, I'm trying fucking hard to control myself here…"

He leans across the bed, and grabs the condom on the bed above my head. My stomach flips as he rolls it onto himself, I'm more turned on than I've ever been in my life, but anxious about Dylan's…size.

Stroking my damp hair from my face, he kisses my closed eyes. "I want you so bad, and I promise this won't be the only time."

"I know," I whisper.

Dylan nudges my legs apart and strokes me again, before pushing against me. I gasp again as the tip of him touches my clit and I swear I'm going to come before he's inside me.

I shift, allowing him to slide towards my wet core, trembling in anticipation of what I've wanted since Broadbeach. Dylan thrusts into me, hard, and I almost cry out. He stills, aware of my tensing, then pulls out so he's barely inside.

"I love you Sky," he says, "I fucking love you."

The emotion is clear in his darkened gaze and I nod, unable to speak. Why am I crying? A tear escapes and he kisses it away gently, before thrusting back into me hard. This time I do cry out, overwhelmed by the new connection to Dylan, wanting more of him but aware he's already given me everything he has - body, heart and soul. He moves slowly at first, eyes still fixed on mine, before increasing the urgency. The pressure builds as the movement bumps my clit. He pulls up one of my legs and I curl it around his hip.

I dig my fingernails into his tense shoulders and he kisses me, the movement of his tongue matching the push of his hips. Everything overwhelms into a world of sensation, as I spiral upwards towards the edge of his galaxy again, eyes dancing with stars. All I can feel is Dylan, inside me, over me, consuming me and I clutch his waist giving into the supernova explosion of my orgasm. Lost in Dylan's world, I'm aware of his hips tensing before he thrusts hard into me one more time, swearing as he comes.

I wind my arms around him, holding his damp body against mine, his rapid heartbeat slowing. Dylan covers my face with kisses and I relax back with my eyes closed. I was right about him from the first kiss - no man could ever make me feel this way apart from Dylan Morgan. He burrows his nose into my neck and slides onto the bed next to me.

"You do things to me, Sky..." he whispers.

I smile and twist my head to kiss his damp hair. "And you are fucking amazing."

He laughs at my language, and we join in cuddling and giggling until Dylan wraps us in his sheets and we luxuriate in each other's arms.

Until he decides to be fucking amazing, again.

Chapter Twenty-Seven

Dylan

The clouds of the last couple of weeks are blown away by my night with Sky. We have a chance to make this work, to continue to meld into the Dylan and Sky we are when we're together. Sure, this isn't magically going to happen but one step at a time, steps I hope she'll take side by side with me.

Replicating the days at the beach house, I cook bacon in the kitchen I rarely use. Singing my Summer Sky song she's yet to hear, I'm aware of someone entering the room behind.

"Last night wasn't very successful, was it?"

I turn, spatula in hand. Steve walks over with tired eyes.

"It was for me." I grin.

Steve huffs and bangs around the kitchen as he pulls out a cup and heads for the coffee pot. "So another night fucking her and everything is okay?"

I stiffen at his use of the word. "We're going to give this a go."

Steve sits on a stool and sips his coffee, face becoming a mask of displeasure. Why isn't he pleased for me? "Great," he mutters.

"What?" I ask sharply. "This is what we want."

"This won't work. Why bother?"

"Because this is what I want, I need to be with Sky to stay sane at the moment."

"Exactly. So when you lose her, it'll fuck everything up."

I'm struck by his words, another reminder this is how things are. Steve doesn't care about anything but our success and the money he makes, and will do anything to protect that. I've seen first-hand how skilful he is at protecting Blue Phoenix's control of the music world, which involves keeping us in line. I allowed him to do some things I wasn't comfortable with because I confused him with a father figure. Steve's no longer a replacement for the Dad who left when I was a kid, and this gradual realisation hit the day before I ran to Broadbeach. For the first time in years, I stepped away, and now I see the control he has but have no idea how to break this.

"That's my decision to make," I growl.

Steve shakes his head slowly. "Well, I hope everything works out for you."

Like I believe him from his tone. "You know what, Steve. I'll do anything to make this work with Sky. And unless you want me fucking off again, I suggest you suck it up."

Steve's pitying look, pisses me off, resolving my determination to make changes and some of those he's not going to like.

I consider the conversation, the words looping in my head as I cross the house towards my bedroom. The bed is a tangled mess of sheets from last night, clothes strewn across the floor. Sky sleeps with an arm over her head, mouth open and I laugh to myself. She'd be mortified if she knew. But she's real; the realest thing in my life since I was seventeen. Placing the tray on the nearby dresser, I stroke her mussed hair from her eyes. Opening them, she wrinkles her nose.

"Bacon?" she asks sleepily.

"Yes. I've been practicing – I reckon I'll be a decent chef in no time." I kiss her forehead.

Sky traces a finger down my arm. "No idea why I never made the connection about the phoenix."

The sensation of her gentle touch along the outline of the blue phoenix from my bicep to shoulder bolts straight to my dick; well, that and the sheet slipping away from her naked tits.

Sky's eyes widen as she becomes aware of my dark-eyed scrutiny and she pulls the covers around herself, pouting.

"Don't hide," I say, and unlace her fingers from the sheet.

She allows me, and I brush a thumb against her hardening nipple, cupping her breast in my hand as I move in and place my mouth on hers. My attempt at deepening the kiss fails as she pulls her head back.

"What about the sandwich?" she says and bites down a smile.

"Fuck, you turn me on," I say huskily, ignoring her.

"Don't you swear at me, Mr Rock God." She pushes my shoulder playfully and I grab her hand, pulling a finger into my mouth. Her pupils dilate as our eyes meet and I remove the finger.

"Sure, you should eat because you're going to need your energy." I cock a brow, just to ensure she understands exactly what I mean.

"Oh? Are we going on a long walk?" she asks innocently. "Hiking around your country estate?"

Fuck, she's sexy, teasing me with her smart mouth. I grab her arms and pin them over her head, enjoying the way her increased breathing pushes her tits up and down. "No, and you know that's not what I mean. I have a couple of weeks to make up for. And we're starting today."

She smirks, rather than the usual girls' yielding reaction to my smooth moves. "Better let me go so I can eat then."

I release her and move back, pushing down the words I want to use but I know she doesn't want to hear. I fucking love you, Sky but please don't rip me apart.

"Are you okay?" she asks, confirming how in tune we are.

"Everything's fucking awesome." I grin, pulling the sheet away from the body I don't want to ever stop touching.

Fuck the bacon sandwiches, there're more interesting things to do with my mouth here.

*****

Sky

Dylan disappears to the recording studio; reluctantly leaving the bed and after a soak in the bath I wish Dylan was in with me, I explore the grounds again. Around the side of the house is a garden of pavers and shrubs, a large rectangular pond is in the centre, overhung by willow trees. I stand at the edge and look down. Koi carp splash to the surface; writhing orange and black bodies. They always grossed me out, these unnatural looking, monstrous goldfish. There's a stone bench beneath one of the tress and I curl my legs under, and open my book.

One fantasy has been swapped for another; I'm cocooned in a different world and not one I belong in. Now Dylan and his overwhelming presence have left, the reality is clawing at the edges.

I stare at the emptiness of the vast estate. The weird family he belongs to - other band members, his manager, even his PA - colours his life in ways I can't imagine.

We never spoke about the 'what happens next'. My heart and body crave to be around him, but I see things like Jem and wonder how I could survive. Jem isn't surviving - and Dylan nearly didn't. Was Dylan once as big a mess as Jem is? Or even worse, is he still like Jem but has this hidden?

Dylan spends all day at the recording studio and I spend mine avoiding that part of the house in case I see any of Blue Phoenix. I'm not ready to embrace the rest of Dylan's life yet.

I took a little time earlier using Dylan's laptop to research ideas for my future. The disconnection from the crap my life has become in Bristol brings clarity, as if I am on some kind of retreat where I can take stock of my life and plan where to go next.

I have the qualifications to study something at university but I have no idea what. Closing my eyes and picking a course by clicking randomly won't help. I sigh and scroll around the site. University would buy me time - and more opportunities. Maybe marketing or some kind of business course? Hell, I don't know.

The shadows grow longer, and only when the temperature drops and goose bumps my arms, do I realise I've been sitting here a while. Crunching footsteps alert me to someone approaching and I glance up, hoping it's not Jem.

Dylan. The setting sun behind silhouettes his tall figure and he bends down to kiss me gently.

"Hey." He sits and wraps his arm around my shoulders, hugging me close. "Enjoying relaxing?"

"Getting a bit bored." I close my book.

"Oh. Sorry. We have to get these tracks finished..."

I touch his face. "Don't apologise to me."

"Okay, I don't want you to..." He pauses.

"Leave?" I ask.

He shifts. "Yeah."

"I'm not staying."

Dylan removes his arm and stares at his boots. "Oh, but..."

"I don't mean I'm leaving today but I can't stay here forever," I say, and take his hand. Dylan doesn't respond and his eyebrows are tugged down. I lace my fingers through his. "Dylan?"

"As long as you don't do what you did last time." He turns the ocean eyes to mine. "Leave without saying goodbye then shut me out."

"No, I won't."

"Good." He lifts my hand and kisses the back, our fingers still entangled. "I understand you want to leave, but do you think going back is a good idea? Maybe you should move somewhere safer than your flat?"

"I don't need to move somewhere safer! I'm going back to my life, carrying on."

Dylan stiffens. "So you are shutting me out?"

"No."

He smoothes my hair from my eyes, cool fingers brushing my warm forehead. "Being Dylan Morgan's girlfriend is complicated though, I don't want you being scared off."

The words skip in my chest. "Girlfriend?"

"You're more than a summer crush now."

His blue eyes shine but I can't resist teasing him. "No, we haven't dated properly yet."

"We've done plenty of other things..." His gaze moves towards my tight vest top.

"So, plenty of people do 'other things' without dating," I say nonchalantly.

"I want to date you. You never gave me the chance."

"We went to Sandchurch"

"And look how that ended. Sky, let me take you out somewhere properly."

"Where? You can't go anywhere public."

"Says who?"

"Your rampant horde of social media toting fanatics."

He shakes his head and rubs a finger along my mouth. "You're funny."

"And you're famous."

He slumps back. "Okay, we'll talk about this later, but I am going to treat you like a real girlfriend, not hide you. How long before you have to go back to work?"

"I'm on a temporary contract. If I don't work, I'm not paid. If I don't get paid, I lose my home."

"I could find you a job?" he suggests.

I bristle. "Remember what you said about not changing me or running my life?"

Dylan strokes my hair. "I didn't think. I didn't mean it like that."

I rub my eyes, tired from my late night in Dylan's bed. "I agreed to be in your life, but I need to do this slowly."

"Sure, I understand. You need to go back home." His semi-pout doesn't go with his words.

"I wouldn't move in with a guy straightaway, Dylan; especially not so soon after Grant. I have to do this one step at a time."

This place is amazing - a dream house - but it's empty. I understand why he wants me to fill the space.

Dylan squeezes me to his hard chest, and I bury my nose against the soft cotton of his T-shirt, inhaling the scent reminding me of Broadbeach and sex.

"So we can try this?" he whispers into my hair.

Seeing Dylan with the dark-haired girl last night slapped reality across my cheeks. I want to try with Dylan and can't stand the thought of him with anyone else.

"Sure, but if you stalk me one more time we're over."

I pull back and when I see the amused look on his face, I want to slap it off. "I mean this. What you did wasn't good. I won't be treated like that!"

"Okay. I promise. It's just..."

I shake my head, indicating he should stop there.

"So you'll wait until tomorrow?" he asks.

I push him in the chest. "Okay, tomorrow."

Chapter Twenty-Eight

Sky

A couple of days later, Dylan insists on accompanying me home, despite protest from Steve and Kim. He dumps my rucksack on the floor and his impression of my small flat is apparent on his face - the moment when people quickly glance around at all the things they think are wrong with something, and then try to hide with a neutral smile.

"Do you like this place?" he asks, shoving his hands in his pockets.

"This is what I can afford."

"I could..."

"Stop," I interrupt him. "Don't even go there."

"You didn't know what I was going to say!"

"I can guess. And I don't want anything implying I'm with you for what I can get out of you."

Dylan seizes me around the waist and runs his nose along my cheek. "Are you sure? Some things you're happy to get out of me..."

"Don't..." I attempt a disapproving frown but I'm not fooling him.

He pouts. "Why not? Aren't you going to show me your bedroom?"

"Jeez, Dylan, we just walked through the door!"

Fingers trace my lower back, sending shivers along my spine. "But all day I've thought of you. About this morning..."

"Well, my bedroom is too messy to receive guests," I tell him, disentangling myself and pushing him away. "Plus, I don't want you to fuck me and leave."

He winces. "I don't fuck you."

"That's how it would feel to me, especially with you going afterwards." I take my rucksack from him and prop it against the wall.

"So no sex unless we share a bed?"

"Correct."

He raises an eyebrow. "Not very adventurous are you?"

Is he teasing me? I shrug at him. "If you want adventurous, you're with the wrong girl."

Dylan laughs and steps towards me, I back away bumping the wall. "I can teach you," he says, fingers playing beneath my short top and across my belly.

One touch and few words is all it takes for Dylan to start hormones charging around my body. I crave his hands on me, to be naked and drowning in waves of pleasure only Dylan could pull me into all the time. Now our bodies have meshed, mine doesn't seem to want to disconnect. I hold my breath and fight the arousal rising.

"I knew I should've seduced you on the beach that night," he whispers against my hair.

I circle my arms around his neck, resting my head against his. "No thanks, I don't want sand in...places."

"Oh? You sound like you have experience?" He grabs my rear and tugs me closer. "Have you? Because now I've got images of us on the beach..."

I gasp in surprise as his mouth meets mine, and delves his tongue into my mouth with one of his skilful, jelly-leg inducing kisses. Immediately we return to the passion of the morning, behaving like two sexually frustrated lovers who've met again after weeks apart, even though the last time I lay beneath Dylan was hours ago. We pull at clothes, drag hands across each other's skin and fight for breath between the kisses leaving my face and lips sore.

I pull away, trying not to pant in an unladylike manner. "You have someone waiting to drive you home in a car downstairs. No way are you leaving your car outside the front of my flat for any longer than necessary." I adjust my jeans, which somehow have become unbuttoned.

Dylan hooks a finger through the belt loop and yanks me close. "You should take them off, not do them back up."

I place my hands on his chest, which rises and falls rapidly. Giving in and letting Dylan do what we wants would be so easy, but I don't want him to leave me afterwards, and I know he has to. Steve demanded Dylan to return straight after bringing me home, and my pull isn't great enough to overcome Steve yet.

"Someone is waiting for you."

"I'll tell them to go," he says hoarsely.

"No." I wriggle from his embrace.

Dylan runs a hand through his hair and adjusts his jeans. "Fuck, you turn me on, summer Sky. You're teasing me..."

I hold a secret pleasure inside that I have this effect on Dylan Morgan. Did I tame a rock star?

"When do I see you again?" he asks. "You will come on our date with me, right? This isn't the end?"

The lust on his face retreats to concern. He's like an insecure puppy, right down to the dry humping.

"No, I want to try this, to get to know you. But that doesn't mean things will work out."

He brushes hair from my cheek. "Such a practical optimist."

I place my hand on his face in return. "I want to try to make this work, but I'm not sure I can be part of the world I saw this weekend."

"Nor am I anymore."

I rub my lips together, a big issue needs resolving not just for him but also for a future us.

"But you have to go back and do rock star things. Don't you have an album to record? Virgins to sacrifice?"

I get a Dylan grin, the one that makes him sexy because he's so natural and happy. "So I can come back and do rock star things to you later?"

I swallow against the thought of what he means. "Tomorrow."

"Fuck, that's forever."

Chapter Twenty-Nine

Dylan

Another night with Sky and the world on my shoulders lightens further. I wasn't too happy she wanted to leave today, but I understand I need to back off. I saw in her eyes what she thinks about my world - and my place in it. I can do this, fix what's around me and walk away. Persuade Sky we can make a go of this - help each other feel our way forward in life. I'll get the album finished then tell Steve I'm not going on tour. Sky gives me the strength to do this; she pulls me away from the hollow Dylan blindly following orders. The one following orders by coming straight back here after taking her back to Bristol.

We use the recording studio at my estate, polishing what we recorded in the Abbey Road studios over the last few months. We're behind schedule for obvious reasons but we're almost done. Daydreaming about Sky being the reason I'm late, I walk through the double doors into the studio area. The sound engineer, Paul, isn't around and voices carry through from the control room.

Jem lounges on the sofa in the area we have set aside for the constant eating and drinking that takes place between tracks. One booted foot resting across his knee, Jem swigs straight from a bottle of Jack. I grab the bottle and slam it on the table in front of him. I don't want to spend all fucking day here waiting for him to be sober enough to get this done.

"Stop being such a fucking cliché!" I snarl.

"Fuck you, lover boy." He picks the bottle back up again, fixing me with a look I've seen a thousand times. I know from the past how well hidden his real state can be. He's high as a fucking kite.

"How the fuck do we get the rest of the tracks down if you turn up to the studio off your face?"

"Don't be such a fucking hypocrite. You pissed off for a week and slowed things down!"

Biting back a retort, I walk into the control room. Bryn rests against the mixing desk and his face is murderous. Liam studies the laptop screen, flicking through the progress of the tracks. Honey's sitting on his knee, tapping a text on her phone. What the hell is she wearing today? Or not wearing. I really don't need to see so much of her tits - or the rose she has tattooed on one.

"Did Jem arrive like this?" I ask.

"Don't think he slept," mutters Bryn.

"I know he's been bad again recently but he's a fucking mess. And the way he spoke to Sky at the party..." Bryn and Liam glance at each other. "What?"

Honey disconnects herself from Liam and sits on the edge of the desk next to Bryn. "She reminds him of Lily."

"What the fuck? And what do you know about Lily?" I flash Liam a look and he shrugs apologetically.

Lily, the groupie who wasn't. The girl from the darkest part of my past. We were off our faces that night and Jem made the biggest mistake of our lives; a week later, I made things a thousand times fucking worse. The aftermath threatened the band until Steve made everything go away.

Jem and me have known each other since primary school, shared our hopes and dreams, and navigated this fucked up journey together. Lily changed things between us and we lost each other. What stories are out there for Sky to find? Unless Jem tells her everything, nothing she reads will make sense. Three years on and the whole mess is a fading bad memory. Only we know the truth.

Sky is nothing like Lily, this situation is completely different.

"Has he seen her again or something?"

Liam snorts. "Do you think I'd ever bring her name up?" He pauses. "You know what the whole fucked up mess did to him, and how he doesn't want girls like her coming into the circle."

"Girls like her?"

"Sweet, innocent but with a huge fucking knife ready to stab in your back. You should know," says Liam

I shake away memories I don't want. "If you knew Sky, you'd know how wrong you are."

"So she's not sweet and innocent?" drawls Honey, smirking.

"She's not an eighteen-year-old school kid!" I snap.

Something hard slams into my back and I stagger forward, catching the mixing desk to steady myself. Jem grabs me by the T-shirt and yanks me backwards. I spin around. Bad timing. His fist collides with my nose, pain splitting across my face and I stagger. Honey shrieks, hands at her mouth as she looks at me slumped against the wall. Jem's a good shot even when he's high; I'll give him that.

Bryn grabs Jem from behind, pinning his hands to his sides. "Don't be a dickhead."

Breathing heavily, Jem stares down at me as I hold my palm against my mouth. "That night was your fault. You were playing the fucking game too. So you're responsible for every fucking thing that happened afterwards!"

Itching to retaliate, I remain slumped, not wanting to fight with him. Pointless fist fights. "Not everything, Jem. You dealt with things wrong."

Holding his face close to mine, the bourbon from his breath is enough to make me drunk on the fumes. "Well, if you don't fuck things up with Sky, I will. I fucking owe you one!"

He stands, and sucks on his swelling knuckles before turning and leaving. Grabbing his bottle on the way out, he slams through the studio door, crashing into an alarmed looking Steve as he leaves.

Steve surveys the scene, eyes flicking between the three of us. I swat at Honey who's staunching the blood from my nose with someone's jacket. Liam's probably.

"Now what?" He pulls himself straight, looking between us like an angry father. "Dylan?"

"Not my fault," I grumble.

"So he broke your nose for nothing? It's one fucking thing after another! Are you two back there again?" He hits his head with his palm. "Fucking great..."

I pull myself upright, snatching the jacket from Honey. "Doesn't look like we'll be doing much till I sort my face out and he sobers up."

I slink off, but before I leave the look Liam gives Honey, and then me, intensifies the situation further.

I should've stayed in fucking Broadbeach.

*****

Dylan

Jem tips his chair back, hand against the boardroom wall staring at the ceiling. I remain standing, while Steve sits with his arms crossed over his chest. The conversation has stalled, although we've not had much of one. Jem refuses to apologise to me, I have nothing to say to him. No change there.

"Can't you see how he's going downhill again?" I ask Steve, indicating Jem.

Jem snaps his head around to me. "Fuck you."

"Can you say anything to me without using the word fuck?"

"No, I fucking can't."

Shaking my head, I turn back to Steve. "Steve?"

"He's okay. Once we're touring he'll settle down. There's plenty to keep him distracted."

"Like what? More alcohol and drugs? What if he kills himself this time?"

"Yada, yada, yada," says Jem, tapping his fingers rhythmically on the table.

"He's okay," repeats Steve.

"Like hell he is!"

Steve flips his phone over in his hands, brow furrowed. "I'm more bothered about you and that Summer chick than you and him behaving like testosterone fuelled teens."

I stiffen. "What's she got to do with anything?"

"Dylan's lovely summer Sky," sniggers Jem.

"She's a distraction you could do without right now, we've too much on in the next few months. Honey trailing around after Liam is bad enough."

"She's in my life now," I say through gritted teeth. "You don't make decisions about my personal life!"

He raises a brow. "Don't I?"

"Steve sorts your shit out, man," pipes up Jem. "Sorts all our shit out, don'tcha Mr Steve?"

Steve smiles at him in a patronising way I spot and Jem doesn't. "Got your back, Jem."

The comment hits me. Jem is a fucking mess. He's spinning like a Catherine Wheel spitting sparks around and ready to burn out, and because of Steve.

He feeds Jem's addiction, lets him have everything he wants then makes all his decisions. He keeps us all in line to maintain the Blue Phoenix brand.

Now I want something that doesn't fit Steve's plan and he's not having this.

"I'm making the decisions about my relationship with Sky! Don't even think of interfering."

Jem mutters something under his breath and I spin around. He may not have a drink in his hand but the odour of alcohol surrounds like a grey cloud darkening by the day. How he can drink so much and stand up, I have no idea. Oh, yeah, right, I used to do the same.

"Say what you gotta say, Jem."

"Nah, gonna say what I gotta say to her. Let her know who she's really dealing with."

I can't show him I'm bothered and give him ammunition, not in front of Steve. The temptation to make his face match mine with an out-of-the-blue punch hovers.

"Jem..." Steve's warning growl interrupts our face off and my fist.

"We're going away at the end of the week, so more of a delay with the album because you can't fucking play doesn't help," remarks Steve, pointing at Jem's swollen knuckles.

"I thought we were getting the album finished up before leaving for the States?" I ask.

I'm planning a date with Sky this weekend, showing her she's more important and I mean every word I tell her.

"You know we're in Belgium this weekend, right?" asks Steve, wearily.

"What the fuck?" I ask.

"The awards night - maybe we arranged it when you were...on sabbatical. I can't remember."

"Someone could've reminded me before I made plans," I snap.

The smirk on Jem's face suggests I was deliberately not told; Steve keeping us in line using every trick he knows. Fuck.

"What do you think Sky will do when she sees the real Dylan Morgan?" sniggers Jem.

"Just because I'm being dragged to a shitty awards ceremony doesn't change a thing about me and Sky."

Jem pauses long enough to watch my irritation mounting. "I wasn't talking about going away."

My fist really wants to connect with this guy's fucking face but I stand instead, and then storm out of the room. A few metres along the hallway, I rest against the wall.

Don't do this, Jem

*****

Sky

The day after I return home, Tara insists I meet her for lunch, wanting the gory run down on my weekend in the house of debauchery. Not prepared to give the final part of myself to Dylan by announcing to anyone outside of us what's really happening, I have to lie to her. Once I'm certain this future is real, she'll be the first to know. Who am I kidding? Social media will be the first to know.

This time we sit in a quieter corner of the coffee shop, in a wooden booth with vintage cushioned seats and expensive fixtures. Furtive glances around the room suggest nobody is looking twice at me. I guess being 'flavour of the month' doesn't last long.

Tara jumps out of her seat when I arrive, and she grabs my hand like an excited toddler. "Tell me everything! Did you meet them all? What happened?"

I extract myself and slide into the seat opposite her. "Tara, I just had my heart broken and you want to rub my nose in it?"

She clamps a hand over her mouth. "Sorry, it's just I've never known a famous person before..."

"I'm not famous!" I hiss.

She jiggles for a minute then decides not to hold back. "Do you mind me asking what happened? Why did you go to his house? I thought you didn't want anything to do with him?"

I fiddle with my cup, not meeting her curious gaze. "Guess I was in denial. When I saw him it was..." Was what? How can I express this without sounding trite? "You know, he's Dylan Morgan and I was mad thinking I couldn't resist him."

"Did you take pictures? Of the house I mean."

"No. Why would I?'

"Sky! I'd die to see the inside of that house! So the band...?"

I tap my fingers and give her my 'frowny face' wishing she'd keep her voice down. "Yes. I met them"

"And?"

"Various levels of dickhead." Unwanted memories of Jem re-enter my mind.

She splutters. "Various levels of *hot*!"

"Um, Tara? Are you listening? The weekend broke my heart?" If this were real, I'd be pissed off by her insensitivity and selfishness.

"Sorry..."

"Maybe in a few days, when I get over this I'll feel better."

Tara rearranges her features into concerned friend. "What happened?"

"Dylan finally understood why we don't fit. As soon as he saw me in his world, compared to everyone around, I think he realised I wasn't for him."

"For someone who was so love struck, that happened fast."

I shrug. "Not like we'd known each other long. Maybe I was just a new toy, and because he couldn't play, he wanted me. Then when I said yes, I was no fun anymore."

"Did you...?" Fighting back the blushing is pointless but I don't answer. "Bastard," mutters Tara softly.

"It's over with," I lie, "Time to move on."

*****

Over the next few days, life returns to the pre-Broadbeach normality. Apart from no Grant, no real job and a relationship with a rock star conducted via Skype and text messages. If I want to see him in between, I track social media. There's at least one new picture of him each day.

Lily Parker. Despite my refusal to be dragged into Jem's games, the name nags at me. Jem is probably stirring something up, but why? When Jem mentioned her name, Dylan didn't react outwardly, but he was holding my hand at the time and his grip tightened. Dylan's words about how I can't normally google potential boyfriends almost guilts me out of searching, but I need to know.

Taking a drink from my glass, I hold the fizzing wine in my mouth and type:

<Lily Blue Phoenix>

Most of the top hits are about different Lilys, who are current fans - Facebook profiles and blogs.

<Lily Parker Blue Phoenix Dylan Jem>

A mix of media reports from years ago are buried several pages into the search results. Most of the stories link her with Jem; Dylan isn't mentioned. There're hints at cover-ups and a refusal by Lily Parker to comment. Flicking from site to site, I come up with nothing. In many cases, I read the same press release repeated across several sites. An uncomfortable feeling something has been 'made to go away' creeps in. I search Lily's full name too but draw a blank. There's little information about her apart from she was eighteen and a student. Somehow, she's evaded the cameras - or someone stopped any pictures being used, because I can't find any images of her. The results are three years old, span a couple of weeks, then fade.

Why is this so bad?

I rub my face and keep digging. I can't find or understand the Dylan connection. Something isn't right here - why is Jem intent on linking Dylan to this? What pieces are missing?

Chapter Thirty

Dylan

I'm terrified I'm going to fuck this up, or Jem's going to fuck this up for me. As Sky sleeps beside me, I stroke mussed hair from her face and kiss her cheek. She murmurs and buries her head in the pillow. Before Sky, waking up with a chick was a no-go. Dylan Morgan the rock star bastard kicked them out once he was done. But I could stay in bed with for Sky days, and never let her go.

I'm exercising massive self-control here, the scent of her strawberry hair and the lingering smell of sex from last night has me so hard it's starting to hurt. I huff, and climb out of bed. At least we had another night to keep me going when I'm away from her, a night revealing Sky isn't as opposed to dirty rock star sex as I thought she might be. *Fuck, stop thinking about sex.*

Instead, I make breakfast, the strange domestic routine I've adopted with Sky and want to continue.

Will she continue? I'll do anything to make this work, and escape the darkness of my life. We can help each other make sense of the world; I can go anywhere and be anything with the strength I find from Sky. Sky's strength to walk away from her relationship with Grant and not fall in a heap amazes me. Her life is a struggle to find what she wants, exactly like mine is; but am I deluding myself if I think walking away from this life will pull me away from the darkness following?

The toast pops in the toaster and I pull it out, pouring hot water into a mug with the other hand. I know how Sky likes her tea - how many sugars. I've never known these small things about anyone before and this proves to me I love this woman. Stupid I know.

Sky approaches behind and wraps her arms around my naked chest, her smooth hands rubbing the muscles then sliding towards my abs as she rests her head on my back. I turn around and draw her to me, running my hands down her delicious curves, before squeezing her ass.

She's in a pink towelling robe. I bet she's naked under there, and I want to find out.

"No bacon?" she asks, detaching my hands from her beautiful backside.

"You don't have any." I slide the plate of toast along the bench towards her.

Sky runs her tongue along her teeth, and she surveys my body. "Do you often make breakfast with just your underwear on?"

I look down at my black briefs. "Want me to get dressed?"

The coy smile she gives me answers before she does. "No."

"Want to go back to bed?" I say quietly, giving her my best seductive smile in return.

She takes a bite of toast then blows hair from her face. "More sex and still no proper date..."

"I'm taking you to London when I get back."

"London? Why London?"

"There's a restaurant I like that's a bit more private than your local Italian place would be."

"Long drive home..."

"We don't have to come home. I have a place in London." 'A place' sounds funny, not the best description for one of the most expensive addresses in the city.

"Of course you do." She rolls her eyes. "Gold plated taps, I hope? I noticed they were lacking in your little house in the country. How many 'places' do you have exactly?"

I slide my hand inside the front of Sky's robe and make contact with her naked breast. I knew it. As I try to undo her robe, she bites her lip and slaps my hand.

"Dylan Morgan, stop trying to distract me!"

Her darkened pupils indicate exactly the effect I'm having on her, the subtle pink in her cheeks turning me on because I know I'm doing the same to her. Fuck, we hardly need to touch each other and my dick gets hard.

Sky's look drops to the hard-on filling my black briefs. "Honestly, Dylan..."

"What can I say? You fucking turn me on," I growl and grab her ass for the third time.

"I get the feeling Jem wants to get between us. Why?"

Talk about a clever way to stop me. *Shit*. I release her then focus intently on taking teabags from the cups and dropping them in her kitchen bin. "Because he's a dick."

How long can I hide this?

"He seems a bit extreme. He scared me."

"When?" I glance around sharply. "What did he do?"

"At your house when he was high, I thought he was going to do something to me. He said something about you trading girls."

Fuck. "That was a long time ago, Sky. I did some stupid shit, as you've seen in your internet investigations."

Sky picks at her toast with her delicate fingers. "I know. Is there anything I need to know about?"

This is my opportunity. But am I going to take it? I spoon Sky's two sugars into her tea and pass her the yellow mug. Picking up mine, I tip my head to the lounge and she follows me through.

"What do you want to know?" I ask, perching on the sofa.

"I know you've had sex with a lot of girls..."

I cringe. "I'm clean. I got tested a few months back and haven't been with anyone since then." I look her in the eyes. "Apart from you."

The cute Sky pink spread across her cheeks and I resist the urge to take hold of her and do things I know will stop her asking questions.

"There are a lot of stories out there, and I know the media makes stuff up, but is there anything not 'out there' you should tell me?"

"Like what?"

She sips her tea. "I don't know, a love child, secret wife, something like that."

My heart fights its way out of my chest. *Now. Tell her now.* "No."

Sky's shoulders relax. "So in Broadbeach all you were running from was your life?"

"Pretty much."

I need to blank the memories of the past, and lose myself in Sky's world. If she won't live in my world, I'm going to live in hers. A wave of her fragrant hair hangs in her eyes and I take hold of the strand, twirling it around my finger.

Sky touches my bruised face with her soft fingers. "Will you tell me what happened? Was this Jem?"

"Possibly." Since I arrived last night, she's nagged me about the result of Jem's punch covering my face, I thought she'd dropped the subject.

"Or your manager?"

"Why Steve?"

"Because of the way he treats you, Dylan. Like a naughty kid. Was he the reason you left for Broadbeach?"

"No, because of everything, I had no control. I told you." I can't help the hardness in my tone; I'm not ready to face this. I need to choose my time.

"And who has control of your life, Dylan?" she asks pointedly. "Not you at the moment."

"Yes, I know, nothing's changed. Can we leave this topic of conversation?"

Silence comes between us, not the usual comfortable silence but one filled with suspicion and unanswered insecurities.

"Has anybody tried to contact you since you came back?" I ask.

"Like who?"

"The media. Fans. Things got a bit crazy back there..."

"Not really, it's you they're looking for; I don't think I'm very interesting on my own."

"Yeah, one thing about Steve, he does a good job redirecting people to where he wants them to go."

Sky sucks her lips together. "Evidently. Like awards nights?"

I stroke her face. "At least the press will follow me to Belgium."

"Hmm."

"You could come?"

Pointless asking, I know, she's taken one step into my world and I can't push her, even though I need her with me. She has no idea how much.

"I don't think so!"

"I thought I'd ask anyway."

Sky snuggles into me, tucking her head under my chin in the spot her head fits perfectly. "You don't go for a few hours, right?"

"Yep."

"And you're distractingly naked?" I shiver as she traces a finger down my six-pack towards the edge of my briefs. Fingers I'd like playing across other parts of my body. "Now I know you won't fuck me and leave me, can you show me some more of your rock star sex?"

Despite the fact I'd be a hundred percent content with sitting here and cuddling Sky for the next few hours, so I can hold the memory when I'm alone in the hotel later, there is no fucking way I'm refusing her request.

Chapter Thirty-One

Dylan

I sit in another faceless hotel, in another luxury suite and the panic seizes my chest again. This is two days away doing TV stints, not even the tour, and already the discomfort creeps in. I can't do this.

The hotel apartment is what is termed "well-appointed". Penthouse living with sweeping views across the city. Honeymoon style - enormous bed covered in white bedding that swallows you up when lying down, a huge TV, spa bath - the works. Exactly the sort of place I'd love to be with Sky, but she refuses to come.

I pull open my suitcase, burrowing through my clothes to the small bag at the bottom. The brown leather bag contains my shower gel, shampoo - scents to remind me of who I am so I don't have to use hotel soap and smell like half the other guests.

The small plastic container of pills sits alongside the shell Sky found on the beach the day the sea pulled her under. Popping the lid, I study the tiny white tablets and grit my teeth, annoyed medication is what I have to do to hold things together in public.

This is why this life has to end.

I need my space; a place to get myself sorted. Creativity won't happen when I'm being wheeled out like a puppet for stadiums and a mind calmed by benzos isn't a creative mind: everything is dull. The fans aren't stupid, and I can only put on an act for so long.

One night here, one night Germany. Did Steve deliberately not tell me? He knows about the panic attacks and how I'm turning to medication to get through this bullshit. Pills I didn't need in Broadbeach, with Sky.

Sky, my beautiful, smart-mouthed girl who won't give her whole self to me and for the same reason I can't be myself; this fucking suffocating life.

Is it wrong to hope Jem ends up in rehab and the tour is cancelled? He's my best mate. Or was. We've spent years fucking up our lives and each other's; of losing control and never realising until we'd been swallowed by the false world we created.

A knock on the door intensifies the panic and I take deep breaths, regaining control before I answer.

Liam. With Honey and a brown haired version of Honey in tow - even their tight leopard print dresses match. Uh oh. I narrow my eyes at Liam and he pulls an apologetic face. Talk about pussy whipped...

"You ready, Dylan?" purrs Honey.

I turn and walk over to grab my leather jacket and Liam follows me in with his entourage.

"Who's this with Honey? Strawberry Jam?" I ask.

Liam sniggers but Honey and friend appear genuinely confused.

"This is Tania, my friend. Liam said she could come along."

"Did you?" I ask an obviously coerced Liam.

"Kind of."

"Great, so groupies get personal invites now?"

Tania, who has gawked at me the whole time she's been in the room, breaks her reverie. "I'm not a groupie. I just wanna go to the after party."

Should I be insulted or relieved? "So, you're someone else's groupie?"

"She wants to meet some famous people," replies Honey, flashing her bright teeth at her friend. They both giggle like six-year-olds. "She was going to go with Jem, but you know, he's not great at the moment and I don't want her around him."

"She wants to tag along with us," explains Liam

"How about Bryn?" I shoot back. "Can't she 'tag along' with him?"

"He's currently sobering up Jem..."

I run my fingers through my hair. "Fantastic, just what I fucking need."

"If he can walk, we'll be fine. We're not playing tonight - just getting an award."

Why the fuck didn't I persuade Sky to come?

*****

I call and speak to Sky between the awards and being dragged into the VIP after party. She'd waited up to talk to me before bed and to give me a blow-by-blow account of what she thought of the performances at the awards. Hearing her smart comments is a breath of fresh air in the suffocating night. Escape is possible now I have Sky.

The dimly lit, red-carpeted room is filled with other musicians and their entourages. As usual, I bump into a stream of stars and we gush about each other's work, enthusing how awesome to meet up with each other again. I don't have a fucking clue when or where I last saw most of them, probably when I was high.

Danni-K, the latest darling of the music scene attracts hangers-on like flies. A drunken Jem turns his full attention to her, and her security team is wary. A black-suited guy twice as broad as me and a good few inches taller sticks to her side, throwing warning looks at an oblivious Jem. If there's one thing Jem likes better than multiple groupies, it's getting into the knickers of squeaky-clean stars. Singers, actresses, heiresses... He loves them all and his reputation helps, not hinders.

Having fulfilled my smiling and socialising duties, I slump on one of the black leather benches in a corner. Blue Phoenix get whatever the fuck they want, as organised by Steve, so the metal table holds several of my choice in beer. I grab an open bottle and drink deeply.

My head pounds, as the alcohol mixes with the medication in my system. Steve's around somewhere - I need to arrange a car so I can get the fuck out of here. Fed up of a stream of girls attempting to engage their bodies with mine, I stare at my Converse and the plush carpet. Right now, I'd give anything to be snuggled on the sofa in Broadbeach with Sky.

Someone plonks onto the seat next to me. "Dylan, man, have you met the beautiful, fuckable Danni-K?" he asks, a little too loudly.

I glance up at the starlet; I don't think she heard. Beautiful, yeah. Fuckable? He can work on that one; I'm not interested. Sleek black hair surrounds her heart-shaped face, her huge brown eyes heavily made up and the dark red lipstick contrasting her mocha tone skin. Clueless about fashion even after all these years, I suspect whoever created the tight blue dress slit to her thigh will get a few orders after tonight.

"Hey, Dylan," she says and smiles.

"Hey. Nice performance tonight."

Flicking her hair over her shoulder with a hand containing enough rings to rival mine, she sits next to me, Jem forgotten about. "Thanks. One for everyone to remember."

A theatrical show with enough semi-naked dancers to fill a strip club, and a raunchy number with The Five, the latest boy band sensation. I suspect she's trying to lose her innocent image. She's hanging with Blue Phoenix, so she must be. The Five are here now, teen boys covered in groupies. Wait until they learn... if they last long enough before their star burns out.

I give her a noise of agreement and swig my beer, scanning the room for Steve. Where the fuck is he?

"Hey! D-K. How's about a picture with The Dylan Morgan," says Jem, pulling his phone out. "Just for us - no press."

I snap my head up. Jem has his phone pointing in our direction ready, and there's a glint in his high eyes worrying me. He's lying. Shit, let her say no.

"Sure," she says in her Southern accent and places her head on my shoulder.

"Aww, c'mon, you must wanna get closer to him than that?"

What the fuck? In a stunned moment, Danni-K rests her skinny behind on my knee and wraps her arm across my shoulders. *No. Fuck.* Before I get a chance to move, her hair sweeps across my face as her lips meet mine. Instantaneously, Jem's phone camera flashes.

"Holy fuck!" I yell.

An alarmed Danni-K climbs off my lap, lips pursed. "Sorry, not you - that dickhead," I say to her, aware her security is watching the obnoxious Dylan Morgan who's had his hands on their star. "Give me the fucking phone, Jem!"

Jem holds his phone high in the air and laughs at me. "I told you I'd fuck things up for you."

Chapter Thirty-Two

Sky

Speaking to Dylan before I slept filled me with a giddy happiness that everything he says about loving me is true. Each day I spend with Dylan encourages me to think this is worth a shot; the further we entangle our lives the harder it will be to disentangle. Dylan's right - I can't apply logic to love; especially my skewed logic. The truth is I care about Dylan. I'm passionately addicted to him physically and see part of myself mirrored in him. I could be fatalistic and agree we were "meant to meet", perhaps we were because this situation goes beyond what I admit. If love is craving to be around someone, being soothed by his presence and not having to find the right words when alone with him, then I'm falling in love with Dylan. If I change my definition of love from living side by side in a house in Bristol, to a scary, consuming need for someone I resisted for those two weeks, then I'm not falling for

Dylan - I've crashed into a scary place where I am in love again.

The one thing I can't let go of is the sneaking fear our colliding worlds will explode, taking me with them.

I switch on my laptop and I'm faced with the possibility this has happened sooner than I thought. On my favourite Blue Phoenix stalking blog are pictures of the band at the after party Dylan complained he needed to go to. The most prominent picture is of Dylan with a celebrity singer I've vaguely heard of. My stomach tightens in horror. The image is of a stunning woman in a blue dress, which exposes more of her than the material covers.

Kissing him.

I refresh the picture twenty times, studying the blurred pixels. Maybe they're not quite kissing? The refreshing doesn't wipe away the image of their lips locked or her sitting on his knee.

The alarm I set on my phone to get me out of the house on time sounds, and I rub my eyes. I can't deal with this right now. In a haze, I head for work, fighting tears all the way. I sit on the ordinary bus amongst everyday people leading monotonous lives. This is my life, not the ridiculous Dylan fantasy. I let down my defences, and was screwed over again.

Halfway through the day, my phone buzzes. A text from Dylan. The coward doesn't even have the decency to call me.

<Sorry. Not how it looked. I'll call later.>

I ignore him, shaking so much afterwards that Jenny, my boss, asks if I'm okay. I nod through tears and a false smile, and then switch my brain off.

His intermittent calls and texts through the day are ignored.

<Sky. Talk to me. Nothing happened.>

Ignored.

<Let me explain.>

Ignored.

At this point, I switch the phone off. Then I check my favourite Blue Phoenix stalking site once more. They're in Europe for another day, and amongst their entourage is the girl in the blue dress.

*****

Anger. Hurt. Betrayal. A bottle of wine and a family size bag of crisps. That's what I work my way through. Deja bloody vu.

I bunker down with the wine, crisps and a book. Why does this tear at me more than Grant? Grant was my life for five years; Dylan was five minutes.

I wake with my book on my face and a sore neck as the home phone rings incessantly.

"What?" I snap when I answer.

"It was Jem," Dylan says.

"I think it was pretty obviously you!"

"I meant he took the photo and leaked the picture."

"Oh, so he forced her to sit on your knee and play tonsil tennis?"

"No, Sky, she sat on my knee, gave me a friendly kiss on the mouth and he took a picture.

Two seconds later, I was nowhere near her; I swear. Were my hands on her? No. Were there any other pictures? No."

Friendly kiss on the mouth? What the hell?
"Why would Jem do that?"
"You know why."
"No I fucking don't!" *Don't cry. Don't cry.*
"I'm back tomorrow and I'll come over and explain everything. Not just Jem taking stupid pictures, but what's going on between me and him that's making Jem behave like this. I'll take you out - show the world you're who I want!"

There's a desperation to his tone I haven't heard before, a panic unlike him. Is he telling the truth? He has to understand why I have a hard time believing him so soon after Grant did something similar.

"Why is she still with you in Germany if it's not true?"

Dylan huffs. "Jem. She's with Jem. Everything will come out soon, and then you'll see."

"You mean Steve and her manager will fix everything?" I snap.

There's a long pause; this isn't the time for this.

"I'm tired, Dylan, and I've had a lot to drink. Call me when you get back to England."

"You do believe me?" His question comes straight back without a pause. "You mean so much to me! After fighting for you so hard, why would I fuck this up?"

"Maybe. I don't know, shit Dylan, I'm drunk. Yeah, probably I do believe you."

The sound of Dylan exhaling comes down the phone. "When I get back, we can talk this through? I don't want to be away from you, I need to figure out what to do."

"To do about what?"

"The tour, everything I ran to Broadbeach from. Shit, if I could walk away and be the ordinary person you want me to be, I would."

His logic is skewed, I wouldn't ask him to change for me and I don't want him to. "Be the person you want to be, Dylan," I say softly. "That's your problem right there. You spend too much time being the image of Dylan, rather than the reality."

"I want to create a new reality with you, my current one sucks."

Sometimes his whining about how bad life is as a multi-millionaire grates, but then I consider what he gave up to achieve this - himself. "Dylan, I need to go, I'm really tired."

"But you believe me?" he repeats.

"Yes. Okay…"

"Sky, I love you so fucking much."

He pauses, waiting for my response. This is what he gets because I've had too much wine. "And I'm falling in love with you, despite concerted efforts not to."

He laughs softly. "So you're not leaving me again over this?"

"My heart won't let me walk away," I say, "And my heart was broken very recently, so it's fragile, which is why I'm guarding it."

"I'll give you my heart to take care of, if you'll give me yours to mend."

"If I do, will you be careful with it?" I whisper
"Always, I promise."

Chapter Thirty-Three

Sky

The next morning, I regret telling Tara things didn't work out with Dylan, because now I don't have anyone to discuss this with. My head hurts from the stupid amount of wine I drank to drown my sorrows, and when I remember telling Dylan how I feel, I cringe. Now I'm exposed, raw and able to be hurt more.

I call into work and tell them I'm sick, I don't think this contract is going to last long. The job was only a week of data input anyway, not the kind of thing I can do today with a head thumping with hungover dehydration.

I retreat to Tara's and my coffee haunt, sit beneath The Great Gatsby pictures and ponder the Dylan situation over several cups of coffee. What holds me to Dylan and allows me to believe him when in a normal situation I'd kick his backside out of my life? Overreacting is more my style, but I allowed myself to believe him. Why? Dylan tells me I overthink things, but not overthinking is what led me to the Grant situation. Besides, when I'm in close proximity to Dylan, rational thinking isn't something that happens a lot.

He may be famous, wealthy and have the sexual prowess of any billionaire in any book I've read; but underneath everything, he's Dylan. My Dylan from Broadbeach, who looks at me as if I fell from the stars.

How can I have spent five years with Grant and felt a fraction of what I do for Dylan after less than a month? This inexplicable desire to be with him; the sick feeling when we're apart. The teenage crush feelings we recreated by the sea have stuck - maybe they're not teenage. I sip the coffee. Dylan doesn't understand how I gave myself to someone else's life for years, and why I can't do this again. However, I know this is different. If I walked away from Dylan now, I'd spend my life asking why. I don't think Dylan will try to change me - he's too busy trying to change himself. Perhaps that's part of what we recognise in each other, our lives have travelled in different trajectories, and now we're pulled onto the same course. I remember Dylan's words on the beach, how he's sure we met at the moment we needed each other.

Deep down, I believe him about Danni-K. My experience of Jem suggests he'd do something like this, his attitude to my relationship with Dylan makes no sense, but the vitriol in his words the night of the party would match this kind of action.

But I need to see the truth in Dylan's face, not just hear the words.

I'm aware a girl at a nearby table has been here as long as I have, nursing one cup of coffee the whole time. This isn't illegal, although the cafe owners might not be too happy, but she keeps staring at me. Not the odd glance where you accidentally meet someone's eyes, but full on staring. On alert for crazed fans, I study her when she's not looking. She's around my age and has long blonde hair, which she wears loose across her shoulders, a natural Scandinavian blonde. Her piercing blue eyes are huge in her oval face and her long, slender legs are curled beneath the table.

Sometimes, I think she's about to come over and talk to me, but if I meet her eyes, she looks away. I can't figure out what she's doing. The longer this goes on, the more convinced I become that she knows who I am. My current situation has me paranoid; one run-in with the paparazzi and fans and I'm on high alert. I shake the thought from my head.

I finish my latte and pick my bag up, ready to leave.

"Are you Sky? Can I talk to you?"

I look up in surprise as the tall, blonde girl hovers around my table. Her face is paler, hands trembling slightly. I glance around. The cafe is half-full, if she is a crazed fan I'm pretty sure I'll be safe.

"Um, okay."

"Would you like another coffee?" she asks, pulling a purse from her oversized brown leather handbag.

"I'm leaving."

"I need to talk to you about something."

"What?"

"Dylan."

I drop back onto the wooden chair and sigh. "Are you a fan?"

She laughs softly. "No."

"Then what?"

"I'll order coffees." The girl disappears to the counter and I stare at the chalkboard advertising drinks and cakes, a little dazed already.

She returns with a number attached to a metal stand, which she places on the table, then sits opposite me. I'm stunned by how pretty she is in such an understated way. Her face is clear of make-up and her plain blue summer dress matches her cornflower eyes.

The girl plays with the sugar dispenser. "I heard about you and when I found out you'd decided to have a relationship with Dylan Morgan, I knew I had to warn you about something."

I stiffen. "Heard about me from who? Nobody knows whether I'm with Dylan or not." I scan my mind; the only people who know are part of the Blue Phoenix entourage.

"It doesn't matter."

"Yes, it does; because they've obviously told you where I live!" I snap back. "Did Jem tell you?"

When she inspects her short fingernails, I get my answer. What the hell is Jem's game now? "You're in a relationship with Dylan Morgan." Her words are a statement, not a question.

"Fine. What do you have to tell me?" I ask. "I've read most of what's on the internet about him; I doubt there's much new you can add? They pretty much dug all the dirt."

"Sometimes, things can be covered up." She looks up, eyes wide. "For a price."

Whatever she's alluding to, I've no idea, but if she's the sort of person who can be paid off, I'm not sure I'll believe anything she tells me.

"A price?"

"Yes, and then there's the impossibility of taking on Blue Phoenix's lawyers and winning."

"Who are you?" I ask.

The girl looks down at her shaking hands curled around her bag. When she looks back to me, her eyes brim with tears as she draws a shaky breath.

I know who she is.

"My name's Lily Parker and three years ago Dylan Morgan raped me." Her voice cracks and is barely a whisper.

The room lurches, her words piercing my heart. "I don't believe you, what sort of sick joke is this? Are you jealous or something?"

"I'm telling the truth. I might be carefully buried at the bottom of the internet, but I'm there. Me, Dylan, Jem and a lot of missing pieces."

I fight the tight-chested panic. No, she's a fan trying to split me up with her favourite star. "This is bullshit!"

The waitress delivering our coffees looks between us curiously as she places the china cups on our table.

"Dylan's bad news, Sky. He may have cleaned up his act, but any man who can do something so sickening to a woman will never change. Not really."

"I don't believe you," I repeat, standing on wobbling legs. "I don't want to listen to your lies."

She doesn't move, and places her shaking hands on the table. Her nails are chewed. Is she telling the truth? She can't be. No way. "I'm going! Don't you dare follow me!" I hiss.

"Ask him or Jem. One of them will tell you the truth."

In my experience, when people lie, they can't meet your eyes and Lily is staring straight into mine with eyes full of pain.

I have no more words.

I stumble out of the cafe, into the bright summer sunshine. Jem told me there was a story; a story Dylan refused to tell me. Everything Jem said, all of Dylan's reactions swim around my mind. No. Not true. Not Dylan, the man who wouldn't touch me without permission. Nausea grips my stomach, forcing bile upwards - is Lily the reason for his cautious behaviour when we met?

A few hundred metres along the road, I have to stop. I lean against the metal pole of the road sign, tears blurring my vision. What if this *is* true? I pull out my phone and call Dylan.

*****

Dylan

Sky ends the call and I stand on the balcony of my hotel room, beneath the bright sunshine, as I watch my world cave in.

My shock at her discovery takes away any words of explanation I have. I need to explain so much, but nothing will come out of my mouth except a hollow denial. Sky didn't demand answers or scream at me, but spoke in a low voice asking for honesty. When I couldn't reply, she told me that until I can tell her the truth I should stay away from her.

Nothing I could say would undo the damage because who I am is who I'll always be. My choices shaped me, carved me into the man I am. I can never walk away from the Dylan Morgan I created that night. After all this time, I have my punishment - I've lost Sky because she's discovered I'm not the man she thought she knew. How I ever thought I deserved something as good as life with Sky, I'll never know.

Jem has what he wants - he's ruined my chance with Sky, as I ruined his with Lily. His obsession with Lily ripped into our friendship; Lily's obsession with me tore us apart.

After three years, the ugly has been resurrected. I left it too late to tell Sky the facts when I had so many chances to. An insane part of me planned to ask Lily to explain to Sky what happened, in the hope Sky would understand. Lily's actions prove she doesn't forgive me, and that her story hasn't changed.

I don't think Sky will accept the truth, and I don't think the truth is any better than what she thinks of me now.

Coming in June 2014

Falling Sky (Blue Phoenix #2)

For more information about my new releases subscribe to my newsletter:
http://eepurl.com/Po81D

More Contemporary Romance
by
Lisa Swallow

The Butterfly Days Series:
Because of Lucy
Finding Evan

About The Author

Lisa is an author of new adult romance and writes both paranormal and contemporary, often with a side of snark.

In between running a business, looking after her family and writing, Lisa sometimes finds spare time to do other things. This often involves swapping her book worlds for gaming worlds. She even leaves the house occasionally.

Lisa is originally from the UK but moved to Australia in 2001 and now lives in Perth in Western Australia with her husband, three children and dog

Facebook
www.facebook.com/lisaswallowbooks

Twitter
www.twitter.com/lisa_swallow_au

Website
www.lisaswallow.net

Amazon
www.amazon.com/author/lisaswallow

She can be contacted by email at:
lisa_writes@ymail.com

Acknowledgements

I'm not great at these and there are so many people who have helped me with my journey so far I'm sure I'll miss one of you.

Firstly, my beta readers Louise, Laura, Katie, Selena and Bec - thank you for all your feedback. As always, the book would not be the same without your input.

Also, a thank you to the EWG cultists who critiqued early chapters.

Thank you to the wonderful Becky and Peggy from Hot Tree Editing for their work on polishing my story.

The amazing cover is a collaboration between Najla Qamber Designs and Lindee Robinson Photography. A big thank you goes out to them for creating something so beautiful.

Thank you to Willow's Formatting for her professional and helpful service.

There are many bloggers and readers who've helped me out over the last few months in particular. Tash and Rose from Forever Me Romance have been wonderful in organising the cover reveal and blog blitz. Many other readers and bloggers have helped me pimp out Summer Sky and my other books, in particular Dzintra, Angela, Danielle, Michelle, Heather, Dawn and Karen. There are many authors I could thank too but again I'm scared of leaving people out!

To everyone who has supported me over the last year of craziness by buying, reading or just believing in me when I doubted myself… thank you!

CPSIA information can be obtained at www.ICGtesting.com
Printed in the USA
LVOW06s1802220614

391149LV00003B/267/P